The Invitation

MICHELLE DAVIS

The Invitation by Michelle Davis

First Edition 2021

Printed in the United States

ISBN: 978-1-7344619-2-3

Library of Congress Control Number: 2021920949

For more writings by Michelle Davis, please visit:
www.michellemdavis.net

"*The path of awakening is not about becoming who you are. Rather it is about unbecoming who you are not.*"

—ALBERT SCHWEITZER

"*The spiritual journey is the unlearning of fear and the acceptance of love.*"

—MARIANNE WILLIAMSON

A

VALENTINE SURPRISE

February 12

Nicki's key easily slides into the wrought iron lock of the rustic wooden door located on the east side of the house. She always enters this way. While the surrounding hemlocks naturally seclude the majority of this newly built modern mountain home, its front entrance remains visible from the street.

Of course, Wyatt doesn't care. Nicki pauses for a moment, wiping snowflakes from the tip of her nose. She inhales the cold mountain air then watches her breath reappear as white puffs that dissolve into the snowy night. She's the one who treasures her reputation and is resolved to preserve this well-crafted image. Nicki runs her perfectly manicured fingers through her shoulder-length bleach-blonde hair, reflecting on how she's struggled to establish herself, her business, and her life. The owner of a successful antique shop on Market Street, she spends Mondays, when her store's closed, volunteering at the local animal shelter. After work, she coaches the girls' high school soccer team in the fall and the softball team each spring. However, what Nicki might be best known for are the warm smiles and uplifting acknowledgments she offers to everyone she greets. There's barely a person in Hawley Falls who has anything but kind words to say about Nicki Keating, or her husband, Billy. And she'd like to keep it that way.

Nowhere as conservative as it used to be, her Pocono hometown is definitely not progressive. Many of the trucks parked downtown host faded Trump stickers and rifle racks. Bingo remains a viable option for Saturday nights, and the mayor leads the Fourth of July parade, tossing pieces of candy to spectators sitting on street curbs. Though many believe this community is built upon the traditional family, there are too many single moms working more than one job to make ends meet. Like Nicki, most girls marry right after high school, except for those lucky few who escape to attend college. And each Sunday, the local Presbyterian church literally bursts at its seams with law-abiding church folk, despite the fact many of these parishioners don't act quite "Christian" during the rest of the week. Most all of the residents were born in Hawley Falls, and most likely the majority will die there.

Even today, the unspoken ethos in this northern Pennsylvanian town remains the same. No matter how bad things are, regardless of what's happening in the family, you do not discuss it. Secrets remain secret. Nicki's parents preached this mantra until the fateful day their Bronco was hit by a Jersey trucker hauling trash to the local landfill.

Thank God they'll never know my secret.

These thoughts quickly dissipate as soon as she returns to the present and pushes open the heavy side door that leads to Wyatt's kitchen. Nicki hangs her slightly wet jacket and purse on the industrial metal standing coatrack by the door. Entranced by that oh-so-tantalizing sensation she feels whenever she enters his house, she takes a big inhale in anticipation of what is to come.

However, this evening, she notices an unfamiliar yet delightful fragrance in the air. Nicki scans the room, as usual admiring the distressed wood adorning the western wall of Wyatt's immaculate kitchen. Complete with Viking appliances, black granite countertops, rift oak cabinets, and stunning wrought iron pendent lights, the kitchen exudes a refined taste. She should be used to the grandeur by now, but every time she sets foot in his home, it's as though she's entering a magical land, one where style, elegance, and class rule.

Nicki reflects upon Wyatt and how everything he touches turns to gold. His recording studio in Manhattan is skyrocketing. In the past three weeks, he'd signed two up-and-coming musicians. Plus, last month, the SoHo art gallery he recently invested in had made the front page of the *New York Times*'s Arts section.

Smiling, Nicki also acknowledges the impact Wyatt's had on her. She's no longer a grown-up version of the Hawley High prom queen. No, Nicki's developed into a sophisticated woman—one who knows what she wants and plans on getting it, all of it, no matter what the cost.

Sure, she began her path to improvement before she met Wyatt. Nicki had made changes to her wardrobe and bought the antique store, revamping it to feature mostly upscale items. After all, more and more New Yorkers were buying vacation homes in the area, and they wanted chic mountain modern, not the Pocono country style she'd grown up with.

Despite her personal transformation plan, Nicki needed guidance. And the moment Wyatt walked into her shop, she knew she'd found her ticket out. Not only did Wyatt leave her antique store with a carful of unique accents for his new home, but he also found a woman, twenty years younger than he, ready to meet his every need.

Dressed in slim-cut black pants, a soft cashmere tunic, and black boots—so opposite from the form-fitting synthetic sweaters, low-end designer jeans, and replica UGG boots she used to wear—Nicki lets her mind shift to tonight, envisioning Wyatt uncorking one of his cellared wines as they casually prepare an intimate Valentine's dinner together, albeit two days early.

Once she found out Billy was scheduled for the evening shift at the fire station, Nicki texted Wyatt to let him know she would be free this Friday night. Billy's shift began at five o'clock, so there wouldn't be enough time for him to come home to change out of his FedEx uniform. Nicki knows how much Billy hates to be late, so she felt confident he'd head straight to the fire station. This would give her extra time to finish up at the store before she prepared for tonight without worrying about her husband stopping home and wondering why she was dressed up.

Besides, she told Billy she'd be spending the night with her best friend, Debbie. Billy understands Valentine's weekend is tough for Debbie, who's thirty-five, single, and perpetually sad about not having a man in her life. Nicki said she promised to hang out with Debbie tonight so she could spend the fourteenth with him. Plus, Nicki claimed if she slept at Debbie's, she wouldn't have to worry about driving home after having drinks. Of course, this made sense to Billy.

Nicki sighs then crosses her fingers, praying Billy never asks Debbie about this. But she knows he won't. Billy trusts Nicki. That familiar pang of guilt punches Nicki in her gut, causing her to realize the lying must end. As usual, she ignores the signal, claiming she's waiting for the perfect time to come clean with Billy.

She consciously returns her focus to the present and with it, more pleasant thoughts. No doubt Wyatt brought aged sirloins from Citarella, the gourmet market two blocks from his Upper East Side apartment. Nicki hopes dinner will end with those amazing heart-shaped Portuguese custard tarts from the bakery he took her to that weekend she told her husband she was visiting her cousin who lives in Brooklyn. Nicki certainly dropped enough hints about the tarts to Wyatt when they spoke on the phone last night. That, and what she'd do to him after dessert.

Nicki emits a sigh. A tinge of shame returns as she reflects on the most recent lie she told Billy. Claiming she needed a walk to calm her jitters from too much coffee, she quickly left the house then sneaked into the backyard shed so she could telephone Wyatt.

Sure, a part of her continues to love Billy. He's sweet, Hawley Falls sweet. Nevertheless, Nicki's aspirations are much higher than settling for a nice guy who has no desire to leave this Podunk Pocono town.

The last time she saw Wyatt, they'd talked about moving in together. However, first, Nicki must leave Billy and end their seventeen-year marriage. She tightly squeezes her eyes shut, as if to dismiss this idea and all the pain and effort involved. Nicki feels the air leave her chest, but only for a few moments.

She quickly forgets her guilt when she spies what's on top of the kitchen counter. There, on a pewter platter, are two huge sirloin steaks, rub already applied, waiting to be grilled. An empty bottle of 2013 Don Melchor Cabernet is on the counter, its contents in a decanter next to an unlit candle. Taking in the soothing sounds of John Coltrane emanating from the Bose speakers, Nicki smoothes her hair then notices the dark pink peonies in a vase on the granite island. Peonies in February? That was the scent she had noticed.

Like always, Wyatt's thought of everything. It's been two weeks since they've been together, and she's missed him. Maintaining a long-distance relationship can be challenging, especially one that's hidden. But Nicki senses tonight will be special, a night she'll remember forever. Imagining what will occur *after* dinner causes that familiar warmth to stir her body.

The house is quiet. Nicki surmises Wyatt must be working upstairs in his office. She recalls how he complained a bit about a young rapper he's about to sign who has given him constant headaches. She suspects Wyatt's in the final stage of negotiating this contract, and it's wearing on him. Regardless, Nicki knows how to calm Wyatt's stress.

A demure smile comes across her collagen-inflated lips as she decides to surprise Wyatt. Instead of calling out the familiar, "Hey, hon, I'm here," she quietly exits the kitchen and tiptoes into the dimly lit hallway that leads to the home's main living space. But once she enters the high-vaulted great room, Nicki freezes. She sees two wine-glasses on top of the coffee table—the one he bought from her store. White wine partially fills one of the glasses. However, it is the bright red lipstick on the empty glass that catches Nicki's eye. *Why was he drinking wine with a woman? Who was she?* Her heart rate quickens, and her hands begin to tremble.

As this thought sweeps through her brain, something in her peripheral vision causes her to turn her head toward the front entrance. Immediately, Nicki's hand flies to her mouth, preventing her from emitting a bloodcurdling scream.

Crimson's everywhere—on the stone wall, across the iron banister, and all over the glass front door. Splatters of blood violently desecrate the foyer of the immaculate vacation home Wyatt had bought over two years ago, right before they'd met that November afternoon in her antique shop.

In the slowest of motions, Nicki forces her eyes to transition down to Wyatt's body, which is lying lifeless on the hardwood floor. Head cocked to the left, his eyes stare toward the steel-and-bronze chandelier hanging over him. Even in this state, she can't help but notice Wyatt's classic features: a Roman nose, defined cheekbones, and a chiseled chin. However, his thick salt-and-pepper hair, that she so loved to run her fingers through, now hosts a nauseating shade of bright red. As Nicki's eyes fixate on her slain lover, she becomes aware of the slashes on his chest and side. His once-gray cashmere sweater now bears scarlet crisscrosses. Blood trickles from his core, beginning to form a puddle on the hardwood below.

Nicki's torso begins to shake. Slow involuntary spasms transition to full-body heaves, accompanied by unrecognizable guttural sounds. She forces herself to move closer, toward Wyatt. Hesitantly, she touches his cleanly shaven face. His skin remains warm.

It's then Nicki feels a rush of cold air. She turns to see the front door is slightly ajar, allowing the wintry wind to snake its way into the foyer. Whoever did this failed to shut the door when he left, after he murdered Wyatt.

A tornado of thoughts floods her head. *Who did this? Why Wyatt? Could it be related to his work?*

Reflexively, her attention shifts from her dead lover to herself. *Will the killer come after me next? Does he even know I exist? Why am I saying he? It could be a woman who did this—that would explain the lipstick. What do I do? I should call the police. But they'll ask questions. They'll want to know why I had a key. My God, I could be a suspect. And if I tell them the truth, well, I can't do that. Then Billy would find out—everyone would know my secret.*

In situations where the body and mind find themselves overwhelmed by opposing forces, people behave in inexplicable ways. And that is exactly what Nicki Keating does. She runs, understandably distraught over the violent death of her lover. Nevertheless, that's not the root cause for her retreat. She's terrified of being discovered, found out for cheating on her husband and losing her meticulously created identity. Without second-guessing herself, Nicki sprints into the dark, freezing snowstorm, desperately searching for an escape route. But to where?

THE BEGINNING
December 18

"**H**oney, I can't hook this. Would you help me?" I ask, standing in a midthigh floral cotton robe as I struggle with the clasp of my diamond necklace, a treasured piece that was once my mother's.

"Of course," Tom says softly. Seconds later, he easily manipulates the tiny clasp with his nimble, highly insured fingers.

"You know, we *could* skip tonight and have that alone time we never seem to find. After all, Patrick *is* spending the night at Pete's." I look pleadingly at my husband as the tip of my right index finger seductively traces the perimeter of a button on his crisply starched tux shirt.

Tom ignores my playfulness. My husband is all business tonight. "I know you hate these things, Marlee, but we need to go." Tom offers me a warm smile. "Besides, it's only once a year, and from what the office manager said, it looks like mostly everyone's attending. Even Michael's coming ... and he's bringing a date," Tom says, raising his slightly graying eyebrows before moving to the bathroom mirror to straighten his black bow tie.

"Well, then ... that alone might be reason to go. This may be a first for Michael," I say as I follow Tom into the master bathroom, a slight smirk forming on my thin lips. Facing the mirrored wall over the sinks, I awkwardly pull a strand of coppery-brown hair from behind my ear, trying to "frame my face"—I think that is what my hairdresser called it when she insisted on adding a few layers to what she claimed was "too long for my age" hair. However, I wanted to grow it again. Letting out a sigh, I acknowledge how much easier it would be to pull it back into a ponytail, my go-to style. But that would not be acceptable tonight.

All week I've been obsessing about Tom's office party. Mingling with some of the male surgeons' spouses can be difficult for me. If tonight's anything like past events, it's bound to be filled with awkward conversations and insincere interactions.

At times, I wonder if I have anything in common with these women. At least that's what my nagging inner voice, who I've come to call Margaret, has been telling me all week. Margaret's been living in my head for some time. She means well. And I know her comments are meant to keep me disciplined, safe, someone who doesn't make mistakes. However, Margaret's constant barrage exhausts me. She expects perfection, and when she doesn't get it, well, she knows exactly what to say to shatter any remaining confidence I may have.

Showing up tonight is the least I can do for Tom. He works so hard and asks so little of me. Recently, he's either taking a late shift at the hospital or sequestered in his home office, reading up on the latest studies. I feel guilty about wanting to stay home tonight. Still, thinking about the next five hours overwhelms me.

Perhaps it's because I feel so out of place at formal events. Sure, it can be fun to dress up occasionally. To be truthful, fashion's not my thing. It's people who intrigue me, what makes them tick, not how they look. I guess that explains my profession. After all, for writers to remain authentic, they must be curious about individuals as well as the motivation behind their actions.

Turning my head toward the walk-in closet, I see the newly purchased Stuart Weitzman high-heeled shoes sitting prominently on the top shelf. This mere sight causes my feet to ache. It's as though my soles know how uncomfortable they'll feel by eight o'clock tonight. Since I ran a marathon five years ago, it hurts to wear heels.

Sadly, I admit the black velvet flats that are my go-to shoes for holiday events won't work with the dress I plan to wear tonight.

Straining my neck closer to the mirror, I loudly exhale before reaching into the top cabinet drawer to retrieve the blush compact. Damn, when did I become so pale? Now that I think of it, I haven't been in the sun since Columbus Day weekend, when we went to Cape May. I let out a sigh as I remember those long walks Tom and I took on the beach, soaking in the gorgeous sunshine—that is, when we weren't standing along the sidelines of Patrick's soccer games. His club team was playing in a Columbus Day tournament. However, soccer was the reason we went; it was not meant to be a romantic getaway at the beach. I sense my jaw clench, knowing how much Tom and I would benefit from more time alone.

Nevertheless, the weekend did provide a much-needed break. I distinctly remember leaving for the shore two hours after I submitted that article about holistic healing to Brad, my editor. While I'm thrilled he loved the piece, last week Brad asked me to write a follow-up. Luckily, it's not due till the end of February because I'm not so sure I know where to begin.

"Did I tell you about my next assignment?" I close the compact then turn to look at Tom standing next to me at the gray marble countertop.

Tom shakes his head, unable to properly respond as he brushes his teeth. Or at least that is what I tell myself. Taking advantage of my captive audience, I start to explain.

"Well, since readers appeared to like that article I wrote in October—you remember, the one about the upsurge of holistic medicine and the roadblocks these practitioners face? Well, Brad wants me to do a follow-up. This time I'm supposed to highlight the most successful practices here in the Philadelphia area. You know, share what people are doing to heal themselves ... physically, emotionally, and spiritually." I hesitate to add the last part because I know how Tom feels.

I watch as my husband spits toothpaste in the sink then rinses his electric toothbrush before carefully placing it back into its stand. "An interesting assignment for a doctor's wife," he says as he wipes his hands on the towel hanging from a rack to the right of his sink before smoothing out his thick slightly graying hair. A traditionalist, Tom's skeptical of natural healing, often citing studies that disprove their proposed benefits.

"I guess you could look at it that way." Tonight, I'm calmly standing my ground. We've had this conversation before, and I usually back down. "Actually, I think this assignment will prove to be interesting. I have no idea what's out there and who is doing what. So I need to conduct a lot of research." I pause to apply a touch more mascara, hoping to make myself look a bit more sophisticated. "Who knows, you may come home to Himalayan salt lamps, burning sage, and meditative music playing in the background," I tease as I put the mascara away then gently kiss the back of Tom's neck. Looking into mirror, I can see Tom smiling, but he does not turn toward me. I'm sure his mind is focused on tonight and the never-ending office politics that inevitably surface at these events.

Although my husband and I respect one another professionally, I reluctantly admit I care little about his work and suspect he feels the same about mine. Occasionally we'll talk shop at home, but we've both chosen to keep our careers separate from our marriage, a formula that appears to be successful. Sure, I'd love the chance to run ideas for articles past Tom for his input. After all, if I can convince him, a conservative Republican who thrives on meat and potatoes, to see my point of view, then I know I have a shot of writing a quality piece. Yet, whenever I've solicited his advice, he offers a few kind words, nothing else. And he's made it clear that when he's home he doesn't want to talk about his patients or the office. Tom views our home as sacred turf; it's his time with Patrick and me. I guess that explains his immediate distance as soon as his beeper sounds.

Looking at my watch, I realize I cannot delay the inevitable any longer, so I walk into the closet, take the black cocktail dress that cost more than I wanted to spend off its hanger, and carefully ease into the formfitting dress. Then I put on a pair of simple diamond studs that complement my mother's pendant necklace before grabbing those dreaded black shoes off the top shelf. While the purse I placed on the bureau does not exactly match, it will do.

"You look stunning. You know that, don't you?" Tom says in a tone more declarative than inquisitive.

Although I can often "make it work," Margaret's made it clear—*You will never be beautiful, Marlee.* Instead, my features tend to be wholesome and warm. I'm the type of person strangers feel comfortable approaching. Whether asking which aisle they can find the organic peanut butter on or inquiring what's the best preschool in the area, random people seem to feel at ease around me. It's as if they instinctively know I'm safe, have the answers they need, and will be open to helping them. I've assumed it's because I don't look intimidating. I guess I'm *somewhat* attractive, though certainly not gorgeous; tall, but not towering; fit, yet far from perfectly shaped. In my high school yearbook, someone wrote, "Marlee O'Brien projects competence, care, character, and control. Should a crisis occur, she's the one you want to be with."

That's who I am in a nutshell. However, a tiny part of me longs to be the glamorous, mysterious, somewhat aloof seductress who doesn't have a care in the world. I laugh at the thought.

***

As we pull out of the garage, flurries gracefully land on the windshield. Perhaps we'll have a white Christmas after all. It's only a week until the twenty-fifth.

Like most women my age, I've been focused on "the list" and checking off each item— shopping, wrapping, baking, decorating— even sending out the last-minute additions to our ever-growing Christmas card list. As intense as this time of the year feels, I believe the chaos actually feeds my holiday spirit. And tonight, as much as I hate to admit it, represents one more annual event that contributes to *our* Christmas. Besides, this is important to Tom, so I decide to adjust my attitude.

On the way to the party, Tom concentrates on the somewhat slippery road as I remain silent, focusing on tonight. Instead of hiding by the shrimp bowl and consuming one too many glasses of red wine, I'm going to challenge myself to meet three intriguing and authentic females who contribute to this world in some unique fashion. Of course, this exercise will force me to exit my comfort zone and initiate conversations. And I'll need to know when to gracefully excuse myself in order to search for the next possible candidate.

I feel a grin emerge on my face. This actually might be fun. What if I thought of it like a game or, better yet, an assignment? That's it—I'll pretend Brad asked me to do a piece on the most genuine spouses at tonight's office party. Suppressing a slight giggle, I congratulate myself for having thought of such a bizarre approach to quell this ridiculous anxiety I have regarding tonight. I hope it works.

***

Twenty minutes later, we arrive at the Bellevue, one of downtown Philadelphia's top hotels. The party's being held in the Conservatory. Jefferson Hospital's Orthopedic Department rarely splurges on its physicians. However, tonight is always the exception. With over seventy surgeons in this unit, plus office staff and all of the spouses, the place is bound to be packed. In an effort to calm the butterflies reeling inside of me, I remind myself to focus on my "challenge."

After getting out of the car, I stand up a bit straighter, pull my shoulders back, and prepare for this self-assigned adventure. Tom places his hand at the small of my back and leads me into the hotel lobby.

As soon as we enter the Conservatory, I'm drawn to the elegant fountain located in the center of the ballroom. This is certainly no ordinary fountain. Its water, a luminous shade of green, rises up a clear tube strategically hidden within the tiered pale pink poinsettias. Once at the top, it cascades over the tube's rim, flowing into a shallow pool below. My attention then shifts to the far corner of the enormous room where a forties-style swing band, band members dressed in white dinner jackets and red cummerbunds, plays "It's the Most Wonderful Time of the Year." I feel my jaw relax, unexpectedly soothed by these festive surroundings. Since I was little, I've been captivated by the magic of this season.

Then, out of the corner of my eye, I spot a tall, slender man with silver, wire-framed spectacles and a grimacing look approaching us. Without even a small effort to acknowledge me, he steps a bit too close to Tom and begins spouting a tirade of complaints. Reluctantly, Tom offers me the "sorry, I've got to deal with this" look as he excuses himself then ushers this man toward an unoccupied area of the room. Remaining within earshot, I overhear part of their conversation. It looks like this man's bending Tom's ear in an attempt to gain backing to his proposal for a new surgical procedure. Watching Tom's tense body language, I sense my husband doesn't share this man's passion. Tom looks trapped. I walk toward them then gently place my hand on Tom's arm.

"Honey, I hate to interrupt ... you two appear deep in conversation," I say as I flash a sweet yet contrived smile, "but the babysitter's texting me with a question about the remote." I speak with a tone designed to convey helplessness tinged with embarrassment for obviously not comprehending the workings of a television remote.

"Excuse me, Doug, can we catch up later in the office?"

As we walk away, Tom puts his arm around my shoulders, pulling me toward him as he whispers, "Thank you. When did you become such a crafty liar? We haven't had a babysitter for years."

"Well, that's all I could come up with. You looked miserable, and I thought you'd appreciate a way out," I say, somewhat proud of my ingenuity. However, it's Tom's compliment that pleases me most.

"Doug's one of those guys who's brilliant but has a negative social IQ. He's excellent with knee replacements, one of the best. Still, everyone in the office pretty much avoids him. He can't take a hint. Plus, Doug can be insulting, though I doubt that's his intention," Tom says as we weave our way through the crowded room.

We pass by the fountain as we head to the bar located at the back of the large atrium. Tom steers me toward a couple standing in line waiting to order drinks.

"Marlee, I'd like you to meet Jared and Sophia Robbins. Jared's our top shoulder guy, and Sophia's a physician." Tom fails to share more. My guess is he's never asked Jared about Sophia's specialty.

Before me stands the most stunning couple. Jared's tall and lean, and his white hair and perfectly trimmed beard project a certain sophistication. While he appears somewhat older than Tom—and his wife—his warm smile and crystal-blue eyes have a youthfulness to them. Something tells me his patients have the utmost trust in him.

The woman by his side is breathtaking, standing nearly as tall as her husband. I'd say she's at least five foot nine without the amazing stiletto heels she's wearing. A part of me becomes envious, wondering how she can actually walk in those shoes.

"It's a pleasure to meet both of you," I say, entranced by the woman's emerald-green eyes. Something inside tells me these two are unlike others I've met at these events. I look closely at Sophia. Her jet-black hair is swept into a tight chignon, and her olive complexion hints at a Mediterranean lineage. Dressed in a burgundy, strapless silk gown that's perfectly fitted, she exudes pure grace.

As the men remain in line for the bar, Sophia and I move to an open high-top table where it's not so crowded.

"Jared speaks so highly of Tom. I can tell he has a great deal of respect for his work." Her voice is deep yet compassionate, no doubt a useful tool for her practice.

Unsure of what this elegant-looking doctor might possibly be interested in, I only say, "And Tom admires your husband too."

"I think they share a lot of the same philosophies regarding office politics." Sophia winks, and her Audrey Hepburn–like nose twitches somewhat, giving me a bit of assurance that she may be one of the "good spouses."

"Do you deal with the same issues in your practice?" I ask, curious to learn more about Sophia's medical specialty.

"Actually, there are only four of us at our office, so naturally things are simpler. However, I am friends with other internists who work at larger practices, and they claim to have the same issues as our husbands. What about you, Marlee … Do you work?" Sophia asks as she casually tilts her head in a curious manner.

Noting this might be the first time anyone's asked me that question at one of these office parties, I pause before answering, truly appreciating the interest.

"I'm a journalist. I freelance for the *Philadelphia Inquirer*. I mostly write articles for the Health and Science section. It's only part time," I say with a slight shrug of my shoulders. "It's perfect … at least for now."

"How long have you been writing?" Sophia's eyes glimmer, and she appears genuinely interested.

"I believe the paper published my first article when our son Patrick was ten, so six years ago," I say, sighing after realizing how much time has passed. Instinctively, my hand travels to my temple, as if surprised that it's been that long. "Actually, I've been writing for various companies since I graduated from college. My first job was for a pharmaceutical firm, scripting its sales literature. Then I heard about a position at Jefferson. Apparently, the administration was directed by the board to create a Patient Advocacy Department, and the hospital required someone with experience in health care who knew how to write. I applied and, luckily, was hired shortly afterward. That's when I met Tom." Momentarily, I flash back to when we first bumped into each other in the hospital's cafeteria.

"I would love to read your work. What topics have you written about for the *Inquirer*?" Sophia asks, bringing me back to the present.

"Pretty much everything … the pros and cons of vaccinations, the latest birth control options, the environmental hazards from traffic on the Schuylkill Expressway, and the top addiction facilities in southeast PA. Most recently, I wrote about the challenges holistic medicine faces," I say, appreciative someone tonight is actually interested in my work.

"I definitely want to read that article," Sophia's eyes widen as she leans closer. "The topic fascinates me. My medical training in Milan focused on traditional methods. However, there is so much more. If only more people could open their minds to different ways …" Her voice trails off. "Well, I believe it would promote healing on multiple levels." Sophia looks at me, her frosted pink lips open as if wanting to say more.

I cannot help smiling, knowing not only have I identified one authentic female, but I've also found a doctor who is truly interested in holistic medicine. And I was right about her Mediterranean ancestry—Sophia's from Italy. Tonight's certainly proceeding differently than Tom's previous holiday parties.

I look up and see our husbands approaching the table. Tom hands me a glass of pinot noir.

"Jared, Marlee is a journalist for the *Inquirer* and has recently published an article addressing holistic medicine and its challenges. I cannot wait to read it. You know, this *is* the future of medicine," Sophia says with conviction as she gently places her hand on her husband's arm.

Feeling a bit self-conscious, I begin to blush, unaccustomed to receiving praise, let alone attention, at Tom's office events.

"I have to say it was well written," Tom chimes in as an unanticipated grin comes over his cleanly shaven face.

Could he actually be proud of you?

Margaret's dismissive, if not surprised. Still, this is the first time Tom's complimented me about that article.

"Of course, I have doubts about methods that lack the proper studies to back them." He pauses for a moment and takes a sip of his scotch before continuing. "Perhaps they work, at least for some people," he adds, safeguarding his prior statement as he clears his throat.

I'm shocked. Never in a million years would I expect my husband to utter such encouraging words about holistic healing. In fact, he's only expressed reservations about this topic. I can't remember him ever insinuating possible benefits to these practices. But I don't call him out. Instead, I lock onto his eyes and give him a quick wink, my way to say, "Thank you."

"I will most definitely check it out," Jared says, raising his white eyebrows. Something in the tone of his voice tells me he will.

"Sophia, do you and Jared have children?" I ask, directing the conversation away from me. As the words come out of my mouth, I begin to cringe inside. It's then Margaret reappears in my head.

Why did you ask that? What if they're unable to have children?

Margaret's tone is degrading, causing my throat to constrict.

To my relief, I watch as Sophia's face begins to glow, her left fingers momentarily graze the elegant gold cross hanging on a delicate chain around her slender neck. "Yes, we have two ... Lizzy and Max. Lizzy works in retail in New York City, and Max is a senior at Brown. It is difficult when they leave home." Sophia blinks her eyes before continuing: "I guess that is what happens when they grow up." I notice Jared squeeze Sophia's free hand as she says this. "You said you have a son?" she asks, as she once again tilts her head in interest.

"Yes, he's our only child," I say, envisioning Patrick and reminding myself that at any moment our easygoing son who has so far stayed out of trouble could find himself in multiple situations that do not end well. It's one of the reasons I pray every night before going to sleep.

As our conversation continues, I know I've identified the first of three intriguing and genuine women. But if I want to complete my challenge, I must find two more.

As if he could read my mind, Tom says, "Hey, there's Michael and his date. This is the first time he's brought a woman to one of these events." He winks at Jared who seems equally amused. "We've got to go and meet her. It's been great seeing you both." Tom casually pats Jared's shoulder as he excuses us.

Quickly and sincerely, I add, "I've truly enjoyed meeting you, Sophia." To which Sophia warmly smiles as she places both of her soft, slender hands around mine, graciously returning the sentiment.

As we approach this younger couple, a tender sensation comes over me as I lean toward Michael and give him a hug. Besides being absolutely gorgeous—Michael resembles Matt Bomer from the TV show *White Collar*—of all of Tom's coworkers, Michael Sutton's my favorite. In a strange way, my feelings about this up-and-coming surgeon waver between a schoolgirl crush and a mature woman's desire to nurture. I first met Michael when he joined Tom's practice as a resident. Since then, my husband's taken it upon himself to mentor the young surgeon. Michael frequently comes to our home for dinner and has even celebrated holidays with us and what remains of the extended Ryan and O'Brien families. Michael is from Tucson, and Jefferson's orthopedic on-call schedule makes it difficult to travel, especially for residents and newer surgeons.

After releasing Michael from my embrace, my eyes reflexively dart to the gorgeous woman by his side. I try not to judge whether this female is *good enough* for Michael. Unsure if this relationship qualifies as "serious," I still find a part of me is secretly thrilled he's finally brought a date to one of these parties.

Michael's certainly not shy; he's actually the opposite. This dark-haired, fit orthopedic surgeon has a swagger that appears to be a magnet for beautiful women. No doubt Michael's one of the most sought-after bachelors in Philadelphia. There rarely seems to be *one* woman who he sees, and he certainly does not show up with any of them at office functions. It's as if Michael prefers the freedom bachelorhood grants and has consciously chosen to remain single. But tonight, I sense something different.

Michael warmly shakes Tom's hand. However, I'm focused on the woman, standing to his right, who most definitely has not reached her thirtieth birthday. Immediately, I'm drawn to her turquoise catlike eyes, which glisten more than the twinkle lights positioned around the atrium. I reluctantly acknowledge a tinge of jealousy regarding her youthful beauty and seemingly perfect body. Several inches shorter than I, Michael's date undoubtedly doesn't wear anything larger than a size 2.

In an unexpectedly natural manner, Michael introduces us to *his girlfriend*, Juliette Greene. Intensely curious about this woman, who's wearing a short, sexy, little black dress and is apparently more than *just a date*, I need to know how she's snagged Michael. Sure, she's gorgeous, but Michael's dated models before. What makes this one so special?

Are you jealous she's with Michael?

Margaret's unexpected comment causes me to cringe. Damn, she may be right.

In an effort to learn more about Juliette and how she earned the title of *Michael's girlfriend*, I begin to engage this woman standing closely by his side. In no time, I discover Juliette owns a yoga studio in downtown Philly, lived in an ashram in India for six months, and received a doctorate in philosophy from Yale. My mind's spinning. Where did Michael find her?

Unable to resist the urge to understand more, I unashamedly monopolize Juliette as Tom and Michael talk about work. After several minutes, I notice both of our glasses are empty. Trying to appear nonchalant, I suggest we leave the men and go to the bar to grab another drink.

"So how did you two first meet?" I ask as soon as we're alone. Casually, I untuck a strand of hair behind my ear, once again trying to "frame my face" as I look attentively at Juliette.

"It all started at my cousin's annual Halloween bash. He has a pretty sweet apartment in Rittenhouse Square. It's about a block from my studio." Juliette's tone is upbeat, uninhibited, direct. "Anyway, he had been bugging me to come to one of his parties, and honestly, I had no excuse to not go this time ... except for the obvious ... I didn't want to wear a costume." Juliette rolls her eyes, and immediately I relate to this woman. As much as I love Halloween, I, too, hate to dress up.

She continues speaking as we both hand our glasses to the bartender who generously refills them with wine. "Finally, he shamed me into coming, so I showed up in my yoga clothes. Figured why not? After all, it's who I am, right?" She lets out an uninhibited laugh. "Anyway, I notice this cute guy hanging by the bar. It was kind of hard not to see him." Juliette heaves out a bit of a sigh as she runs her fingers through her stylishly tousled golden hair.

"There must have been three or four girls, all in somewhat slutty Halloween outfits, vying for his attention. I sensed this was a typical Saturday night for him ... surrounded by a medieval wench, a French maid, and a life-size kitty cat." Juliette pauses as she tries to suppress a laugh but fails. A quirky smile unapologetically appears on her face. "He must have sensed me watching because before I knew it, Michael left the women and came over to introduce himself to me. Well, that was it." Juliette's expression shifts, becoming serene as we walk away from the bar toward an open high-top table.

Interestingly, Juliette's not gloating as if she were better than those women at the party. Instead, it's as though she knew she and Michael were meant to be together, a fate of sorts.

"That's a great 'how we met' story, Juliette. Makes you believe in true love." I dangle the bait as I nonchalantly lean against the table, attempting to give my feet a break as I wait and see if this intriguing yoga instructor with a doctorate in philosophy bites. Unable to grasp a solid read on this woman, I'm debating whether she is *right* for Michael.

Who the hell are you to determine that?

Laughing casually and totally oblivious to the chastising voice lurking inside my mind, Juliette lets her head fall slightly backward. "True love ... we'll see about that. All I know is it's working, and for the first time in forever, I like who I'm sleeping with." Juliette's turquoise eyes glow, and an ethereal look comes across her face. "I know it sounds strange, but for a while, it became more about the sex than the guy. It's not like I didn't care about them—I certainly did—or I would not have dated them in the first place." She pauses, and I can see her shoulders slide down her sculpted back. "I think I was searching for something else, like a spiritual experience." Juliette sighs then her eyes shift upward to the glass windows in the atrium. "I learned that requires more than physical attraction. There has to be a deeper connection, you know what I mean?" She takes a sip of wine then sets the glass on the high-top. "Then I met Michael, and well, things kinda came together." Juliette's face softens as she looks at me, as if trying to ascertain if I understand.

"Yes, it's been some time, but I totally recall that feeling," I say, thinking of my early twenties. "I would always fall headfirst, and then after a few months, I'd see the real person. I usually didn't love what I saw, so I'd retreat. I remember it was different with Tom." I pause, wondering if I truly believe my own verbiage.

"Exactly! With Michael, it was kind of like we had a tentative dance, unsure as to whether or not we wanted to continue to the next song or get off the dance floor," Juliette says as she chuckles and shakes her head.

I nod, becoming more confident this woman is authentic and perhaps deserves to be with Michael. She may even be good for him.

It's then Tom and Michael join us. Juliette and I listen to the guys rehash tales from working together at Jefferson. However, I'm more focused on Michael's behavior and his unusual attentiveness toward Juliette than I am on their old stories. I notice the way he looks at her and how they hold hands beneath the table.

I glance at my watch, surprised to see it's close to ten thirty. My feet are killing me, and tomorrow's schedule is packed. Patrick must be at soccer practice by eight o'clock. Surprisingly, I'm actually having fun at Tom's holiday party and am in no rush to leave. Plus, I haven't met the third interesting woman of the night. However, my sensible side overrides my desire to complete "my assignment," so I give Tom the look, the one that says, *It's time to go.* As usual, he pretends not to notice. Then, as I'm about to deliver the second signal, the nudge under the table, a couple I don't recall ever meeting approaches.

"Marlee and Juliette, this is Jonathon Thompson. He's our new head of orthopedic surgery," Tom says as he rises to greet the man and woman who are now standing next to our table.

Jonathon, a somewhat balding man with short, dark coiled hair who looks to be in his late forties, offers a genuine smile as he shakes our hands then introduces his wife, Annie, to the group. Jonathon shares Annie is a psychologist, specializing in teens, and works at a practice located downtown near Ludlow and North Twenty-First Street. Annie gives us a pleasant smile, but I can't help noticing how drained she appears. This petite brunette dressed in a conservative long sleeve black cocktail dress bears dark circles under her eyes. I watch as she tries to cover up a slight yawn. No doubt her caseload doesn't meld well with late-night events such as tonight. Annie appears to do her best in her role as the department head's wife. Although she attempts to be cheery, her sallow complexion tells me she would much rather be in bed, curled up with a good book.

Noting our party's growing, I see a larger table, one with actual seating, is now available. "Let's all move over here where there's more room," I say, as I gratefully sit down on an empty chair.

Graciously, Annie nods then takes a seat next to me. She's sipping on what appears to be club soda and lime. "How nice to get off of my feet. It's been a long week, and I'm wiped out," she says before quickly adding, "But, of course, it's nice to be here tonight." Annie pauses, looking extremely uncomfortable, as if she's unsure how to proceed.

"I can't imagine how stressful your job must be. Working with troubled kids, you've got to have a ton of patience," Juliette says after joining us, perhaps in an attempt to break the ice. "Sure, we're all busy at times, but I bet you're operating at a whole other level."

I readily agree. "Yes, I mostly control my schedule. I presume your day depends on your caseload and which patients need to be seen."

Annie sighs. "It can be overwhelming, but I love my clients … They're everything to me … except, of course, for Jonathon."

She looks lovingly toward her husband who appears to be enjoying his conversation with Michael and Tom. "Still, with both our schedules, we barely see each other." Annie's chin drops toward her chest, and her smile fades. It's at this moment she appears tiny, like a young girl.

However, it's more than her actions that draw me to this observation. There's a timidity with how she expresses herself. No doubt she's extremely dedicated to her profession and is probably an excellent psychologist. Regardless, it's as though Annie has no life outside of work. She didn't mention any children. And if her husband's as busy as Tom says he is, Annie's accurate in claiming they spend little time together. Instantly, my heart fills with compassion for this woman. It's as if she's an innocent soul striving to do what she feels she must to help others. Unfortunately, somewhere in the process, she began to miss out on living her own life.

Annie is my final interesting woman of the evening ... Sophia, Juliette, and Annie ... mission accomplished.

Twenty minutes later, the men finally take Annie's and my repeated hints it's time to go, accepting the women are tired and the night's over.

The four of us say goodnight to Michael and Juliette as we head toward the hotel's entrance. Tom searches his inside left jacket pocket for the valet ticket while I glance back at the young couple who remain at the table. I watch as Michael leans toward Juliette, his expression softening as he places his arm around his *girlfriend*.

After the valet retrieves our car, we say goodnight to Annie and Jonathon. But something inside tells me this isn't goodbye till the next holiday party. No, she, Juliette, and Sophia are most definitely different from women I've met at previous events. Could we possibly become friends?

What makes you think that? Remember, you don't do "friends" very well, Marlee.

I let out a sigh, acknowledging Margaret's analysis. She could be right. Perhaps tonight was merely four women, bored at their significant others' holiday party, who entertained one another. I ease into the passenger seat and kick off my high heels.

GAME DAY

January 2

Eyes barely open, I reach my right hand toward my phone to turn off its alarm. I sit up, leaning back against the upholstered headboard. Searching my emails for information about today's tournament, I say a quick prayer it's been canceled due to the forecasted storm. What I'd give for a chance to sleep in on a Saturday morning.

However, weekend tournaments are part of travel soccer, and Patrick's team is scheduled to play this morning at a new indoor facility in Maryland. As much as I enjoy watching my son as center midfielder during his high school games, I dread his club matches. His club coach, who I'm not a fan of, prefers to play him in goal. And that is one thing I cannot bear—I hate it when my son wears that damn goalie shirt.

The mere thought of him being the last line of defense causes my jaw to clench, resulting in a throbbing sensation on the left side of my face—the exact feeling I have right now. I emit a loud sigh in acceptance there's no cancellation email in my inbox. It must not have snowed much, or at least not in Maryland, so the tournament is on.

Reluctant to get up, I slide under the covers and pull the comforter to my shoulders. Basking in the warmth of the down bedcover, I turn to my left and cuddle up next to Tom, all delay tactics to avoid the cold walk to the bathroom. Tom doesn't stir with my touch. However, it's our border collie, Roxie, who gently paws my leg, signaling it's time for me to get up. Knowing I cannot avoid the inevitable, I leave my husband in our cozy bed and begin my morning routine.

Luckily, I remembered to set the coffee pot's timer last night. I hear the soft percolating noise coming from downstairs, along with the faint aroma of French roast rising from the kitchen. Forcing myself into the shower, I fully embrace the hot water as it streams from the shower head, hitting the spot between my shoulder blades, the area that's usually tight. Roxie waits patiently on the fuzzy bathroom mat, knowing before long, she'll have her bowl of kibble.

After pulling on a pair of jeans and a light blue sweater, I begin to head downstairs. On the way, I stop at Patrick's door, ready to pop my head in and wake up my son. Of course, it's not necessary—Eminem's playing loudly through the shut door. I keep walking.

This is Patrick's pregame ritual. Unlike most kids his age, Patrick's an early riser, especially when it comes to soccer. And I can't recall him becoming anxious prior to games. Instead, he puts himself into a zone, no doubt a habit that will serve him well later in life. Still, I'm baffled a boy his age possesses such discipline. Shaking my head, I slowly descend the stairs, Roxie at my heels.

***

Within forty-five minutes we're parked outside the Jameses' home, located only a half mile from ours. The sun is beginning to rise. Looking around, I see there's only a slight dusting of snow on the ground and the roads are clear. I suppose the storm veered north of us.

Natalie James and I take turns driving to away games. While we are not close friends, it's nice to have company on the ride, as Patrick and Natalie's son, Matthew, usually listen to music through their headphones the entire trip. Plus, when the belligerent parents start acting up during the games, yelling at the refs and each other, I'm grateful Natalie's next to me. Both Natalie and

I are enthusiastic about this sport, but we know what is and is not appropriate parental conduct during U-17 soccer games. Usually, we're in the minority.

"Morning," Natalie says as she jumps into our eight-year-old Audi, careful not to spill the contents of her mug. It makes me chuckle, as Tom constantly teases me about my messy car. Although it's not even seven o'clock yet, Natalie's looking good. Her short auburn hair is partially covered by a stylish beige knit hat, and she's wearing slim-cut jeans and black leather boots.

"OK, what's your latest concoction?" I ask, knowing Natalie does not drink coffee, tea, or Diet Coke in the morning, like most of the other moms who struggle to arrive on time for these early away games.

"It's maté … See the cool mug and special spoon you use? Actually, maté is amazing … It has so many nutritional benefits. Plus, it's fun to drink," Natalie says in an upbeat manner as she takes off her puffy coat and fastens her seatbelt. Matthew mutters a brief "Hi, Mrs. Ryan," as he climbs into the backseat next to Patrick.

Natalie prides herself on knowing the latest health food craze. Though far from preachy, she's quick to share knowledge about her newest find. Last month, she was raving about the benefits of mushroom coffee. And in October, she was a walking encyclopedia regarding intermittent fasting. Natalie enrolled in an online course for some sort of certification. Slightly embarrassed, I admit to not always paying attention when Natalie goes into her health monologues. I silently sip on my strong black coffee, hoping my soccer mom friend will weave what I missed into the conversation.

"Do you want to take a sip? I learned about the wonders of maté, a form of tea, from one of the women I met in my new course … you know, the one I'm taking through Colorado Technical University for my Ayurveda certification."

Bingo! I knew she'd remind me.

"No thanks, I'm good with my coffee." I pause, momentarily wondering if perhaps I am missing out on some wonderful benefit. "So when will you be finished with the program? And what will you do with the certification?" I ask, looking both ways before pulling the car out onto the street.

"Actually, I'm halfway through the coursework. My goal, besides improving my own body's balance, is to become a coach of sorts, you know, assist women in finding their optimum health through Ayurveda. Perhaps I'll try to team up with a local medical practice. Did you know Ayurveda has been around forever? It's not like it's witchcraft or anything." Natalie laughs with a wave of her hand as she rolls her eyes. I'm amazed with the energy she has this morning. Could it be the maté?

Something clicks, and I'm reminded of my assignment. Understanding Ayurveda—whatever that is—could be useful when I finally sit down to write the article, the one I've been ignoring. But it's not due till the end of February. I have plenty of time.

***

The boys win their first two games. After a quick lunch at a nearby diner, the four of us return to the frigid indoor sports center for their third and final match. They're playing the top-ranked team in the tristate area. Knowing the arena is also used for ice hockey, Natalie and I are bundled up, equipped with heavy blankets and warm ski gloves. Nevertheless, I'm freezing. I expect in no time, however, the fear of my son in goal will soon cause droplets of sweat to appear on my forehead.

Despite my trepidation, I know Patrick is a good goalie—that is beside the point. For me, it's pure hell watching him, especially against teams like this one. With ten minutes to go, the game is tied at 3–3. Patrick holds his own, preventing any of the opposing players from scoring another goal. When the buzzer sounds, I sink back into the ice-cold metal bench. I know what's next—a penalty shoot-out. As the players line up to attempt the winning goal for their team, I squeeze my eyes shut, scrunch my nose, and pull the fleece blanket tightly around me, burying my face into its soft fur.

"Tell me when it's over, Natalie. I can't watch." Shoulders hunched near my ears, I shiver as my left temple and jaw violently throb.

"OK. You know the buzzer will ring when there's a goal."

"That's what I'm afraid of … someone scoring against Patrick."

"Don't worry. He'll be fine," Natalie says in a reassuring tone as she gingerly rubs my shoulders. She's used to being my eyes whenever the team goes into penalty kicks.

Hearing the crowd's loud reaction after each kick only magnifies the uncertainty and throbbing sensations. Worst-case scenarios, spoken in Margaret's voice, ping-pong through the recesses of my brain.

He could dive into the goalpost trying to save a ball.

He better watch out for the upper left side … his weak spot.

And you know he will feel total responsibility if his team loses this game.

A shrill buzz echoes in my ears. The game's over. A brief silence precedes a loud applause.

"Who won?" I tentatively ask, peeking my head out from the blanket as I open one eye at a time.

Natalie's smiling ear to ear, a good sign. She tilts her head toward the field. Summoning the courage to look, I witness my son, carried on top of two of the players' shoulders, beaming ear to ear.

"Guess it worked out?" I say as an awkward grin emerges on my face, embarrassed I resort to this behavior whenever there is a shoot-off.

"Marlee, Patrick was awesome! He had amazing saves. I wish you could watch your son. You know, needing to bury your head in the sand … or a blanket … it's kind of ridiculous. Do you realize you're clenching the left side of your jaw?" Natalie asks, shaking her head as she stands and begins to gather our belongings.

Acknowledging my soccer mom friend is 100 percent correct, I let out a long sigh, wishing I had the fortitude to watch my son during shoot-outs. Usually, I can handle all sorts of parental things: broken bones, bloody cuts, calls from the school—the normal stuff. But watching Patrick with those gloves on, being the last man of defense, well, that's my Achilles' heel. Unsure whether I'm terrified he'll sustain an injury or worried he'll bear the brunt of a loss, I find it easier to shrink, go within, and shield my eyes from the field. Watching is too damn painful.

The drive home proves to be more festive than the trip to Maryland. We stop at Friendly's for a celebratory ice cream despite it being the first Saturday in January.

When we pull up outside of the Jameses' home, Natalie leans over to me and says, "Seriously, you drive yourself nuts with this goalie stuff. I think I can help you. I've learned some things in my course that may be beneficial. Would you be willing to hear about them?"

Caught off guard, I agree without considering the implications of my answer. "Sure, that would be great."

"OK, I'm going to hold you to it. I'll call you later this week once I come up with a game plan," Natalie says with a tone of satisfaction in her voice before shutting the car door and scurrying inside.

Shit, I've opened up a Pandora's box. How will I get out of this one? Knowing there's time to devise an excuse, I shift my focus to the next thing—making dinner for a hungry boy. Tom is on call, so tonight it's only Patrick and me.

***

After doing dishes and putting the leftover pasta and salad in the refrigerator, Patrick heads to the basement to play video games. Somewhat tired, but not wanting to watch television, I sit at the kitchen counter and leaf through a copy of *Bon Appétit* as I wait for Tom to come home from his last rounds at the hospital. While perusing through delicious-looking recipes, one catches my eye: braised short ribs. After I read through the ingredients and directions, a part of me would love to try it out; however, it seems silly to go through all of the work for only the three of us. Maybe I'll invite some people over. Hmmm … Do we owe anyone? I don't think so.

While I'm in the midst of this thought, my phone pings. It's a text from Tom.

> Tom: *Be home shortly… catching up with Jonathon and Jared. Both enjoyed meeting you at the party. And Jared said Sophia asked for your cell so she could text you.*

Why not invite Sophia and Jared for dinner? I felt a strong connection when we met last month. Plus, this would give me a reason to try the short ribs recipe. As my attention returns to the magazine, I note the recipe serves eight. Eight? I'll also invite the Thompsons … and Juliette and Michael—that is, if they're still together.

Excited, I envision this newly evolving dinner party. My mind begins to wonder what salads and desserts would go well with short ribs. I walk to the pantry, pull my favorite cookbook from the shelf, and begin paging through it for those tried-and-true recipes. After retrieving a packet of sticky notes from the junk drawer, I mark several options. Next, I grab my laptop from where it's charging on the kitchen counter, open it, then look at the calendar for available weekend nights. In the midst of searching for Tom's call schedule, I quickly lose focus, and my attention shifts to the mark on the dining room wall.

You can't have people over unless you fix that.

Margaret's speaking, loud and clear.

Critically eyeing the long scratch Patrick made last May as he rushed through the room carrying his lacrosse stick, I make a mental note to fix the nicks on the woodwork and walls with the extra paint stored in the garage cabinet. Lost in these thoughts, I don't hear the garage door open. I jump a bit when Tom, who walks into the kitchen unnoticed, kisses the back of my head.

"I had the best idea," I say, turning to wrap my arms around Tom, kissing him softly on the lips.

"If you promise to greet me like this every time I come home, then I guess the answer's a definite yes," Tom says in a surprisingly refreshing manner after having rounds on a Saturday night.

"Good," I grin, opening the magazine to the page with the picture of the fabulous-looking short ribs, "because I want to have a few people over for dinner to make this recipe, and I thought it might be fun to invite your friends from work."

"Wow … who is this woman in our kitchen, and what did she do with my wife?" Tom playfully asks, raising his eyebrows as he moves toward the pantry and grabs a bag of pretzels.

"No, I'm serious. What if we invited the Robbins, the Thompsons, and Michael and Juliette, assuming they're still a couple?" I know Michael a bit too well. None of his past relationships have lasted more than a few weeks.

"I'd say it's a great idea. What made you want to do this?" Tom asks, taking a bite of a sourdough pretzel as he looks at me suspiciously.

"Let's just say I enjoyed meeting all three women." I walk over to Tom and help myself to a pretzel from the opened bag. "I know I went kicking and screaming to that party, but for the first time ever, I had fun."

"OK. When you have the date, let me know, and I'll text the guys." Tom walks to the bar area, grabs a glass from the overhead cabinet, and reaches into the ice maker. "Can I get you something?" he asks as he tosses several cubes into his glass then removes a bottle of scotch from the liquor shelf.

"No thanks, I'm good," I say as I take a sip from a mug of tea that I made after dinner. "Could you ask for the women's cell numbers? It's probably easier that way. After all, women usually respond much quicker to these things than men. Besides, most females keep the couple's social calendar," I say as my husband sits down next to me at the kitchen counter.

"I'm glad you like them," Tom says, placing his hand on top of mine. "Lately, it's as though your only focus has been work ... and taking care of us. You haven't spent much time with friends," he adds.

I nod knowingly. But I've needed time. It made sense to pull back as I try to figure out the friend thing. Still, I continuously beat myself up for having trusted those two women. I thought they liked me. We were inseparable, at least for five years we were. But then everything changed—and in a flash, all of my faith in friendships vanished.

Staring at the kitchen counter, I return to the moment when I overheard them making sarcastic comments, judging the new body I was so uncomfortable in, inferring it was my choice. How could they not have understood what I was going through?

Although my scars from breast cancer are barely noticeable, the internal wounds still exist, no doubt requiring more time to heal. I suspect these painful gashes go much deeper than this isolated event. Of course, I still struggle with that feeling of being incomplete, losing my breasts—a significant part of myself, my femininity. The jagged lines across my chest represent more than the transformation my body, and mind, went through. It was the abandonment by women whom I trusted, friends whom I assumed would be there for me, that rocked my world. They judged me, inferred I was happy to have reconstructive surgery, enjoyed the attention. I let out a huge sigh, still unable to comprehend why they said those things. Yet that was not the first time I misjudged friends, assuming they were loyal when they were anything but.

However, there was something different about Sophia, Juliette, and Annie. It's as though an unknown voice within, definitely not Margaret's, is telling me it's time to trust again.

***

Before going to bed, I add all three cell numbers to my address book then text Juliette, Annie, and Sophia, inviting them to come for dinner this upcoming Saturday. Within the next half hour, each responds. As luck would have it, everyone is free.

THE DINNER PARTY

January 9

The short ribs simmer, casting a rich, gamey aroma throughout the first floor of the house. I pause, reminiscing on how we came to own our home ten years ago.

One of Tom's partners, who knew we were outgrowing our townhouse in Haverford, told him about an old farmhouse in Radnor his wife, Lori, was about to list. Apparently, the owners, both in their early eighties, were behind on taxes. Luckily, this elderly couple's children became aware of the situation, paid the back taxes, and moved their parents to a retirement community. Not interested in taking on the major renovations necessary to restore this home, their daughter, who played tennis with Lori, convinced her parents to list the farmhouse with Lori.

Before the house could make it to the classified section of the local newspapers, we called Lori, requesting to see the property. By chance, she was free to show it that afternoon.

When we arrived, it became clear this stone home built on an ignored, yet potentially magnificent, four-acre lot was more than we could have imagined. Both the hidden beauty of its unique features as well as the incredible possibilities for the property prompted us to put in a bid, hoping our "best offer" was good enough. Luckily, it was. Ninety days after closing, we began a massive refurbish. Finally, after seventeen months spent watching this charming yet delipidated building turn into a magnificent home for the three of us, we moved in.

Glancing around the kitchen, which so naturally flows into our family room, I feel a sense of pride ripple throughout my body. I made it my mission to incorporate classic stonework, oak hardwood floors, and authentic ceiling beams to create a warm and enticing space. To this day, I believe it's the appliances in the kitchen that make it truly special. Enhanced by gorgeous modern lighting, this is a true chef's kitchen. The architect and I figured out how to incorporate two traditional ovens as well as a steam oven, a Sub-Zero refrigerator/freezer, two dishwashers, warming drawers, and a pullout microwave drawer into the blueprints. My fingers graze the concrete countertops. Honestly, if I were to do it again, I wouldn't change a thing.

Some may think it's a bit over the top, but unlike many built in Main Line homes, this one is a working kitchen. Cooking's my creative outlet. Sure, some days my only goal is to put dinner on the table, nothing more. However, when time permits, I find chopping, dicing, braising, and simmering therapeutic. One of my favorite pastimes is to sit on the sofa poring over a pile of recipe books. And instead of spending free afternoons shopping for clothes or accessories, I prefer to peruse local gourmet shops, experimenting with various cuts of meats, exotic spices, and locally grown produce. I know it sounds strange, but I find peace when I'm in the kitchen.

But as much as I often lose myself in the intricacies of preparing entrées, sides, and appetizers, I rarely make desserts. Baking has never been my thing. It could be because I had to watch my weight growing up. Perhaps I avoid baking so I don't have tempting treats around. Regardless, Patrick and Tom are not big fans of sweets, so I don't feel compelled to have freshly baked treats for dessert or after-school snacks. Of course, in case someone has a craving, there are usually Oreos and chocolate bars in the pantry and ice cream in the freezer. That's pretty much the norm in the Ryan household. But not tonight. This afternoon, I'm attempting a family heirloom recipe: my great-grandmother's chocolate cake.

I look down at my watch. It's one o'clock. Knowing today would be busy, I deliberately woke early this morning so I could get in a decent run. Then, as soon as I was showered and dressed, I began the short ribs, wanting to ensure I had ample time to prepare dinner without rushing.

Yesterday, I took care of all the shopping—picked up the meat from the local butcher, purchased flowers and fresh vegetables at Whole Foods, and bought wine and a few bar items at the state store. Now, as Coldplay's "Sparks" streams in the background, I begin to mix the butter with the eggs, sugar, and flour, carefully ensuring I whisk out any lumps before I add the buttermilk and melted chocolate. It's certainly not the healthiest dessert, but when made properly, it's sublime.

***

Two hours later, the three layers of chocolate cake cool on wire racks as I slice sweet potatoes, parsnips, brussels sprouts, carrots, and beets. After carefully placing the root vegetables on a large roasting pan, I drizzle olive oil on top then add my favorite seasonings. Next, I turn my attention to the polenta, adding the dried grain to boiling salted water, stirring it as it slowly thickens. All that's left to do is to set the table and ice the cake. I let out a sweet sigh as I take in this afternoon's accomplishments.

Before I know it, everything's done, and I'm curled up on the sofa with a copy of the latest James Patterson novel on my lap. Though instead of reading, I look out the bay window into the now barren backyard. A lone cardinal sits on the recently filled bird feeder hanging from a dogwood branch. As it nibbles at the sunflower seeds, the beautiful bird appears content, seemingly unaffected by the cold, damp day. His bright red feathers stand out against the darkening gray sky. Minutes later, the bird flies to a low branch of a nearby sugar maple tree. I keep my gaze on him. Strangely, he appears to be staring back at me. As my eyes remain locked on the cardinal, my mind begins to wander to earlier days.

Why did she say that about me? I thought she was my friend. This isn't my fault. It's not what I wanted—this happened to me. I can't believe she insinuated I chose implants. That it was deliberate …

The book falls to the ground when my body jolts, startled by the sound of the front door shutting. Patrick must be home. I check my watch. It's close to four thirty. I must have fallen asleep. Tom's working today, but he promised to be back by five. I stretch my arms and peer outside, only to find the cardinal's flown away. As Patrick comes into the room, I uncurl my legs and stand so I can hug my son, who appears to grow taller with each passing minute.

"Mind if I go to the movies tonight and then sleep at Matt's? Mrs. James said she would drive us to our nine o'clock practice tomorrow morning."

"Of course you can," I say as I kiss Patrick's forehead. I take a moment and look closely at my sixteen-year-old man-child. In two months, he'll be eligible to take his driver's test. And once he passes, I'll probably rarely see him. "Make sure you guys don't stay up too late. Don't want you getting sick and missing school. Midterms are in two weeks," I say, knowing it is the last thing I need to worry about. Somehow, we've been blessed with a son who's responsible and mature. I give him a hug then coax him into the kitchen promising a slice of the chocolate cake I made for this evening, knowing it is the one dessert he loves.

He offers me a warm smile as he says, "Sure, Mom."

As I cut into the freshly iced cake to feed my son, my heart fills with joy. From the beginning, there's been something special about Patrick. When I watch the interactions between his friends and their mothers, it's clear our connection is unique. Patrick understands me, as if he can sense what I need. It's sweet how he allows me to baby him whenever I'm feeling maternal or the way he sheds light on a situation I'm struggling with. My son most definitely has an intuitive spirit about him.

However, as I languish in this thought, that all-too-familiar lump appears in my throat as I realize that before long, he'll be off to college. Then it will only be Tom and me. People say being an empty nester is like a renewal of marriage vows, perhaps a honeymoon of sorts. I don't know. It's been so long since it's been only the two of us. Has Tom changed? Have I? Have we?

You both have.

Damn that voice.

***

Sophia and Jared are the first to arrive, followed by Michael and Juliette. Thirty-five minutes later, I'm greeting the Thompsons at the front door, both of whom look extremely out of sorts.

"I'm so sorry we're late," Jonathon says somewhat sheepishly as he offers me a caramel-colored gift bag containing a bottle of wine. I take their coats then he quickly ushers Annie toward the others. Clearly something is wrong with Annie. She appears flustered and is talking incessantly, more like chattering in circles. I detect a rift between the two of them. Hoping to help calm or possibly settle Annie, I suggest she come with me into the kitchen to check on dinner. As soon as we're safely away from the others, Annie breaks down.

"It's my fault we're late. Jonathon's furious with me," Annie says as tears stream down her cheeks, falling on her embroidered silk top.

"Annie, relax … There's nothing to be upset about. Everyone else just got here." I fib a bit as I offer Annie a tissue from the box sitting on the kitchen counter.

"I had a really difficult day," Annie says as she wipes her eyes. "The kids I see, their lives are filled with such trauma. I kept going over the allotted time during my morning appointments … It's as though I can sense how some of my clients are feeling when they walk into my office. Often, I know their problems before they tell me. These kids' lives are so troubled. And their pain is deep. How can I not spend extra time with them?" Annie pauses, as if expecting me to respond. "Before I knew it, the entire day became backed up. Even though I worked through lunch, I got home late." Annie looks at me with puppy dog eyes. "I know that's no excuse. Everyone works hard. But *I'm* always behind, constantly trying to catch my breath. I can't keep it together, Marlee." Annie rubs her forehead. "Then after I got home, I accidentally fell asleep on the sofa … I'm so sorry." Annie hangs her head as she continues to wipe her tears.

Gently, I take hold of Annie's shoulders and in a motherly fashion say, "Everything's fine. It's best you had a nap. You feel better now, don't you?"

The corners of Annie's mouth rise a bit as she nods her head, resembling a timid little girl. Instinctively, I give her a hug.

"I want you to enjoy yourself tonight, so try not to think about work. OK?" I say in what I hope is interpreted as a supportive tone.

"Thank you, Marlee. Seriously, not many women understand how I feel. After all, both you and Sophia work, and you are moms on top of that. And Juliette has her own business. Plus, look at this house." Annie steps back then twirls around, seemingly captivated by the size and craftsmanship of her surroundings. "It must take a ton of effort to maintain this beautiful home. And your kitchen … I bet you're an incredible cook." She takes in a big breath. "Sure, Jonathon and I have an amazing apartment in Rittenhouse Square … but it's only the two of us. We wanted to have children, but I don't believe that's going to happen." Annie bites her lip as she says this, as if embarrassed to reveal such personal information. "Jonathon and I try to spend Sundays together, go to brunch or catch an exhib-it at the museum. That's the only day we're both at home." Annie's eyes fall to the oak hardwood floor.

"I think it's amazing how devoted both you and Jonathon are to your patients. Not everyone has your ethics, you know, don't you?" I instinctively place my hand on my hip as I offer Annie another perspective on her life, a mothering habit I've no doubt picked up from talking with Patrick. "And I'll let you in on a few secrets. First of all, my son is sixteen. He's rarely home. Sure, there's time and energy involved with being his mom, but he makes it easy. Sophia's son is in college, and her daughter lives in Manhattan," I say before pausing. "And regarding this house, well, I have a housekeeper who comes every Thursday, and Tom employs a yard service to take care of the outside. Yes, I love to cook, and I spend a lot of time in the kitchen, but not every day. Sometimes, like everyone else, I resort to ordering pizza." I tilt my head and give Annie a knowing look.

Annie continues to appear dejected as she pulls a stool out from under the kitchen counter and sits down.

Figuring I may as well continue to plea my case, I say, "And though I work part time, I'm in control of my schedule, so I have tons of flexibility. Annie, you're a psychologist … and your pa-tients depend on you. I can only imagine how draining that is." I do my best to calm this overwhelmed woman whose chin is now propped on top of her cupped hands, elbows resting firmly on the kitchen counter.

Annie's silent, as if trying to take in everything. Finally, she looks up at me and says, "I wish I didn't feel their pain so much. I know I mentioned this earlier, but it's true … I often sense what my clients are experiencing." Annie then wipes a few remaining tears. "Some of these kids have it really rough." Annie's head drops, and the strong connection she feels with her patients becomes clear.

"You know, if you truly want to help them, *you* must take care of yourself."

"I know ... you're right. I guess I haven't been getting enough sleep." She lets out an exhale. "I should know how important rest is. I'm constantly telling my patients to make sure they allow themselves downtime." With this statement, I sense a bit of relief in her voice, and her face appears to soften. I swear I hear a chuckle come from her lips.

"Then you should take your own advice." I offer her a quick wink.

As Annie's about to speak, Tom walks into the kitchen and hands her a margarita. "Jonathon said this was your favorite."

"Oh, thank you, Tom." After taking a sip, she says, "It's delicious ... Just what the doctor ordered." Tom glances my way, apparently aware he's interrupted a serious conversation.

"Go join the others," I say to Annie as I move to the oversize slow cooker on the far counter and give the short ribs a quick stir. "We can talk later," I add, offering the warmest smile I can muster, hoping to convey how much I truly care.

Before Annie leaves the kitchen area, she walks over and gives me a genuine hug. "Thank you for listening," she says, her sad brown eyes glistening with newly formed tears. Something tells me Annie is deeper than she first appears.

"Absolutely. That's what friends are for," I say responsively as Annie moves to the adjacent living area. I can't help but flinch when the words come from my mouth. What do I know about friendships? However, I suspect Annie doesn't have too many females in her life either.

While everyone enjoys cocktails and appetizers, I put the finishing touches on the meal. I then glance at the dining room table, set perfectly for a wintry night. The table runner's adorned with fresh pine cones, conifer boughs, and ivory candles floating in glass vases. I fill the large glasses using the pitcher of purified water. Knowing I'm as prepared as I can be, I feel a new sense of confidence as I move into the next room and join our guests.

As I walk toward the others, I allow myself to wonder whether these women could become my friends. Can I trust them? Instead of hearing Margaret's usual caustic warning, I feel optimistic. Maybe things *will* be different.

Thirty minutes later, I ask Tom to offer our guests the choice of an aged cab or a crisp sauvignon blanc with dinner. Tom attends to the wine orders, and I head to the kitchen to begin assembling dinner, nestling the short ribs in polenta then carefully placing roasted root vegetables around the perimeter of the ceramic dinner dishes. Sophia joins me, offering to carry the plates into the dining room.

Once everyone's gathered around our rectangular wooden dining table, Tom makes a toast, thanking our guests for joining us this evening.

"So you can cook and write," Jared kindly says as his fork pierces a piece of tender beef.

"Merely two of her many talents," Tom says, glancing in my direction. My heart skips a beat when he says this.

"It's what I like to do," I humbly say as I fidget in my chair, a familiar habit whenever the attention is placed on me.

"Well, we certainly appreciate your gifts," Sophia chimes in. "These short ribs are amazing ... and the polenta reminds me of my mother's. She makes it whenever we visit."

"Where does your mother live?" Juliette asks, most likely unaware of Sophia's heritage.

"She and my father live in Florence ... where I was born." A dreamy expression flashes over Sophia's face as she talks about her hometown. She's wearing the same cross I noticed at the holiday event. The light from the candles causes it to glisten.

"Florence … it's so far away. You must miss her," Annie says, her eyes conveying deep compassion for Sophia and her parents living on different continents.

"At first it was difficult, but we make it a point to travel to Italy every summer. And my mother and father come here each December so we can celebrate Christmas together. We've had this schedule since our children were young. It's allowed them to know their grandparents." Sophia and Jonathon exchange a glance, as if in confirmation of their agreement to maintain a long-distance relationship with her parents.

"Your kids are lucky to spend so much time in Europe," Juliette adds. "If I *ever* have children, I will definitely make sure we travel as a family."

Tom can't resist smirking at Michael. "Did you hear that?" he asks in a less than whisper.

Everyone laughs, including Michael whose cheeks are now a soft shade of crimson.

"No, seriously." Juliette, who is dressed in a bronze sweater dress, appears unfazed by the teasing. "It's important for kids to see what the world's like and how others' lives are so different from ours."

"I agree," Annie shyly offers. "We didn't travel when I was young. I still haven't been many places," she says as she lets out a sigh. "There are *so* many countries I would love to visit." Annie draws out the word *so*, revealing how much she wishes this were true.

"Then you need to make it a priority," Juliette says as her turquoise eyes light up. "I know you're busy at work, but you must have vacation time scheduled. You two should go to India. I lived there for six months." Juliette pronounces this in a direct manner as she flips back her flaxen hair.

"It may be best for us to build up to traveling to India," Jonathon says in a gentle tone before he takes a sip of water. "Perhaps we could start with London, or Paris, or Italy. I'm sure Sophia could guide us." He sets his fork down then softly drapes his arm around his wife, who's seated to his right. Annie's entire body softens with Jonathon's reassuring touch. Their spat certainly didn't last long. Of course, I wouldn't have expected it to linger. Jonathon appears to have a soft side, especially when it comes to his wife. I'm sure he was merely irritated and embarrassed about being late.

It's then I notice Juliette's shoulders drop a bit as Jonathon dismisses her idea of traveling to India.

"India is one of the countries I hope to visit someday," Sophia says, apparently also aware of the change in Juliette's body language. Seemingly adept at reading people, Sophia leans forward, closer to Juliette who is directly across from her, and says, "Please tell us about your time there."

Juliette's expression brightens as she begins to recap her travels through this developing country. Captivated by tales of life in an ashram, the seven of us listen to stories of sunrise devotions, simple vegetarian meals eaten by hand, and endless days of silence. After several minutes, Annie turns to Sophia, who is sitting next to her, to ask about growing up in Italy. I watch as Sophia appears delighted to share poignant stories and enticing tidbits about her native country. Annie looks absolutely mesmerized when Sophia describes life in Florence. Maybe Jonathon can convince his wife to travel after all.

After a short lull in the conversation, Jared looks at me and says, "I read your article about holistic medicine and found it fascinating. Considering our specialty, we don't encounter a lot of requests from patients for alternative treatments, but there have been times when I've been asked my opinion regarding nonsurgical options for orthopedic issues."

Hearing her husband speak, Sophia takes a break from discussing Italy and adds, "Annie, what are your thoughts? Do you suggest alternative healing methods to your clients?"

"My initial reaction centers on the placebo effect. If my patients believe certain practices will help them, then perhaps they will. And there are new studies coming out every day in support of nonmedical options. I've tried tapping and had some success with it, especially with my younger clients," Annie says then unpacks tapping, speaking in a strangely confident manner. She explains the progression of tapping points, then demonstrates the practice. Her shyness magically disappears when she is in her professional persona.

"Well, as proud as I am of Marlee for writing that article, I admit I'm a skeptic. I choose to rely on scientifically researched studies, and until I read more evidence in favor of the validity of holistic practices, I will remain a bit leery," Tom announces as he stands to refill wineglasses. My heart sinks a bit.

"Don't knock it till you try it, Tom," Juliette speaks in a somewhat demure manner. "You may think I'm biased because I run a yoga studio, but what I saw and learned in India, well, let's just say I have no doubt about the impact of these methods. You'd be amazed with the healings I've witnessed." She sits back in her chair, and a smug look appears on her face. Sophia picks up on the uneasiness and shifts the conversation to the latest sold-out performance at the Kimmel Center.

As the meal progresses, conversation flows as if we've been couple friends for years. The eight of us genuinely interact. Unlike the small talk that happens so frequently at dinner parties, our discussions have substance. Too often at these events, people are insecure, jockeying for the position of "top dog," but not here, not tonight. The men, having established a strong relationship through work, enjoy their evening together outside of the office. And we, the women, have no difficulties intermingling. Quite the opposite—what talent one of us lacks, another possesses. Despite our difference in age and occupations, we somehow reinforce one another, promoting feelings of positivity and curiosity, not the "less than" sensation that can easily occur when among new acquaintances, or even women who claim to be your friend. No, tonight a lightness fills the room. Friendships are forming, meaningful relationships built on fundamentals such as trust, curiosity, and true interest rather than hinged on familiarity, commonality, and circumstance. Could these women be different?

After consuming healthy portions of the chocolate cake, the guys grab their coats then proceed to the deck to smoke some of Tom's cigars, Cubans stored in the wooden box in his office. Luckily, a warm front's coming in, and the temperature hovers in the low forties. While the men smoke outside, we quickly clean up the dishes before transitioning to the family room. As we gather in front of the stone fireplace to enjoy the warmth of the crackling fire, I offer coffee; however, everyone declines.

"There's something special about winter nights like this," Juliette shares. "As much as I love summer weather, nothing beats hanging around a cozy fire with fabulous women."

"I know," Annie says as she leans back into the sofa. "It's wonderful. In fact, I haven't felt this relaxed in ages."

"If you like this, then you would love being at my family's mountain home. It's only two and a half hours away. When you're there, you feel like you're on your own island, far away from the everyday responsibilities," I say as I prop a comfy taupe throw pillow behind me. I then try to remember the last time I was at our mountain home in the winter.

Sophia looks at me in a knowing manner, as if she understands. "How special this must be for you, Marlee, to have a place to go. It sounds heavenly."

"We rarely use it." Automatically, I feel my body sink into the cushions. "I haven't been there since our annual family reunion this past August." I pause, thinking "family reunion" is a bit exaggerated. It was only the three of us who visited my aunt and uncle. "The house belonged to my mother and her brother. When Mom died, Uncle Pete took charge of it. It became a lot of work to maintain the property, so he and his wife, Aunt Sue, moved in, making things easier on all accounts. Still, the house is unoccupied half of the year when Uncle Pete and Aunt Sue are in Sarasota. They love the Florida winters." I smile, thankful they can get away from the cold and damp Pocono weather. "None of my siblings live nearby. And even if they did, they don't seem to have any interest in the place." I frown, not only because we no longer gather as a family at the Poconos, but also because we no longer gather. "Uncle Pete tells me to use it." I shake my head. "Unfortunately, it doesn't seem to happen. Somehow Patrick's soccer and our busy schedules consume our weekends." It's as though I drift away as I share this piece of my family history, my soul yearning for the warmth of this cozy mountain home.

"Well, it sounds pretty freakin' amazing," Juliette says as she leans back and stretches her arms over her head.

Having a sudden urge to return to this home, without thinking, I say, "I have an idea. I know we all don't know each other that well, but would you be interested in spending a weekend there … at the mountain home?"

"I'm in. You tell me when," Juliette commits without an ounce of hesitation.

"What a kind offer, thank you. I would love to go, Marlee," Sophia adds, genuinely appreciative.

Two down, and the only one yet to respond looks somewhat frozen.

"Oh, it sounds so nice." Annie's eyes momentarily light up, only to quickly dim. "I'd hate to say yes and then find out things are too busy at the office." Immediately, Annie's petite body stiffens, her face pales, and her forehead, which has been relaxed for most of the evening, now furrows. I'm amazed to watch Annie so quickly retreat into her protective shell.

"Annie, you deserve your time too. And this would be a fabulous opportunity for you to get away and escape all of the crap at work. You can figure out a way to make this happen … *if you want to*," Juliette says with a "what's it going to be" look, forcing Annie's hand.

Sophia and I remain silent, patiently waiting for Annie's response.

Finally, Annie sits up straighter as she declares, "You're right, Juliette. I guess I *can* take time off. Jonathon's always encouraging me to do so. Because he constantly works, I figured I might as well do the same … but this sounds *so* nice." Color returns to Annie's face, and the lines on her forehead relax. Within moments, she appears years younger.

"When would you ladies like to go?" I ask. "Presidents' Day weekend is only five weeks away. Does that allow you enough time to adjust your schedules? Plus, it's a three-day weekend. Sunday is Valentine's Day, so if we leave after lunch, we'll be back by late afternoon." Being Juliette and Michael recently began dating, I don't want to mess up any Valentine's Day dinner plans.

The women unanimously agree to the proposed date before the conversation transitions to the challenges Annie faces in her practice.

"So many of the kids are incredibly overwhelmed. It wasn't that way when I first started," Annie says, a tone of frustration in her voice.

"What do you mean?" Juliette asks.

"My patients don't only complain about emotional issues. Many also suffer from physical ailments. Of course, this only complicates things." Annie shifts uncomfortably on the sofa as she stares down into at her hands.

"Now that you explain it, it makes total sense," Juliette says. "Stress is one of the reasons my business is growing so quickly. Most of my clients live hectic lives, trying to balance way too much … and, unfortunately, many don't possess the tools to do it. Coming to my studio gives them a short period of bliss. That's how I decided on its name."

Sophia smiles upon learning the origin of Bliss. "I, too, agree. Many of my patients not only battle physical illnesses, but they are also anxious, often bordering on depression." Sophia exhales then stares into her half-full glass of wine as if the answer resides at the bottom.

"This is exactly why my editor wants me to write a follow-up article about holistic practices in this area. Health care providers cannot deal with both the physical and the emotional aspects that are occurring simultaneously. There has to be other options ... not in place of ... but in addition to." I stop, tucking a loose strand of hair behind my right ear. "Of course, I need to conduct a lot of research if I want to write a decent article. I admit I don't know much about the topic." I unconsciously bite my lip after letting out a big sigh.

"I can help you, Marlee. Come to the studio. You can try one of the classes I offer, learn a bit about yoga and meditation. I teach a combination class on Friday mornings at seven thirty. If that doesn't work, there are lots of other classes you might like. I'll text you our schedule," Juliette says as she takes her phone out and begins tapping on the screen. "I also have an instructor, Sabrina, who works with gemstones and specializes in crystal healings. I'll copy you both on a text so you can connect. And I'm becoming certified in energy healing, so if you like, I'll give you a quick tutorial. In fact, I'm happy to do a healing session with you."

"Wow ... thank you," I say before continuing. "I think I can make a Friday morning class work." I pause, as I consciously avoid committing to Juliette's offer to do an energy healing session with me. Actually, the thought kind of scares me.

"My massage therapist incorporates Reiki ... a form of energy healing ... into her massage practice. I find it incredibly soothing. This may be something you want to explore. She also offers sessions that are purely Reiki. Meeting with her may prove beneficial for your article. And of course, if you decide to try a Reiki session, it will help you personally," Sophia says with a knowing smile and a curious slant of her eyes.

There's something about the way Sophia gazes at me that makes me feel as if she can see deeply into my core and understands some of the challenges I've faced. It is as though she's prescribing Reiki as a way for me to heal. But that's ridiculous. We've only recently met. How could she know anything about my past? Immediately, I dismiss the thought.

"I definitely want to meet her, Sophia." My face brightens at these prospects. In fact, I need to learn all about what's out there, anything that's related to holistic health. I perk up as I share more about this assignment with my new friends.

"You know, all of this could help me with my practice. It would be wonderful to be able to refer my patients to reliable holistic practitioners. I think we're prescribing too many drugs for emotional issues. There must be better options," Annie says, a tone of conviction in her voice.

"I agree. Our daughter suffers from migraines. We have tried everything traditional medicine offers. Right now, she is ready to explore alternative methods. Jared and I feel helpless because we are not aware of everything currently available."

"What about acupuncture?" Annie asks. "It's helped one of my patients."

"I do not believe she has tried that. Thank you, Annie. I will share your suggestion with her." Sophia speaks with grace and calmness.

"Actually, one of my client's mothers is a certified practitioner. She frequently does acupuncture on her son. I've noted a big difference since he started these treatments," Annie says.

"Really?" Annie's got my attention. "Could you possibly connect me to her? Acupuncture is one of the healing modalities I find fascinating. And if you trust her, that's all the vetting I need," I say, wondering if I am crossing a boundary with Annie.

"I am meeting with her son on Monday morning. I will ask his mother if I can share her information." Surprisingly, Annie appears fine with this idea.

"Perhaps we may all be able to help you with this assignment. Plus, trying different methods of healing will also benefit you personally," Juliette says with a knowing tone.

First Sophia, then Juliette suggests I'd benefit from holistic healing, causing me to wonder if my lack of confidence is more evident than I thought. But instead of reading too much into their comments, I allow myself to feel the genuine sincerity from these women, who are most definitely different from others I have known. Their interest in me and my assignment is only one more sign these relationships are meant to be. Surprisingly, I don't hear Margaret countering my assessment.

As if on cue, the men come in from the deck, the smell of cigars lingering with them. Then before long, the night winds down, and we say goodbye to the three couples, leaving Tom and me alone.

"Have a good time?" he casually asks, as if he knows the answer. Tom begins to clean up the bar area.

"Yes, these women are amazing. Each one possesses a unique and distinct personality. Kind of like bouillabaisse ... Although each ingredient is delicious, when combined, they create a mesmerizing stew."

"I think you're taking this chef thing a bit too far," Tom teases me for my choice of words. Regardless, I believe this example perfectly describes tonight's symbiotic relationship.

"Sophia, Annie, Juliette, and I ... the four of us ... are going to the mountain house over Presidents' weekend. And everyone's offered to help me with my article. Isn't that incredible?" I say as I dry a large ceramic platter.

"Really... all of that happened when we were outside?" Tom smiles before adding, "I guess it is pretty incredible." He then dumps the extra ice from the ice bucket into the sink before asking, "Even Annie?"

"Yep." I give him my biggest smile.

"You were able to convince her to go away for a weekend? Jonathon told me he's tried to take her on a vacation, but she constantly gives excuses why she can't leave." Tom shakes his head in amazement.

After we go upstairs, I head to the bathroom to brush my teeth. Staring in the mirror as I remove my makeup, I notice an unusual glow on my face. I actually asked three women, whom I barely know, to the mountains for a weekend. As I gently scrub my skin with a washcloth, I sense something shift inside me. Could I genuinely be excited about a weekend in the Poconos with Sophia, Annie, and Juliette? Normally, the thought of time away with women would induce anxiety and unending comments from Margaret—who has been incredibly quiet tonight. However, I don't feel worried or uneasy. Though I have no idea what these three days will be like, something tells me I'm going to learn a few things, perhaps grow in unexpected ways.

THE UNAVOIDABLE
The Week of January 11

Sitting at my desk, I look vacantly at the blank screen in front of me. It's more than being unsure of how to begin this article—I've no clue about the middle or ending either. Despite all of the online research I've conducted, as well as the introductions promised Saturday night, I'm at a complete loss. What's my message? And then there's tone—should it be direct and factual, or perhaps more down to earth, personal?

You never should have accepted this assignment. What were you thinking?

Damn that voice. As I slouch back into my chair, my chin falls toward my chest. Maybe *she's* right. I know so little about holistic medicine, only what I've found online, and of course what I wrote about in the first article. However, that piece focused on its rising popularity, not what it is and how it affects people. Where do I begin?

In an attempt to avoid the empty Word document staring back at me, I write a quick text to Annie inquiring about the acupuncturist she mentioned Saturday evening. While I'm at it, I text Sabrina, introducing myself and asking if she would have some time next week to meet. As soon as I hit *Send*, the phone rings.

"Hi, Marlee! How's it going?" Before I can say a word, Natalie continues without waiting for my response. "The boys play in Conshohocken on Saturday. Want me to drive? It's nice because the field's not far away, and the game doesn't start till ten."

"Sure, Natalie, that would be great," I say, my mind continuing to focus on possible openers for the article.

"Oh, and I've been researching methods to help you handle your stress when Patrick's in goal. I think they'll make a difference in how you'll feel," Natalie says in a rapid-fire fashion.

A big neon-green "YES" sign flashes in my brain. Natalie's taking that course in something beginning with an *A*. Why didn't I pay more attention when she was explaining it to me? "That sounds great, Natalie. Thank you so much," I say before taking a big breath, knowing this could go either way. "Would you want to get together for coffee tomorrow ... so you could share your ideas with me? And I'd like to know more about the course you're taking." I unconsciously gulp, hoping I won't regret asking my exuberant friend to enlighten me on her newest endeavor. However, I'm desperate to learn something about holistic healing, and from what Natalie's said, at least what I listened to her saying, it sounds like this thing, whatever it is, might qualify.

"Absolutely! How about tomorrow at ten?"

∗∗∗

Against my better judgment, I join Natalie at a corner table at the Starbucks on Lancaster Avenue. Seated with a latte and apricot scone in front of me, I listen to my soccer mom friend as I hold my pen over an opened notebook. Natalie begins explaining the background to this ancient practice.

"*Ayur* means 'life' and *veda* is translated as 'science' or 'knowledge.' So, loosely, it's the science of life. Ancient Indian sages, from India not Native North Americans, created this system of holistic practices to promote maximizing health, detoxing the body, and recognizing your individual *dosha*'s needs. Ayurveda stresses the mind-body connection to staying healthy and disease free. The ultimate goal is to balance the body, helping it function at its optimum level."

I furiously write as Natalie continues speaking.

"There are lots of things you could do right now to help improve your physical well-being, but I'm only going to recommend a few simple daily practices, OK?"

Knowing Natalie's not asking, she's telling, I nod my head.

"First thing each morning, I want you to scrape your tongue before you brush your teeth. This gets rid of the toxins that accumulate on the tongue's surface while you sleep. Plus, it will help your breath smell fresher without all of the gunk on it."

As inconspicuously as possible, I put my hand in front of my mouth, lick the palm, and then casually take a whiff to see if my breath stinks. Thankfully, I cannot detect any foul smell, and Natalie doesn't seem to notice what I'm doing. She's too busy referencing the books she's brought along to help "educate" me.

"Then afterward, you brush your body with a body brush … in little circles before massaging oil all over," Natalie says in a nonchalant, matter-of-fact manner. "And when you're doing this, you put some sesame oil in your mouth and swish it around … like this." Natalie begins to inflate her mouth, making her look like an oversize goldfish.

"What?" I ask as my eyes become wide, and my mouth remains open a bit too long, which I guess is OK because my breath doesn't smell.

"No, I'm serious. Be sure to buy the organic sesame oil. And you're bound to find the body brushes and tongue scrapers in most drugstores if they aren't available where you shop for groceries. Remember, start with your feet then calves, making small strokes, and then move up your legs. Do your entire body … and make sure you move toward your heart. Then take the sesame oil … you may want to warm it first … and massage it into your skin. Again, begin with your feet, then your ankles and calves, and move upward," Natalie says as she uninhibitedly stands up and begins demonstrating on her own body with a make-believe brush. "If possible, you should shower afterward. The hot water helps the oil penetrate into your skin. And don't forget about the oil pulling … That's the name for swishing the oil in your mouth. Oh, and when you're done … after fifteen minutes or so … spit it in the kitchen trash can. It's not good for the garbage disposal."

I have no idea how to respond to these preposterous ideas. Seriously, I cannot see myself doing any of this. I put my pen down and close my notebook. Unfortunately, Natalie's still on a roll.

"Then, I want you to sit silently for ten minutes and drink a glass of warm water with lemon. It will help you to settle your mind. And on Saturday mornings before a game, sit for at least fifteen minutes. And if your thoughts go to someone scoring on Patrick, then change your thoughts … Instead, picture him stopping goals. Got that?"

"Yep," I say, biting my lip to keep me from saying a resounding *hell no*!

"Oh, and try to eat only whole, unprocessed foods for breakfast. Like cooked quinoa with fruit and nuts. I know you like your coffee, but try to limit it on those mornings, OK? I think it gets you super amped up."

Natalie's hit a nerve. No one messes with my coffee consumption, especially on Saturday mornings if we've been out the night before. Plus, quinoa for breakfast? That sounds horrible. However, I remain silent, allowing Natalie to continue, as I resume jotting down her prescribed practices.

"Trust me, you'll begin noticing differences in your mood and skin tone right away. Plus, the oil pulling helps you to avoid colds, especially this time of the year."

Convinced Natalie's completely lost it, and extremely conscious of how the other patrons keep glancing in our direction, I quickly agree to her zany ideas before she returns to showing me how to do the brushing or oil swishing again. "OK, I'll try this," I say. "Though I can't promise anything."

"You've got to believe in it, Marlee. These practices will lessen your stress and promote a well-being in your body. I promise. However, you must have faith in Ayurveda to gain its full benefits. Promise me you'll stop on your way home and buy a tongue scraper, a body brush, and sesame oil so you can start first thing tomorrow morning ... plus lemons, lots of lemons. And remember, for it to be beneficial, you must make it a daily practice. It takes time to build up the positive effects in your body."

"Natalie," I hesitantly say, expunging the visual of her air brushing and self-massaging, "I was wondering ... would you be able to share more about Ayurveda with me?" Clearly, I've hit rock bottom on the desperation scale if I am willing to subject myself to more of her "recommendations."

Natalie immediately perks up and begins explaining the three *doshas*, or body types. "These are *Vata*, *Pitta*, and *Kapha*. Most people are a mixture of the three." She looks at me intently, eyeing me up and down. "I'm going bet you're mostly *Pitta* ... with a bit of *Vata*," she says, scrutinizing every inch of my visible body. Clueless to what she's referring to, I know this is valuable information for the article, so I sit there, intently focused on taking notes.

Simultaneously, my brain begins outlining a possible framework for this assignment, hoping it will work.

Ha! Sure, go ahead and tell yourself that.

Thirty minutes later, I say goodbye and thank Natalie as I head to my car parked in the Starbucks lot. Before I proceed to the grocery store, I add the body brush, tongue scraper, sesame oil, and lemons to my shopping list I keep under "Notes" on my phone then quickly scroll through my cell's inbox. I pause when I see an email from Sophia.

Marlee,

This morning I had a delightful massage with Elena, the woman I spoke of who practices Reiki. When I told her about you and your assignment, she offered a complimentary session so you could feel the impact of Reiki for yourself. Below is her contact information. I believe you will benefit from meeting with Elena.

Have a beautiful day,
Sophia

Elena Holmes
ehliftenergies@comcast.net
610-256-3899
www.liftenergies.com

Sensing a blend of gratitude mixed with nervous anticipation that Sophia thinks "I will benefit from meeting with Elena," I click on Elena's website. Immediately, a calmness settles over me. Elena doesn't look like a flake at all. In fact, from the information on her website, she appears very professional. After perusing through her site, I compose an email to Elena, thanking her for her kind offer and asking when she would be available to schedule an appointment. Before I lose my nerve, I hit *Send*.

***

While I'm putting the last of the reusable grocery bags on the kitchen counter, I hear a ping on my phone. It's a text from Sabrina. She is free next Wednesday at ten. After confirming the time with Sabrina, I realize I didn't hear back from Annie. So I decide to give her a call.

"Hello," answers a timid voice. I wonder how she interacts with her teenage patients and their parents, because socially, Annie borders on awkward.

"Hi, Annie. It's Marlee. I hope you are doing well." I do my best to project enthusiasm.

"So nice to hear from you. I'm OK ... Another long day. Guess that's par for the course."

"Annie, I'm not sure if you saw my text ... I was wondering if you had a chance to ask your patient's mom, the one who does acupuncture, if I could meet with her?"

"Oh ... well, um ... no, I haven't." I hear Annie take a deep breath. "Actually, Marlee, I thought it might be a bit awkward. I've known this woman for years, but I don't think I can ask her. She might interpret it as violating our confidentiality. I think the margaritas and wine made me say that."

I take a moment and consider the professional and ethical situation Annie faces and acknowledge her concerns are truly valid. "No worries, Annie. I totally understand. Is there anyone else you know who's involved in some type of holistic healing?"

The phone goes silent. I assume Annie's thinking.

Finally, Annie says, "Well I'm not sure if this counts, but my neighbor, Roberto, asked me to try his breathwork class at his studio downtown. He thought it would help to center me." I hear her heave out a long sigh. "Jonathon and I have had dinner with Roberto and his partner, Malcolm. Yet going to a breathing class ... whatever breathwork is ... well, honestly ... I don't think I could do that." The inflection in Annie's voice confirms her last statement.

"Annie, this man sounds perfect! I've read a bit about breathwork and its benefits. Some people claim it's a life changer. Would you ask Roberto if I could meet with him? Of course, I'm happy to pay for a class," I say, a tone of desperation weaving through my voice.

"Are you sure you want to do this?" a tentative Annie asks.

Something tells me her neighbor may be happy a journalist wants to learn more about what he is doing. "Please assure Roberto this article will be in support of breathwork, not one scrutinizing the practice."

"OK, I'll do it." Although her voice sounds shaky, Annie promises to ask Roberto if he'd meet with me.

"Will you text me as soon as you talk with him?" I ask, hoping Annie doesn't back out.

"I will. I promise," Annie says, and I believe she means it this time.

The phone goes silent. All of a sudden I feel like a five-year-old, waiting to see if all of her friends can come to her birthday party. Only this is not a child's celebration; this is research for an article for the *Inquirer*.

That's when something inside, certainly not Margaret, tells me there's a higher purpose than merely writing this article. Surprisingly, this does not cause me concern. Although unsure of the message I'm receiving, I sense a bit of optimism, perhaps even inspiration. Confused by it all, I shake my head then proceed to place the perishables in the refrigerator.

After putting the groceries away, I glance at the newly purchased body brush and sesame oil sitting on the kitchen counter. Sighing, I pick up the brush and tentatively pull up my sweatpants, exposing the lower half of my leg. Slowly, I begin moving the head of the brush in small circles. Unexpectedly, my calf relaxes as I move the brush clockwise.

If I want to understand what this holistic thing is all about, then I've got to take a risk and try it out. Body brush and sesame oil in hand, I go upstairs to the privacy of our bathroom and replicate Natalie's modeled movements over the rest of my body. Afterward, I pour some of the oil into my hands, rub my palms together, and begin to massage my feet, then calves, then thighs. Surprisingly, it feels nice, even more than nice. I inhale the sesame scent as I lose myself in the calming motion of my hands pressing into my sore muscles around my neck. Slowly, something inside begins to unwind. It's more than physical, but I cannot properly describe the calming sensation.

After I wash my hands, screw on the top of the sesame oil bottle, and put on my sweatpants and top, I hear my phone sound. It's a text from Annie, along with a card containing Roberto's contact information.

Annie: *Ran into Roberto on the elevator, and he said he'd be happy to meet with you.*

Quickly, I respond after adding the card to my address book.

Me: *Thank you! I will call him this afternoon. You're the best!*

Energy surges within, as I cannot wait to meet with Roberto. He, along with Elena and Sabrina, sounds fascinating. Again, an unfamiliar feeling within suggests there's more to learn than merely information for an article. Unsure as to where this is leading, I decide to shift my thoughts to next month's weekend at the Poconos. If there is *another purpose* for me to be writing this article, I'll figure that out later.

Yesterday I emailed Uncle Pete to make sure it's OK for us to stay at the house. His response led me to believe he and Aunt Sue were thrilled their favorite niece and her friends would be visiting. Grinning ear to ear, I allow my mind to begin planning the meals and activities—all of the details I love to dig into. This girls' weekend is exactly what I need.

I question my use of the term *girls* as we are all grown women. No one says "womenfriends"—the term's *girlfriends*. Could this be because we're all girls at heart?

Girlfriend is a term I rarely use. For me, it brings up images of cliques, queen bees, and wannabes. Maybe that is why some girlfriends are anything but real friends ... because they act in the immature girl mode. Now if we said "womenfriends," perhaps females would better understand what is expected of them in this role. Instead of resorting to pubescent behaviors like talking behind another's back after smiling to their face or spreading false rumors merely to be mean, they'd be loyal, caring, and compassionate.

There you go again, being judgmental. What makes you think it was their fault? You're the one who doesn't know how to be a good friend.

Shaking my head as if to reject images of failed past friendships, I do my best to ignore Margaret's harsh comments, reminding myself not all females are like some I've known. There are solid women out there, ones who make fabulous friends. Yet I couldn't find them. Instead, I tended toward the ones who appeared fun and popular. However, something always went wrong. I wonder if I've subconsciously picked the wrong women as friends. I rub my temples, attempting to clear this depressing thought from my brain. Could Sophia, Annie, and Juliette be different? Or will they ultimately reveal traits similar to the others? What if Margaret's right— what if *I'm* the one incapable of being a true friend?

RESEARCH
Week of January 18

Icircle February 22 on the calendar hanging over the desk in my office. Knowing I must submit the article, the one I have yet to begin, in a month causes uncomfortable rumblings in my stomach. Having established a game plan to be 99 percent finished before leaving for the Poconos, so there will only be final edits when I return, I cannot shake the unusual fear centered around this assignment. I've written numerous articles about topics I'm unfamiliar with, but I've never felt this way before.

I take a tablet of lined yellow paper from the middle desk drawer and begin to map out a plan, creating a checklist of items to do. Then I attach a date next to each task, signifying when it must be finished. Hopefully, this schedule will give me some peace of mind. However, though the steps and deadlines make sense on paper, it's as if a piece is missing, and it's driving me nuts that I can't identify what's wrong.

Perhaps I'll figure it out this upcoming week when I meet with all of the healers. Tomorrow, I have a session with Elena to help me better understand the benefits of Reiki. Then Wednesday I meet with Sabrina to learn about crystal healings. The following day is the private breathwork class with Roberto. Combine that with what I'm learning from Natalie about Ayurveda and Juliette's promise to introduce me to yoga, meditation, and energy healing—which I guess I'll try—I *should* have a strong foundation for the article. However, I'm still unsure. It's as though I'm using a piecemeal approach to something that instead requires a well-laid-out and logical plan.

I pull my hair back into a ponytail using the scrunchie that was wrapped around my wrist and dive into the assignment. The first step to writing articles involves research. Although I've done a lot the past two weeks, I diligently read up on each of these specific healing practices I'm about to encounter. Sifting through articles, I scribble notes then review what I've written, highlighting areas I find confusing. Several hours later, I have a list of bulleted questions for each of the practitioners.

This is all bullshit, and you know it … Do you actually believe you can write anything the least bit convincing? Besides, don't you realize you'll lose your readers' respect if you claim these woo-woo practices really work? Plus, what about Tom? You know he doesn't believe in this. And have you considered his partners' reaction? Why are you doing this, Marlee?

Margaret's sharp words catch me off guard, causing me to pause and ask if there is any truth to her warnings. Am I foolish to think I can pull off this article? But more importantly, could submitting this assignment in any way impact my relationship with Tom?

However, another sensation within, one most definitely not controlled by Margaret, projects an entirely different message. Instead of warning me to halt and reevaluate what I'm doing, it gently encourages me to proceed.

This is what you are meant to do. Use your voice. Speak your truth.

I snap out of this confrontation between internal voices when I remember I must register for Juliette's yoga/meditation class at Bliss. After pulling up Bliss's website, I'm prompted to create an account before I can sign up for the seven thirty class this Friday morning. Once I've typed in the required fields and allowed access to my credit card, I receive an email confirming I'm registered for the class. One more item completed on the endless checklist for this assignment.

It's then I notice the familiar tightness in my shoulders. With both elbows on my desk, I drop my head down between my arms and begin to massage my neck and upper back. Unsure of the cause for this muscle tension, I know it could be anything—my deadline, Tom's inevitable reaction to the article, or the uncertainty that surrounds our upcoming weekend in the Poconos. Nevertheless, there are deeper concerns, fears I hold tightly within and wounds I am not yet prepared to reveal. I lift my head as I glance toward my office ceiling. Staring at the bland whiteness of the plaster, I wonder if there is any validity to these holistic practices. Can they make a difference in people's lives? And if so, could they help me? Am I able to heal? Or are my scars too deep?

***

Curious and admittedly nervous about meeting Elena and experiencing Reiki, I hesitantly open the glass door to an office building located off of Lancaster Avenue. I assume I'm at the correct address, as the sign outside matches the Lift logo from Elena's website.

The door leads into a small seating area complete with an inviting ivory leather love seat, a glass-and-metal coffee table displaying yoga and meditation magazines, and a welcoming beverage station offering a variety of herbal teas as well as a water jug filled with cucumber and lime slices. A bowl of cashews sits by the empty ceramic mugs.

How lovely, I think as I pour myself a glass of citrus-scented water and scoop several nuts onto a napkin before settling on the love seat. A vertical tapestry of lotus flowers painted in a rainbow of colors catches my attention. Assuming this artwork represents the various chakras, information I learned during my research, I study each unique flower, noting a calmness settling over me. *Hmmm.*

Several minutes later, a tall, stunning woman with thick, wavy dark hair descends the staircase adjacent to the waiting room. She's dressed in jeans and a button-up shirt. In fact, she looks pretty, um, "normal." As this woman, who appears to be in her late thirties, walks toward me, her distinctive eyebrows arch in a knowing fashion, and the sepia hue of her face radiates warmth.

"Marlee," she says as she extends her hand toward me, "I'm Elena. Welcome to Lift. Let's head upstairs." Elena gracefully begins to climb the stairs and I follow, unsure of where all of this is headed.

She invites me to join her in what I presume is her office, a pale yellow room filled with plants and gorgeous indigenous artwork. In the middle is a massage table, angled across the room's diameter. Elena tells me to relax on the table as she sits at a beautifully hand-painted wooden desk. A long thin console filled with various gemstones catches my eye. I recognize the amethyst and the rose quartz from my recent research. Cream-colored woven blinds cover only a portion of the windows, allowing exactly the right amount of sunlight to cast a soft glow about the room.

"Is this your first experience with Reiki?" Elena asks as she picks up a clipboard and pen from her desk.

"Yes," I say as I carefully hop onto the table. It feels strange to lie down, so I prop myself up with my elbows.

"One of the beautiful things about Reiki is you do not need to do anything. Please, lie down and relax." Elena reaches for an iPhone, and within seconds, soothing music comes over the loudspeakers.

I allow myself to rest into the soft cotton blanket covering the massage table. I take several deep breaths before shutting my eyes. I feel Elena place something on my chest.

"I'm putting various gemstones on and around you. They will serve to amplify the energy you will feel today. You may sense my hands hovering over your body. I will also be directly touching you at times. If anything becomes too overpowering, please let me know."

Feeling like I'm about to take off on a wild roller-coaster ride, or perhaps a rocket ship destined for some unknown destination, I sense my neck and shoulder muscles tense, causing one of the stones Elena placed on my chest to fall to the table.

Elena softly laughs. "Nothing will hurt, Marlee. It may feel as though various intensities of energy are flowing through you." And with that, she replaces the stone on my sternum. "Most people actually like it."

Silence follows and then an amazing stream of electricity courses within me. When Elena places her hand onto my stomach, the current increases. I feel pops occurring in my core. Something is definitely happening, though in no way can I explain what it is. These energetic pulses continue. They then begin to move, traveling throughout my body, as if they are controlled by the movement of Elena's hands.

"What are you feeling?" I sheepishly ask, knowing she is most likely getting information from my body.

"Energy work is like peeling back layers of an onion. We all have sad memories we've repressed for years. These negative emotions are stored in various parts of our bodies, our chakras, and cause blockages. Energy work helps to open these blockages, releasing the pain inside."

"So Reiki balances your chakras by getting rid of stored muck?" I ask, remembering this particular point I had wanted to clarify during today's session.

"Yes, Reiki can do that. Although at times we require more intensive energy healings to deal with our past traumas," she says as she moves her hand to the center of my torso. "Reiki has limitations, but there are practitioners, like shamans, who are capable of so much more."

"Like what?"

"Soul retrials, past life transgressions … It's truly amazing what energy work can unveil and how it can heal." With that pronouncement, Elena moves her hands to right above my belly button. "What I'm working on right now is your third chakra … This is how we view ourselves … our confidence and self-esteem. It is where we can repress feelings of inadequacy, of not being good enough."

Immediately, my mind goes to my childhood. I was the youngest of six, and my siblings tormented me on a daily basis. They constantly magnified any and all flaws, making public all of my mistakes and imperfections. As a result, I grew up incredibly self-conscious. In fact, even today, I continue to struggle with my self-image.

"Well, you're going to find lots of blockages there," I joke as I let out a slight laugh. Still, there's nothing funny about it.

"All of this is totally normal, Marlee. Each one of us holds a great deal inside. That's what's beautiful about energy work. It can make you feel better … physically and emotionally."

"Physically?"

"Yes, the deeper we bury our emotions, especially the strong, negative feelings, the more likely they are to embed themselves into our physical bodies. If we continue to internalize these thoughts, over time, they can develop into physical ailments."

"Like what?" I ask, a tone of concern rising in my voice.

Elena must have picked up on my apprehension because she says, "Well, suppressed sadness can present as asthma. And control issues we deny can show up in your bladder. The key is to understand how our illnesses are connected to our emotional states. In no way should we ignore physical symptoms or not seek medical attention. However, it's important to consider possible underlying reasons for what you may be feeling. For example, if you keep getting bladder infections, you should ask yourself if you struggle with control."

"I think I understand what you're saying," I say, then drift off for several songs. There's something about the feeling of the energy moving throughout my body—it's incredibly soothing and freeing at the same time. I feel another pop. Could one of my blockages be clearing? I remain quiet for the rest of the session, enjoying the sensation of electricity pulling, releasing, and then pulling again.

"I've been studying energy for ten years, and the more I learn, the more I realize how little I know." Elena momentarily lifts her hands then resettles them on my ankles. "As we end our session, I want to ground you, so you don't feel too floaty."

"Elena, what was the pulling I felt?"

"That was me taking out some of your fears. It was easy … You were ready to release them." She smiles as she begins to remove the stones, setting them on the table behind her.

I continue to lie there, soaking up the last few moments of our session.

"How do you feel?" Elena asks as I slowly sit up.

"Amazing," I say, sensing a lightness and a newly found energy within.

"We released a fair amount today. It's important for you to drink water. Take it easy. And please let me know if something doesn't seem right. If you text me, I can send you some energy to balance whatever is off." I acknowledge this with a nod, yet I have absolutely no idea how Elena could send energy to fix something I was feeling.

I offer to pay for the session, but Elena refuses, reminding me she wanted to share her work with me. Due to my newfound intrigue and because I feel so damn good, I ask if we can schedule another session.

Ten minutes later, before pulling out of my parking space, I glance in the rearview mirror to ensure there are no oncoming cars. It's then I do a double take, noting how rested I appear. In fact, my eyes have an unfamiliar sparkle to them. Could this be due to energy work? Unwilling to credit this new glow to Reiki, I put the car in reverse and proceed to drive home. However, I cannot shake the possibility that energy could be responsible for this look of grace and ease.

***

Since I avoided telling Tom about this week's "research appointments," I keep today's session to myself. After all, I know how he'd react. And to be honest, I don't want to go there right now. Plus, if Margaret's words have any credence, I'd hate to spark any rifts between us. Besides, I feel incredible after the session with Elena. All I want to do is relax and let it all soak in.

***

Later that night, while Patrick's in his room doing homework and Tom's watching a Sixers game on TV, I decide to head to bed earlier than normal. For some reason, I crave time alone. After kissing Tom goodnight and knocking on Patrick's door to do the same, I change into my favorite lightweight cotton nightgown, prepare for bed, then crawl under the covers. At first, I reach for the remote, a habit whenever I'm the first to bed. But not tonight. Instead, I lie motionless, nestled in the cool sheets, and return to this afternoon, to how I felt during the Reiki session.

After several moments, the memory of that current, the flow of what I presume was energy, returns. Though I can't actually feel the sensation, I most definitely recall how it affected me, especially in my core, the area Elena referred to as my third chakra. She said it was how we see ourselves. I sigh, knowing this is certainly not my strong suit. Of course, others, especially those outside of my family, would be surprised to hear me say this. In fact, people think I'm self-assured, confident, perhaps even a bit distant.

I let out another sigh, acknowledging this facade is only a front, a mask of sorts I've relied upon for many years. The truth remains that self-esteem is not one of my strengths. Going through breast cancer, and all of the corresponding consequences, certainly didn't make it any better. Reflexively, my left hand moves to my temple, then jaw, as if in anticipation of the tension that frequently forms there whenever I think about that part of my life.

There's only one picture of me, without hair, that I've kept. Tom loves it. He says I look beautiful. Of course, whenever I see it, something inside me cringes, making me want to hide. It's not the vision that upsets me; it's the fear of people feeling sorry for me, pitying me for going through chemo, losing my hair, and being sick. I did not want others to perceive me as weak.

I force myself to exhale. That was eight years ago. I'm better now. I look like I did before the diagnosis, except for a few more wrinkles. However, the scars are not only on my chest. There are open wounds inside, yet to be healed lacerations that probably occurred way before the cancer. Perhaps they caused it, who knows.

Not wanting to think about his anymore, I grab the remote on the nightstand and turn on an episode of *Sex and the City*, one I've seen at least three times. But it's OK. It numbs the pain.

***

Sabrina, the yoga instructor who also does crystal healings, doesn't have a traditional office space like Elena. Instead, she works out of her home. I enter her address into my GPS and head east toward Manayunk.

This small community next to the Schuylkill Expressway has a unique quaintness about it. As my phone announces, "You've arrived," I spy an empty parking spot outside of a three-story duplex. Within moments of my ringing the buzzer under 218A, a young woman with platinum-blonde hair and dark-rimmed glasses answers the door. Jubilantly, she invites me to follow her up the stairs, then inside her apartment where she offers me a seat at a round kitchen table covered in a deep indigo tapestry.

After several minutes of small talk regarding how we both know Juliette, Sabrina asks, "Would you like a cup of chamomile tea?"

"That would be great," I say, taking in my surroundings. Her apartment is small yet meticulous. Sabrina has a definite flair. She must have eight orchids, all blooming, strategically located throughout her living space. And there are gemstones everywhere, many of which I have not come across during my research on this topic.

Sabrina fills a teakettle, turns on the gas burner, and then takes two large stoneware mugs from the cabinet. She removes two tea bags from a canister on the counter before placing one in each cup.

"So, as you know, I work with gemstones," Sabrina says when she sits down next to me.

"Yes, although Juliette didn't explain much. I'm pretty much a newbie at this."

Sabrina smiles. "It's simple. Each stone has a unique frequency, a vibration of sorts. This energy it emits corresponds with the body's chakras and other energy systems, connecting to various aspects of life we hope to either amplify or diminish."

More energy, I think to myself.

"And the location of the stone is important?" I ask, once again referencing some of the information I had read earlier this week.

"Gemstones can be worn, placed throughout the house, or carried in your pocket or purse. You can even place one in your bra if you like." As she smiles, two adorable dimples appear. "I like to think of the crystals as the body's tuning forks. Similar to aligning an instrument to the proper tone, gemstone energy attunes various areas our environment ... including our body ... for a particular outcome so we can function at a higher level."

"When you say it that way, it makes sense, kind of takes the mystery out of it."

"Actually, there is a great deal of science behind gemstones. The key is knowing the healing properties and frequencies of each stone so it can be properly applied," Sabrina says as she hands me two of the crystals sitting in a tray at the center of the table. "For instance, black obsidian is dense. Because it allows little light to pass through it, this crystal vibrates at a very low frequency, making it more of a stabilizing stone. At the opposite end is clear quartz, which has a very high vibrational element, causing a more stimulating effect."

As Sabrina rises to take the now whistling teakettle off the stove top, I take turns holding each of the gemstones in my hands, noting the different vibrations each gives off. The quartz emits lighter pulses, while the black obsidian feels dense and has a heavier sensation. I watch Sabrina as she gracefully pours the steaming water into the mugs before returning to the table, setting my cup of tea in front of me.

"Would you like honey?" she asks. I shake my head no. "My job is to understand my clients, what their needs are, and which areas of their life they want to enhance or diminish. Then I determine which stones will help them achieve their goals. Make sense?"

"Totally," I say as I sip my tea.

"So how can I help you, Marlee?" Sabrina asks, her hand cupping her chin as her elbow rests on the kitchen table.

Somewhat stunned with the directness of her question—I'd rather she tells me what would be beneficial for me—I pause. What do I need? I have no idea.

Several moments pass.

Sabrina doesn't press me for an answer; instead, she patiently waits in silence. However, in my mind, there's a timer ticking, and my response is most definitely required before the bell rings. I take a deep breath, searching for something missing in my life. What do I need? Everything seems fine with Tom and with Patrick. My husband and I have a solid relationship. It's not perfect, but what marriage is? I admit I'm nervous about my son going to college in a year and a half. But there's nothing I *need* regarding that. And thankfully, my health appears to be good. My career is on track, and I like writing for the *Inquirer*. Then finally it comes to me. Friends. I'm missing close female friends. Yes, I have many acquaintances, but people I trust, well, that's another thing.

Against my intention, I travel back to sophomore year at Cardinal O'Hara High School …

For the first time in what seemed like forever, I felt like I belonged. I was popular. My friends were the pretty girls, the cheerleaders, the ones the seniors asked out. I wasn't sure how I found myself as part of this crowd, but I was, and I finally felt important—like I mattered. Then one November afternoon, I learned otherwise.

Cramps—it was that time of the month. I was in the girls' bathroom, sitting in a stall, hoping I didn't get my period, as I had forgotten to put a tampon in my purse. It's then I heard them. The three of them—the ones whom I thought liked me.

"Can you believe Marlee? My God, what was she thinking, showing up to school in that shirt?" Susan Phillips said. I could easily recognize her nasally tone.

"I know, it's like she's trying to prove she's special or something, buying the same exact top Caroline Shippers wore last week."

That had to be Nancy Roberts. She told me she thought I looked great in the shirt. I felt the lump in my throat growing by the second.

"But that's not all … Marlee is so boring."

The third voice belonged to Maggie McDonough. And that's when my heart sank into my stomach. I'd confided in Maggie. Told her my deepest secrets.

"When I asked her what she did this weekend ... because she never showed up at Mike McCarthy's party ... she told me she and her parents went to the movies. What a liar! I know she didn't go to the movies. She was too chicken to go to Mike's after she heard his parents were out of town and his older brother bought him four cases of beer."

Maggie laughed, then the other two joined her. I pictured them rolling their eyes in disgust, all without missing a beat as they examined themselves in the mirror, applying lipstick and perfecting their hair before they hiked up the skirts of their school uniforms to reveal more of their thighs.

"And to think we told her she could hang out with us? Really? That's got to stop. So who is going to let her know?" Susan asked the others.

"Probably best if we ignore her, you know, forget to tell her where we're going after school, or make sure there are no empty seats near us at lunch," Nancy said as I heard three sets of feet walking toward the door.

The door shut, and once again, it became silent in the second-story girls' lavatory at Cardinal O'Hara High School. After hearing their conversation, I knew I couldn't return to eighth period chemistry and face those three, so I took my only option. Slowly, I emerged from the stall, ensuring no one was left in the girls' bathroom. Then, awkwardly, I headed to the nurse's office, telling the school nurse I had horrendous cramps and needed to go home. I listened as Nurse Murray made the call to my chemistry teacher, explaining I was in the health suite and would not be returning to class.

The security and status I thought I'd achieved crumbled before me. No longer was I Marlee O'Brien, one of the popular sophomore girls. Instead, I returned to plain old Marlee O'Brien, the nondescript, quiet girl who read a lot and did well in school.

I chastised myself for having believed I could be more. Those past several months, I had ignored who I was: a shy, awkward, smart fifteen-year-old who's naturally a loner. Why couldn't I accept myself? Why was I constantly trying to be somebody else?

I snap back to reality when Sabrina sweetly asks, "So have you thought of something I might be able to help you with?" No pressure is insinuated in her voice. My guess is Sabrina's only trying to bring me back to the present moment.

Without thinking, I blurt out, "Friendships, solid friends. Not the women whom you see at dinner parties or who are your kid's friends' moms … I'm talking about the kind of females who are loyal … and there for you, no matter what." There, I said it.

"I can help with that," Sabrina gingerly says as she stands up and places her hand on my shoulder, offering me a reassuring look before walking to a large closed cabinet nestled between two windows. When she opens the two doors, I see shelves filled with beautiful crystals and containers filled with gemstones, carefully categorized and perfectly organized.

Several moments later, Sabrina returns, sits down at the table, and places a beautiful deep blue stone in front of me.

"What *is* that?" I ask as I carefully pick up the multicolored, unevenly shaped stone and rub my thumb over its porous surface.

"It's blue barite, a sixth chakra crystal. This raw pocket stone can help mitigate fears and worries. It's also known for supporting friendships because it encourages honest and direct conversations and interactions. It's especially helpful if you are shy because it assists you in sharing your feelings with others." Sabrina looks me directly in the eyes as she knowledgeably recites this information.

Something tells me I underestimated Sabrina. She understands more than I first thought.

Sabrina explains when and how to utilize the barite. Then she adds it will help me become more intuitive in my relationships, realize negative thinking patterns, and accept inner truths. Immediately I think of Margaret, wondering if this stone could tame the voice in my head that constantly berates me. When Sabrina claims this stone will also assist in achieving my dreams, even connect me to the spiritual world, I'm unable to suppress a smile. Perhaps this is exactly what I need.

Sabrina suggests I keep the barite in a pocket, but then warns me about its delicate nature, recommending I may prefer to throw the gemstone in my purse. However, by having it near my body, in my field, I'll have an extra boost of confidence, especially in uncomfortable situations.

I ask Sabrina how to place gemstones in a house. She explains it depends on the location of the house as well as what energies we feel are missing.

As much as I hate to admit it, I'm kind of hooked. By the time I leave, I've scheduled an appointment for Sabrina to come to the house to do a personalized energy clearing. Of course, I intentionally choose a time when Tom will be at work. Despite knowing he'll have some sarcastic comments when he walks in and sees a crystal on the bedside table, I'm committed to exploring this healing modality. But knowing Tom, if having a gemstone near our bed leads to more sex, I think he'll be OK with that.

***

The week's final holistic healing appointment is this afternoon. However, I'm nervous about this one. Maybe it's because the session is with a male. More likely, it's due to the apprehension I have toward this whole breathwork thing. What will it be like? Will I have some big release like I've read about? If so, what am I releasing? Will it hurt? Will I make noises? Why did I sign up to do this?

I begin to second-guess my willingness to take on this assignment. Reiki and gemstones are one thing, but breathwork is an entirely new level of woo-woo.

Being Roberto's studio is located downtown, I make sure I allow enough time to navigate my way into the city. Once I hit the Blue Route, I see traffic's moving quickly. Twenty-two minutes later, I pull into an open-air parking lot adjacent to Rittenhouse Square. Roberto's studio is two blocks northwest, requiring only a short walk. Midblock, I notice his sign, "Breathe"—how appropriate. I wonder if I'm being foolish for having requested a private session. However, after seeing a YouTube video of a breathwork class, there's no way in hell I want others to see me doing this.

The studio appears simple with white walls, hardwood floors, and a long, thin table adorned with candles, reminding me of some type of altar. I see a man sitting on top of a round burgundy cushion in the corner of the room. Eyes shut and head lowered, this intriguingly handsome guy appears to be in some sort of meditative state. As the door shuts, a chime sounds, causing him to slowly open his eyes. Once he makes eye contact with me, a welcoming smile appears on his bearded face. He then stands and walks toward me. Instead of offering his hand, he bows, hands pressing together at his heart. That's when I notice his man bun. Damn, this guy is kind of hot. Perhaps breathwork won't be bad after all. However, then I remember Annie said *he and his partner, Malcolm,* live in their building.

"Marlee, I'm Roberto," he softly says, his smile now turning into a boyish grin.

Unsure exactly how to greet this man standing in front of me in striped baggy pants and a loose-fitting black tunic, I mimic his bow and reply, "Nice to meet you."

"You're new to breathwork, correct?" Roberto asks.

I nod.

"Let me set up a space for you," he says as he disappears into a small closet, soon returning with two folded multicolored blankets, a bolster, and a yoga mat. Carefully, he puts the mat on the hardwood floor and folds the first blanket in half, placing it at the top of the mat. Then he takes the bolster and positions it closer to the other end.

"Please, lie down. Allow your legs to rest against this bolster," he says as he gestures with his hand toward my newly created crib of sorts. After I position my legs on top of the bolster, I lean back, allowing my head to sink into the soft woven blanket.

"Comfortable?" he asks as he gently covers me with the second blanket.

Once again, I nod my head yes. I'm beginning to feel a bit, well, awkward right now, as if I'm a little girl being tucked into my bed at night by a stranger. As I lie on my back, snugly cocooned, my eyes dart around the room, and my pulse quickens. Is he going to play music or something? What is going to happen?

As my uneasiness begins to build, Roberto pulls his bolster closer to me, sitting down with shins crossed in front of him. He then begins to explain what I will be doing as well as what I might experience.

"We spend so much of our day taking shallow breaths. I am going to teach you another way to breathe. It will require you use your diaphragm instead of your chest to inhale." Roberto then shifts the angle of his body and proceeds to show me exactly what I am to do. "And you will breathe through your mouth, not your nose. Let your belly rise as you take in air. Don't be shy … Let it fully expand. Top your breath off at your chest, then let it go. Quickly, not as a slow exhale." He repeats the process several times before inviting me to join in.

This method of breathing feels incredibly awkward. I've spent my entire life sucking my stomach in, and now some man is asking me to distend it in a grotesque fashion. This is wrong, unnatural. Yet I try, reminding myself why I am here—for the experience so I can write the damn article.

Roberto goes on to explain it is normal for the hands to cramp, in a lobster claw fashion. "Don't be alarmed if this happens."

Right as I'm getting the hang of this new way to breathe, Roberto stands and walks to his phone, which is plugged in by the table resembling an altar. After momentarily touching the phone's screen, a beautiful pulsating sound fills the room. These rhythmic beats help me relax and breathe as he directed. Roberto leans down and takes something out of a wicker basket before walking over to where I am lying. As he gets closer, I see he's carrying a small, tie-dyed beanbag, the size of an eyeglass case. Carefully, he lays it over my brow. Small bean-like objects nestle into the crevices around my eyes.

"*Feel* the music as you breathe. The melody will guide your breaths. Listen to my voice." And so, eyes lightly shut from the weighted bag, I do my best to follow Roberto's verbal cues to inhale fully, hold, then gently exhale. The song changes four times, and with each shift, the beat increases. Yet I try to keep up with the rhythm, forcefully drawing my breath in and allowing my stomach to fully expand. It's hard work.

Halfway through the third song, something shifts inside of me. It's as though a tidal wave forms in my core, rises to my throat, and then crashes down past my heart, ribs, and stomach, landing at the base of my spine. This circular movement continues, gaining strength and momentum. My body begins to arch in alignment with the internal frenzy. The music grows louder as Roberto's voice magnifies in intensity. This revolving wave isn't only crashing; it's now exploding, leaving no parts of me untouched. I envision my chakras being swept clean, uprooting blockages hidden within. However, it is my unexpected tears that catch me off guard. Starting slowly, in silent, steady streams, they quickly begin cascading down my cheeks, spilling over both sides of my face onto the blanket that covers me.

"Don't stop breathing," Roberto says encouragingly.

So I continue to breathe, and to cry. Normally, I'd be self-conscious of my emotional outburst, but for some unknown reason, I'm not. Instead, I accept the tears and attentively focus on my breath.

Several minutes later, a new song begins. Its rhythm becomes slower, more deliberate than the others. Slowly, my body sinks into the blanket, muscles letting go, softening, surrendering. When the music ends and the room becomes silent, I soak in the sweet sensation, trying to comprehend what happened.

Roberto allows me several minutes to bask in the serenity, then slowly guides me back to the present moment. I notice my clenched hands truly do resemble lobster claws. Bit by bit, they begin to uncurl. He touches my ankles, similar to what Elena did, no doubt to ground me.

When I finally sit up, he hands me a tissue to wipe the streaks left by my salty tears. "How do you feel?" he asks.

Unsure of the answer and certainly incapable of intelligently conveying anything through words, I remain silent. Roberto only smiles, placing his hand gently on my shoulder then sitting down on the floor next to me.

"Every person has a different reaction to breathwork, especially the first time. Some release tears, shedding layers of sadness. Others scream, expressing repressed anger. And some people don't show any visible reaction to the practice. Regardless of the external effect, a great deal changes inside," he explains, speaking with his hands as well as his words in a reassuring manner.

"I felt like a tidal wave was taking over my body," I say as I open and close my hands, gradually gaining more movement.

"That's a common response," Roberto says in a soft and calming voice. "Take it easy for the rest of the day. Drink a lot of water. And if you begin to feel a bit, well, untethered, take your shoes off and walk barefoot on the ground."

"To ground myself?" I ask, noticing some of the similar post-session advice I received from Elena.

"Yes. And if it's too cold to go outside, take your shoes off and sit with your feet solidly on the ground as you envision roots growing from your feet into the floor. Either method will help you regain your balance."

A few days ago, I would have thought the man sitting next to me, in what I would have referred to as pajamas, had lost it. But after my experience in this studio, as well as the sessions with Elena and Sabrina, well, there may be something more to all of this. I certainly cannot explain what's been happening inside of me, at least not in a logical manner. All I know is how I feel. And, right now, that's pretty freakin' amazing.

***

The rest of the day, I notice I'm a bit flighty, as if my head is elsewhere. I don't mind it. In fact, I like this sensation. It's as though a part of me continues to float, in a relaxed, ethereal way.

The thought of making a meal is surprisingly the last thing on my mind. Normally one to look forward to preparing a freshly cooked dinner, I allow myself a pass, deciding I'll order Thai instead. I spend the afternoon on the sofa, lost in my thoughts. For once, I permit my mind to soar, without limits, and the effects are delicious.

At one point during my random thoughts, I pause to wonder what my life would be like today had I not had cancer. Most likely, I would have continued my ridiculously fast-paced life, focused on doing, accomplishing. Remembering those days, it's now apparent I never took time to breathe and relax. Most likely, I shunned the idea and instead pushed myself harder and harder as I mindlessly transitioned from one "to-do" to the next. Talented at multitasking, I'd flit between projects without taking a moment in between to reflect.

Of course, the mastectomy put everything on hold, forcing me to pause so I could physically heal. Naturally, I made it a priority to take better care of myself. That's when I began altering a few things in our diet, like cutting back on fats and red meat. And I made sure to exercise more. Knowing I would have to take Tamoxifen for at least five years was an extra incentive to work out—in no way would I let myself gain weight from that medicine. Yet extra pounds were not that drug's biggest side effect. It threw me into menopause, within days of first taking it. Again, the left side of my face begins to throb. Unwilling to go there, I shift my thoughts to tomorrow's meditation and yoga class at Bliss. Instantly, I feel myself relax.

Then I remember Juliette's "energy healing" offer, whatever that entails. I don't know why, but something about it scares me. Working with Elena was one thing. But Juliette is Michael's girlfriend. And she knows me. Do I want her digging into my inner thoughts? Nevertheless, I'd hate for her to think I'm not grateful, as that may hurt her feelings. I push this dilemma from my head, knowing I'll deal with it later.

***

It's on my drive to Bliss the next morning that it hits me—why are thoughts of cancer resurfacing? That is a part of my life I prefer to keep in the past. Thinking about it only causes pain and fear that it could happen again. Are these recollections reappearing because of this week's sessions? Did Reiki or breathwork stir things up? Or could it be the blue barite? I thought holistic healings were supposed to help you. If this is the case, then why would they dig up painful memories?

Twenty minutes later, I walk into Bliss. Immediately I see Juliette, who's fully engaged with clients, registering them for class on her laptop. As I look around, it's obvious yogis and meditators come in all sizes and shapes, young and old, men and women. Several moments later, it's my turn to check in.

"It's wonderful to see you. I'm glad you signed up for class," Juliette says with a welcoming smile on her face. Her tone and mannerisms are calm and even, distinctively different from the animated and quick-witted woman I met at the holiday party and then entertained at our home.

"Thanks. I'm excited to try this," I say, though I'm not so sure what *this* will entail. However, something tells me it cannot be as intense as the breathwork.

"Come, take one of the spots in the front near me," Juliette says with a slight wink as she grabs a rolled mat from behind her then leads me to an open spot. After I sit down crossed-legged on the rose-colored yoga mat, I watch as Juliette stares at me, squinting her eyes. She then walks to the shelf holding yoga equipment and returns with a cushion and two blankets.

"Let's set you up like this," she says as she folds the two blankets then places the cushion on top, motioning for me to sit down. Once seated, I squirm a bit as I try to make myself comfortable.

"See how your knees are lower than they were when you were sitting on just the mat? This is a much better position for your spine."

My eyes travel around the room, noting most people are only using a cushion. Several have one blanket. No one else has two. Juliette seems to notice my reaction.

"Marlee, stop worrying about everyone else." Her voice returns to the tone I'm more familiar with. "This is about you and what you need." Again, *what I need*—why does this phrase keep repeating?

I nod, silently vowing not to compare myself to others, though I know that's a joke. So I sit up straight with a forced smile on my face. No doubt Juliette recognizes my fake expression as she gives me a bit of a smirk before gracefully settling onto her cushion and beginning class.

The next thirty minutes fly by. I am unsure where my mind went or what it was doing during this time span. All I recall is Juliette's calming voice guiding us to breathe. Between cues directing the class to focus on our inhales and exhales, she acknowledges it's natural for the mind to drift, comparing our thoughts to clouds that appear from nowhere and then float by. Instead of obsessing about these thoughts, she asks us to label them as the emotion they represent—fear, frustration, anger. I try to follow her instructions, yet I can't help but become fixated at times.

When she rings a bell and tells us to slowly open our eyes, I'm amazed at how calm my body and mind feel. Following those around me, I place my cushion and blankets to the side of the mat in preparation for the yoga portion of the class. It's then I notice the amazing prints on the wall of the studio. Some are of an unusual-looking elephant. Others depicts a goddess-like woman with multiple arms. Although I'm unsure of what this artwork represents, I do know a part of me finds the pictures intriguing.

When I stand up to begin the yoga practice, something's different. Could it be my feet are connected more solidly to the ground? Or could it be the lack of anxious thoughts, those that usually occupy my mind? Once again, I find myself in uncharted waters, sensing a new way of being.

We begin to move. Juliette leads us through a series of poses—slow movements transition to flowing twists, lunges, and planks. We balance on one leg, bend backward, and touch the floor. Juliette uses words like *Chaturanga*, *Tadasana*, and *Trikona-sana*—Sanskrit for various yoga positions. Most in the class act as though they know what these words mean. I do my best to follow along.

Surprisingly, my body seems to like yoga. Although I certainly cannot bend and turn like the others, I experience a new freedom of sorts. This is so much more than stretching, something I often forget to do after running. Attempting to follow Juliette's instructions, I sense a graceful fluidity. She emphasizes the importance of breathing, telling us to exhale on the more exerting moves and inhale on the easier ones. After thirty minutes of shifting from one position to another, Juliette says it's time to lie on our backs. Finally, uninterrupted bliss as we rest in silent *Shavasana*, or corpse pose. At first, this term unsettles me. Before we sit up, she instructs us to turn to our right and lie in a fetal position, explaining this signifies rebirth following our practice. Instantaneously, I feel a sense of relief—or perhaps it is merely a renewal of sorts.

After completing class with a closing gratitude, I return my cushion and blankets to the shelf. Glancing over my shoulder, I watch as practitioners crowd around Juliette, perhaps thanking her or sharing their reactions to class. Regardless, they definitely adore her. After catching Juliette's eye, I give her a warm smile and a small wave as I grab my belongings and begin to exit the studio.

"Marlee." I pause when I hear her call my name. "Thank you," she says from across the room. "I hope you liked class."

I nod, as I say, "It was amazing, Juliette."

"Don't forget about the energy healing session … I think it could help you … with the article," she calls before turning to refold a messy blanket that had been left on the shelf.

Somewhat caught off guard, I give a quick nod and say, "Definitely, let's talk this week." Then I walk out the door.

I let the idea float out of my mind, similar to how Juliette suggested we allow the clouds representing our thoughts to pass by. I'm surprised with how light my body now feels, as well as the ease with which I could sit for thirty minutes in stillness. There truly must be benefits to meditation and yoga.

That's when the missing piece appears. It's the reason why I couldn't write the article—I didn't believe these practices could work. However, after this week's hands-on research, I now know the truth. Holistic healing is the real thing.

HAWLEY FALLS
February 11

Anticipating long lines of travelers who are also heading northbound on the Schuylkill Expressway for the upcoming holiday weekend, I decide it's best to leave Thursday afternoon. Besides, while Uncle Pete said Aunt Sue cleaned the house before they left for Florida, I'd prefer to arrive first, in case the place needs some tidying up.

My shoulders relax as I think about Eagle's Landing, the name my family calls our mountain home. The last time I was in Hawley Falls was August when we had a mini family reunion—Aunt Sue, Uncle Pete, Tom, Patrick, and me. Sweet memories of the cozy home sitting off the shores of Lake Hawley flood my mind, causing more excitement about this upcoming getaway.

Looking at the three full bags on the kitchen counter loaded with groceries and bottles of wine, I hope I have enough food and alcohol for four women. It's been so long since I've been on a girls' weekend that I'm not sure.

***

I pull out of our driveway a bit after one, a good time to leave as I'll get there before dark. Knowing I may hit some traffic, I'm still glad today's trip will definitely be shorter than my friends' ride tomorrow afternoon.

Sophia offered to drive Annie and Juliette. They plan to depart by midafternoon and should arrive somewhere around six o'clock tomorrow night, which will be perfect, as it gives me the entire day to get ready.

I think back to this morning, how Tom and I made it a point to stay in bed longer so we could have some time to ourselves. My relationship with Tom appears to be better. It's not that it was ever bad in any way—maybe only a bit disconnected at times. Lately, we seem to have more to talk about, probably because I've been immersed in my assignment, not so focused on Patrick or trivial matters. Regardless, I worry what it will be like when Patrick goes to college, when it is only the two of us.

Last night Tom shared with me Jonathon's concerns about Annie and how insular she's become. In fact, Jonathon was shocked Annie agreed to go to the Poconos, adding he hoped his wife wouldn't cancel last minute. But something tells me if she tried to bail, Juliette and Sophia would prevent that from happening.

My thoughts shift to the next few days. Although I've carefully assembled a blueprint for our time away, including a variety of activities combined with ample downtime, I don't know these women well. In fact, the four of us have only been together once. However, my instinct tells me not to worry.

There's always a possibility for conflict. Have you considered that, Marlee?

I ignore Margaret's negativity. No, these women are different. And our Presidents' weekend away will be amazing.

Remember, there are some things that can't be anticipated, despite the best game plan.

***

When I arrive at Eagle's Landing, as usual, I'm struck with the home's presence. In no way is this house elegant—quite the opposite. The rustic building, stained in a dark forest green, hosts a large wraparound porch with wooden rocking chairs and deer antlers nailed to one of the window frames. I look up at the slate roof, reminded of the loud noises it makes during rainstorms. Yet, despite the somewhat old-fashioned woodsy exterior of the place, the interior makes me feel warm and cozy.

As I turn my key in the front doorknob and then walk into Eagle's Landing, a smile emerges. My mom's parents are the ones who christened it with this name. Apparently, only weeks after the house was built, my grandparents witnessed a lone eagle settle on the roof, dangling a dead snake in its beak. As the story goes, they looked at one another, smiled, and promptly decided to call their new home Eagle's Landing. While a part of me questions the truth of this tale, I treasure it nonetheless.

Being this is the Poconos, I make a mental note to check for mice as well as spiders and other insects. I chuckle at the thought of Annie opening a cupboard and accidentally seeing a decaying rodent, leg half severed as it tried to gnaw its way out of its death trap. None of this phases me. Guess it's because I spent summers collecting daddy longlegs to feed the toads I kept as pets. It's all part of life in the mountains—snakes wrapped around the dock ladder, skinning freshly caught perch, even deer corpses hanging from wooden frames during deer season. No doubt there's a certain rawness, but I find a comfort in how life, death, and the in-between seem to be so easily accepted.

I pause to watch the sun as it sets over the mile-long Lake Hawley, casting a gentle glow throughout the main floor. I switch on the lights and survey the place. Overall, everything looks pretty clean. The kitchen, which opens into the family room, was remodeled three years ago. Aunt Sue used an interior decorator from town to help. Her face beamed with pride when she showed us all of its features during that year's summer reunion.

Out of all of Eagle's Landing's charming traits, my favorite is the huge stone fireplace. Instead of a television mounted above the pine mantle—there are small televisions in the bedrooms now, but when we were kids, this home was a TV-free zone—there's a head of a large elk, shot by my grandfather fifty years ago. I remember that thing scared the hell out of me when I was a little kid. As I gaze into the glass eyes of this large beast, I go back to when I was six, forty years ago …

I had woken up in the middle of the night thirsty, so I went downstairs for a glass of water. As I descended the staircase, I swore that elk was glaring at me, its nostrils flaring and eyes glowing a wild orange. After releasing a loud scream, I quickly turned and ran back to bed, hiding under the covers of my bottom bunk in the kids' room. Uncle Pete must have heard my shriek because shortly afterward, he came into the room and sat down on my bed, no doubt needing to hunch over to avoid hitting his head on the top bunk. I remember feeling terrified, my tears dampening the top of my nightgown. Uncle Pete told me not to be afraid of the elk. She was not an evil elk. She was a good elk who watched over the house and all in it. He called the elk Bessy and shared glorious tales of her heroic feats. Slowly, my fears regarding this taxidermy trophy subsided, and I poked my head out from under the covers. After a bit, I calmed down, wiped my eyes, and drifted off to sleep. Uncle Pete has a way about him, knowing exactly what to say to ease others' worries.

The old-fashioned grandfather clock standing in the corner strikes five times, announcing the time is 5:00 p.m., cocktail hour at Eagle's Landing. After all of these years, this chiming continues to startle me. I move closer to the clock, carefully examining its intricate design visible through the glass casing. Looking intently at the gears, my mind drifts off again, this time returning to the summer of '80 …

On the first day of summer vacation, we'd all pile into Mom's station wagon and leave our stone Tudor in Drexel Hill to head to

Hawley Falls, our home for the next two and a half months. I was relegated to the rear-facing jump seat, which usually made me carsick, but no one cared. Mom would give me a paper bag, just in case. Dad joined us every Friday night then would leave Monday mornings, early enough to make it back to work on time.

Each day began the same for us kids: cereal and chocolate milk followed by building forts, fishing, exploring in the woods, and playing games. Of course, my three brothers and sister chose what we did. I merely "tagged along," no doubt bugging my older siblings from early morning till late in the evening. Mom and Dad rarely knew, or cared, what we were up to. And, unless there was gushing blood or a visibly broken bone, you did not disturb the adults. We had to suck it up and take care of ourselves. Teasing, being ignored, or even bullying were not cause for going to Mom or Dad. As a small girl, I learned to figure things out on my own.

Unfortunately, there weren't any neighborhood kids my age. Everyone in the area seemed older, except for the one little boy, Travis, who lived down the street. However, Travis lived here all year long, not only during the summers. It wasn't till later we became close.

Like most older siblings, my brothers and sister knew how to bait me. Their well-rehearsed routines often started with an offer of a treat—most likely a spit-upon cookie or piece of licorice that had fallen on the ground—or asking me to watch a movie with them, only it would be a horror film, which fueled my nightmares. Some days they'd invite me to play a game, typically tag, Marco Polo, or some other activity that would most likely end poorly for me. Eventually, I realized it was easier to stay away. But ultimately, I'd become lonely and seek them out.

One warm and humid July afternoon, the brother closest to my age, Mark, suggested we play hide-and-seek. Thrilled to be included, I eagerly accepted Mark's offer, fleeing to hide in my favorite spot, behind the grandfather clock in the living room.

I waited and waited and waited for what seemed like forever. My tummy rumbled. I hadn't eaten anything since a bowl of Cheerios at breakfast. Then the clock chimed fourteen times, signaling another hour had passed. Something had to be wrong. Finally, I mustered the courage to leave my place of hiding, cautiously sliding out from behind the monstrous piece of furniture, hoping not to be discovered.

That's when I saw them, my siblings, huddled around the kitchen table, eating ice cream, and playing Monopoly, *my* favorite game. Even at age five, I knew I'd been duped, dumped, abandoned. They didn't want me around. For the rest of that summer, and the many that followed, I remained alone—just me, my books, and my journal.

I dismiss this unpleasant memory and head to the car. After bringing everything inside, I put the perishables and white wine in the fridge then store the rest of the food in the pantry closet. As Aunt Sue promised, the kitchen cabinets are stocked with the essentials—coffee, sugar, spices, and even three boxes of pancake mix. I smile as I envision her, clipboard in hand, taking inventory prior to leaving for Florida. A super organized lady, Aunt Sue no doubt has a list of items ready to purchase when they return in April.

I decide to take the only bedroom on the first floor, placing my bags at the foot of the bed. Knowing the upstairs is quieter, I suspect it will be easier for the others to sleep in—that is, if they choose to. However, that's not the reason I prefer this room. The first-floor bedroom is my favorite. It's where I spent my teen years. Once my brothers and sister had graduated from high school, it was only Uncle Pete, Aunt Sue, my parents, and me. Since there were no longer multiple kids living there each summer, they turned the bunk room upstairs into another guest room, but with a king bed.

That's why I slept in this room on the first floor. I was fine with a double. And it was within these faded paneled walls I read countless romance novels, imagining I was the beautiful heroine, pursued by the handsome and intriguing stranger. And I remember spending hours staring out the huge bay window facing right onto the lake, watching the fly fishermen cast their lines toward the shore. I guess the main reason I want to sleep here this weekend is because it makes me feel like I'm home.

Currently frozen, Lake Hawley magnificently reflects the day's last sunbeams from its icy surface. Instinctively, I move to shut the louver wooden blinds, but then I stop. There's no need to close them as this room is in the back of the house. Eagle's Landing is far enough from the lake even those ice fishing cannot see in. Plus, it's winter, so no one will be near our dock. Walkers stick to the road and trails. They rarely go exploring by the lake.

Before long, the sun sets. I put on my coat and go outside to retrieve several logs from the metal rack on the front porch. After carefully arranging the pieces of wood in the huge stone fireplace, I crumple newspaper and strategically wedge it between the logs before lighting a match at the base. Gradually, the fire grows, as does the warmth from the slowly forming embers. I sit down on the gray plaid couch, mesmerized by the darting flames. My eyes become heavy, and I drift off to sleep.

When I awaken, I look at my watch, seeing it's nearly seven. Only then do I realize I haven't eaten since the protein bar I had during the car ride here. Contemplating my dinner options, I choose the path of least resistance. Rising from the sofa, I go to the fridge and pull out the container of quinoa salad with chicken and chickpeas I bought at Whole Foods. I don't mind eating a cold meal. In fact, it's a treat not to cook. Normally, I'm conscious of properly feeding Patrick and Tom. Since it's only me, a cold supper is fine. I spoon the salad onto a plate before opening a bottle of chardonnay chilling in the fridge. After pouring myself a glass, I take my dinner and wine into the living room, set both on the wooden coffee table, then opt to sit right on the floor, leaning my back against the couch.

Looking around, I inhale deeply, close my eyes, and give a silent thanks for having a moment of solitude in this special space. When I shift back against the sofa, I feel something under my bottom. It's then I remember putting the crystal from Sabrina in my jeans pocket this morning. I remove the barite gemstone from my back pocket and trace my fingers around its uneven edges. While I am unsure if a rock can actually influence anything, a part of me hopes this stone will give me the confidence to nurture friendships this weekend. I hold it tightly, wondering if a piece of stone could help me release negative thoughts or become more intuitive, let alone form lasting relationships. Hoping Sabrina knows what she's talking about, I place the crystal into the front pocket of my jeans before taking a bite of salad.

Tonight is the first time I've been alone in this house. God knows I never was as a kid. Once I started college, my mom stopped spending summers in the Poconos. It's then she started to feel unwell. Still, my entire family would convene here every August. Well, for several years everyone did, until Mom passed. I grow somber, acknowledging my siblings no longer care to make the effort. Now it's only Uncle Pete, Aunt Sue, Tom, Patrick, and me.

I consciously stay up late, soaking in the solitude of the mountain home that's been the backdrop to so many childhood memories. After a quick conversation with Tom and several texts to Patrick, I return to the sofa with my iPad and watch reruns of *Two and a Half Men*. I actually prefer Charlie Sheen to Ashton Kutcher as the show's lead. I fill a glass with ice water then open a bag of lime tortilla chips, allowing myself to indulge.

I'd forgotten how much Eagle's Landing means to me, but apparently my body remembers as it naturally lets go. Suddenly, my jaw's relaxed and those shoulders, which are normally hunched toward my ears, have found their proper place on my back. I pull a blanket, no doubt crocheted by Aunt Sue, around my shoulders as I rest my head on a throw pillow and pull my knees toward my chest.

The past several months have been a blur—I've been too busy, perhaps needlessly so. It's as though I'm falling back into some bad habits. Maybe this explains why completing this article's been so daunting. As much as I want to finish it and believe I'm on the right path, I simply can't do it. There's still something missing. For it to be believable, I need more. Unfortunately, I don't know what "more" means. Anyway, I've blocked out the entire next week after we return to complete this assignment. I let out a heavy sigh, take one last chip, wash it down with a sip of water, then allow my head to sink back into the throw pillows as I watch one more show in the series. Finally, after the episode is over, I close my iPad then rise from the sofa, putting the empty chip bag in the trash can and setting the glass in the sink. Time for bed.

As I crawl under the warm down comforter, I think of Tom and Patrick, saying my prayers that both are fine. Then I add one more—I ask that this weekend teaches me about true friends.

***

Forgetting to set an alarm, or perhaps unconsciously choosing not to do so, I permit myself to sleep in. When the bright sunlight streams in through the bay window, I squint as I slowly take in the familiar room around me. My eyes leisurely drift from the watercolor painting depicting fish hanging from a metal stringer to the solid oak armoire used to store extra wool blankets and hand-embroidered quilts. Finally, they settle on the avocado-and-forest-green shag carpet, no doubt a magnet for years of spilt juice, cookie crumbs, embedded dog hair, and God knows what else.

Instead of popping out of bed, I remain under the thick down comforter and interweave my fingers at the base of my neck.

As I arch my back, the top of my head nestles into the soft pillow. Instinctively my legs stretch toward the opposing corners of the double bed, where the covers remain tightly tucked. I stay this way for several minutes, soaking in the tranquility. This is what it must be like to wake up and have no one need you. Patrick is pretty self-sufficient—it's Roxie who demands my attention first thing. And as much as I love our dog, I appreciate the break from her early-morning routine.

Twenty minutes later, I reluctantly rise from the warm bed. After putting on the fuzzy robe I packed, I find my slippers next to the nightstand then head to the bathroom and begin my new routine of tongue scraping, oil swishing, body brushing, and massaging oil into my skin. In less than ten minutes, I'm in the kitchen making a pot of coffee. Of course, first I heat a kettle of water and cut up a lemon. While the coffee's brewing, I sip on the lemon water as I place extra logs from the hearth on top of the ashen remnants in the fireplace, add crumpled newspaper on top, then toss in a match. Instantly it flames, as though a natural continuation from last night.

I return to the kitchen to rinse my mug, ensuring to wash off any lemon remnants, then pour myself a cup of freshly brewed coffee. Mmmm, this tastes so much better than hot water and lemon juice. Nevertheless, if I want to see whether Ayurvedic practices have any impact, I have to honor my commitment. Mug in hand, I shuffle over to the sofa and curl up, wrapping my arms around my knees as I sip the French roast in solitude.

In no rush to begin my day, I remain on the couch, pulling the crocheted throw around me. When my cup is empty, I return to the kitchen to refill it as I heat up one of the muffins I bought at my favorite bakery in Radnor. After spreading honey butter on the warmed blueberry muffin, I dig my journal out of the canvas Orvis bag that sits by the counter before retreating again to the couch.

It's been so long since I've taken time to write for me. Lately, everything seems to have a purpose, a deadline. Somehow, I've lost the desire to freewrite. So, for the next thirty minutes, I allow myself this sacred privilege, jotting down ideas and writing in cursive as opposed to typing on my laptop. I sketch a few images. Before I know it, words begin to flow as my feelings form on paper.

Conscious there are things to do before everyone arrives, after ten more minutes, I go to my bedroom and get dressed, changing into dark gray tights and a comfy black cable-knit sweater. I pull my hair up in a clip, wash my face, and apply moisturizer. It's nice to take a break from wearing makeup.

After putting on my puffy coat, I grab my purse and keys from the kitchen counter as well as a list of items I need from downtown. Remembering how much Annie liked Tom's margaritas, I quickly text him to make sure I have all of the necessary ingredients on my list. Before heading outside, I carefully tuck my phone into my purse.

The cold, crisp air strikes my face when I walk onto the front porch. A layer of frost covers the Audi's windshield. Spoiled by having a garage at home, I'm not used to "warming up" my car—but there is no garage in the Poconos. Once inside the car, I shiver as the cold from the frigid leather seat penetrates through my tights. Five minutes later, defroster on high, the windows become clear as the car begins to warm. I shift the car into gear and head to town.

As I approach the first stop light in town—there are only three in Hawley Falls—I see the liquor store on the corner. Luckily, there's an open parking space directly in front, so I turn on my blinker, and as soon as the light turns green, I parallel park in front of the state store.

The door chimes as I enter, causing the clerk to look up. Although he appears familiar, I cannot remember his name or the particulars about his family. Smiling, I give a courteous nod as I gently pull a small shopping cart from the stack at the front of the store. Within moments, I find the tequila, surprised with the multiple brands available. Picking one of the nicer bottles—cheap tequila often equates to a nasty headache—I place it in my cart then proceed to the wine section, deciding it's better to have too much than not enough.

As I am perusing through the choices of reds, I'm startled by a familiar voice, one I have not heard for years. My body freezes as his smooth tone resonates through my ears. Suddenly, I feel uncomfortably warm. As I turn toward the voice, wondering if my memory is correct and it is who I think, my arm accidentally bumps into a display, causing a large cardboard vodka bottle to topple onto the linoleum floor with a loud crash. The speaker immediately stops talking before looking in my direction. Our eyes meet, and a big grin forms on his face.

"Marlee? Marlee O'Brien, is that you?" this man, who to this day has an uncanny resemblance to Luke Wilson, asks.

I feel my face flush as I lean down to pick up the cardboard Tito's advertisement, setting it upright before saying, "Yes, it's me. Travis?" My head tilts slightly to the left as I give my best "I'm so surprised" smile.

In an instant, I'm in Travis's arms. The feel of his skin against mine combined with his musky scent returns me to the summer of 1993. I was eighteen, a recent graduate from Cardinal O'Hara High School. For those twelve weeks before I began my freshman year at the University of Vermont, I spent every free moment with Travis Keating.

It was only Mom and me that summer, and of course Aunt Sue and Uncle Pete, before they moved to Eagle's Landing permanently. Dad had passed the prior winter, and all of my siblings were out of school and working full-time. Three of the four were married.

I had a job lifeguarding at The Birch Lodge, the one and only resort in Hawley Falls. Travis worked at the hardware store downtown. That entire summer, we spent each evening and days off together—hiking secluded wooded trails, waterskiing behind his family's motorboat, fishing in isolated streams, or swimming in the warm moonlit lake at night.

"Marlee ... beautiful as ever! What brings you to Hawley Falls?" Travis asks as he takes a step back to fully look at me. His dark brown hair, once thick and slightly wavy, is now somewhat thinner and cut short. And I can see his hairline's beginning to recede. Yet those intoxicating golden-brown eyes with flecks of amber still mesmerize me.

"I'm only here for the weekend. Have some girlfriends driving in tonight," I say, trying to sound nonchalant, although I feel myself blushing from the sight of him and my unexpected trip down memory lane. Damn, he looks good. Not meaning to stare, I can't help but observe his lean, muscular build. Suddenly, I wish I'd put on some makeup before coming to town. It's then I notice his eyes glance down at my left hand. His body seems to exude a silent sigh.

Never one to miss a beat, he continues by saying, "Well, if you gals need anything, holler, OK? My number is in the phone book." Of course the residents of Hawley Falls still use phone books. With that, he gives me a wink—the one that used to melt my heart.

"Good seeing you," I say as I lean forward and gently kiss his cheek. This time, it's Travis who blushes. I guess he remembers as much as I do.

After paying for three bottles of cabernet sauvignon, a fifth of Jack Daniel's, and a bottle of Patrón, I turn back toward Travis before exiting the liquor store. He's crouching, a clipboard in his hand and a pen clenched between his teeth while looking at the bottles on the bottom shelf. It occurs to me I didn't ask him what he is doing or how he's been. Guess I was taken aback from seeing him after all of these years. After all, how often do you randomly run into the first guy you slept with? Shaking my head, I continue walking toward the car.

***

Around two thirty, Sophia texts to tell me they are about to leave. Assuming it will take at least three hours, I predict they'll arrive sometime between five thirty and six. I smile, knowing that allows me a bit more time to myself.

The thermometer located on the back porch window reads forty degrees. Unsure if I'll have any opportunity to exercise this weekend, I decide to go for a run. There's a five-mile loop I frequently ran in high school, perfect for a day like today—sunny, cool, and a bit windy. I head to my room to change into running clothes, grab a set of gloves, then lace up my sneakers. Last minute, I decide to take my phone with me, just in case.

Less than an hour later, I'm back, cheeks bright pink from the wind whipping off the frozen lake. Invigorated from the brisk exercise, I decide to do a few sit-ups and push-ups before showering.

As I emerge from the bedroom, clean, warm, and relaxed, I realize I can't remember the last time I had a day like today. My thoughts return to bumping into Travis at the liquor store. He really did look good. And why was I such a klutz? Knocking over that cardboard Tito's sign? I shake my head, wondering why I became so flustered at seeing Travis. Then I remember how it all ended—how *I* ended it. At the time, I thought I was acting stoically, doing what was best. But now I realize what an ass I was.

Regardless, that was a lifetime ago. Glancing in the hall mirror on my way to the kitchen, I'm reminded how little I resemble that eighteen-year-old girl who fell in love with the kindest guy she ever knew. *None of that matters anymore*, I think as I head to the kitchen to prepare dinner for my guests.

AND SO IT BEGINS
February 12

Upon taking the gouda, havarti, and brie from the fridge, I begin assembling a tray of charcuterie. Energy courses through my veins as I artfully arrange the cheeses with smoked meats and nuts. Grabbing another platter from the cabinet, I fill it with fresh fruit, cut-up vegetables, and hummus. Juliette's a vegetarian, and I suspect she may appreciate some healthier options.

After placing both trays on the coffee table by the fireplace, I taste the simmering chili. Deciding it needs a little more kick, I add a bit of cayenne pepper to it before retrieving more logs from the front porch. The temperature's dropped, and the air feels thick and moist, like a wet wool blanket. My bones tell me snow's coming. The full moon, amidst dense clouds, illuminates a portion of the darkening sky. The forecast calls for a light coating tonight, but nothing out of the ordinary for this time of year.

After rekindling the fire, I mix up a batch of Old Fashioneds, taste testing them along the way. Tom suggested I serve his favorite cocktail, and it truly is the perfect drink for a night like tonight. As I muddle the orange, headlights begin to shine through the kitchen window, and I hear a car coming down the gravel driveway. A shot of adrenaline surges through me—the weekend's about to begin. Eagerly, I grab my coat from a peg by the front door and go outside to greet the three women piling out of Sophia's Volvo wagon. They're laden with weekend luggage and canvas bags. Gingerly, I hug each then help them with their totes filled with fresh baked goods, flowers, and no doubt other treats.

"This is so dope!" Juliette's expression catches me off guard, causing me to laugh aloud.

"Your family's home is beautiful, Marlee," Sophia says as she places a pastry box on top of the kitchen counter and hands me a bouquet of gorgeous tulips.

"It's amazing. Oh, Marlee, this is going to be so much fun!" Annie, dressed in a woolen hat and a quilted Barbour jacket, adds. She's looking more relaxed than I've seen her. Thank God Sophia and Juliette got her here.

"I'm so glad we could all be together this weekend," I say before I take the three upstairs and show them their rooms. While they settle in, I put the yellow tulips in a vase of water and place them on the center of the countertop. Smiling at the bouquet, which is as lovely and graceful as Sophia, I sense this weekend might exceed my expectations.

Moments later, everyone's downstairs and gathered in the living area next to the blazing fire. I pour each woman a cocktail then add maraschino cherries to our drinks before placing the half-empty pitcher of Old Fashioneds on the coffee table.

"This is absolutely delicious," Sophia says after taking a sip, then helps herself to a piece of havarti.

"Seriously, how cool is this place?" Juliette asks as she slowly walks around, observing framed pictures from family gatherings throughout the decades, which hang on the wall. "Look. This must be Marlee when she was little. I can tell by the shape of her nose and her smile," she says as Annie and Sophia huddle next to her around a faded photo of me in a metal rowboat, wearing an orange life jacket and courageously trying to maneuver the long, wooden oars.

"How adorable," Sophia declares as she strains her eyes to look deeper at the picture, as if she's searching for something more than what appears on the photograph's surface. "Can you see how

AND SO IT BEGINS 111

content she looks? Something tells me this mountain home means a great deal to you." Sophia breathes a soft sigh of appreciation as she smiles then looks my way.

"Can you imagine coming here as a kid?" Annie asks as she points to where Bessy the elk is mounted on the wall. "If I were little, that would scare the shit out of me if I woke up in the middle of the night and saw that monstrous head."

I have to chuckle. Not only at Annie's choice of words but also because it's as though Annie knew exactly what I experienced as a kid.

Juliette begins to belly laugh. "Annie, I'm shocked to hear you speak like that," she teases.

"Well, it would." There's pure sincerity in Annie's voice, and I sense she possesses a truly innocent side. Perhaps this accounts for the timidity I often hear in her speech.

As we sip our drinks by the fire, conversation flows. Everyone relaxes, especially Annie.

"Juliette, I loved the class I took. You both should visit Bliss," I say to Sophia and Annie, who are sitting next to one another on the sofa. "The first part was purely meditation. It wasn't at all like I imagined it would be. Because of the way Juliette guides you, helping you remain focused on your breath and aware of your thoughts, it's not hard to sit still." I look at Juliette, who is now grinning ear to ear, no doubt happy I'm promoting her studio and praising her technique. "And the yoga was perfect ... not too difficult but challenging enough. My body felt incredible afterward." As if on cue, my shoulders slide down my back as I state this.

"I'm thrilled you liked it," Juliette says in the most heartfelt manner as she places her hands in prayer position at her sternum and does a slight bow. "I realize my classes aren't for everyone. Some people come expecting a big workout."

"I definitely felt like I moved a lot." I pause, remembering Juliette's ability to both calm and inspire, combining the dichotomies of her own personality into her teaching.

"Yes, my classes require effort, but they don't cause exhaustion. There are many styles of yoga that push the participants. And that's great, if that's what you want." Juliette's tone insinuates she does not agree with this philosophy.

"I have a home practice," Sophia says as she folds her hands on her lap. "It is what I do after work. I find it so relaxing, especially when I practice to music."

"I've never tried yoga." Annie's shoulders slump, and she makes an awkward-looking face, as if she's unsure whether she'd like it.

"Come next week," Juliette says. "My studio is only a few blocks from where you live. We have several evening classes, which should fit into your schedule. I think you'd like the Yin class. I love this style of yoga because it's slower paced and allows you to get into your deep muscles and fascia."

Hesitantly, Annie agrees to look at the schedule. It's as though I can see the scared little girl returning in her expression, suggesting she has no intention of following through.

Our conversations shift from one topic to another. I learn Annie cross-stitches when she wants to unwind from work, Sophia speaks three languages (a requirement her parents set for their children), and Juliette learned how to surf in Bali while working one summer at a yoga retreat center. Observing this newly formed cluster of unlikely females, I feel my mouth round upward. I've done it. This weekend is actually happening.

After filling our glasses with what remained in the pitcher, I realize everyone must be hungry. Transitioning to the kitchen, I take the salad of baby mixed greens, tangerines, slivered almonds, and feta from the fridge and place everything on the counter next to soup bowls and salad plates.

"Please, help yourself," I say as I remove the lid from the pot of vegan chili before retrieving the tray of corn muffins warming in the oven and placing them into a napkin-lined basket. I exhale as I eye the meal, graced with the beautiful yellow tulips Sophia brought. A casual Friday supper, exactly as I intended.

Following dinner, the three women take over my kitchen, loudly conquering the cleanup. They instruct me to sit and relax, claiming I've already done more than my share. Alone at the dining table, I eye the interaction in front of me. Soapsuds loom near the brim of the sink, dish towels flash like flags waving on a windy day, and pots clang as they are returned to their proper places. I notice the sweet connection occurring. All's proceeding to plan.

But doesn't it always start off like this?

Annoyed with Margaret, I consciously ask her to leave my brain and grant me a weekend without her condescending comments. Though I know this voice is only trying to keep me safe, *her* warnings are completely unnecessary with these three.

The women return, carrying a bottle of wine, a plate of macaroons, and bowls of lemon sorbet covered with berries. While a part of me misses Tom and Patrick, it feels good to be with friends, miles away from my typical routine.

"I'm so glad you talked me into coming on this trip. You have no idea how much I needed to get away." Annie's cheeks turn rosy, perhaps from the realization she needed this break, but more likely from the cocktails and wine.

"Oh, I think we may have," I say, winking at Sophia and Juliette.

"No, seriously, I can't remember the last time I was with women ... hanging out ... no expectations. It's so freeing." I silently giggle as Annie drains her wineglass then reaches for the bottle of chardonnay.

"You are right, Annie." Sophia speaks next. "It is wonderful to be in the company of bright, caring, and interesting women. I am so happy everyone took time away from their busy lives. And cheers to Marlee for hosting."

Glasses clink.

"Well, I'm certainly glad we're together. Plus, this house needs some life in it." I pause, remembering the noise and chaos of dinners from my youth. "Somehow, I've forgotten how special this place is to me."

Before I can lose myself in the past, Juliette commands the group's attention, clinking her glass. "Well, kudos to Marlee. This place is pretty spectacular ... And to Annie and Sophia. Even though we've only recently met, I feel a vibe, you know, a connection ... kinda like we're meant to be here ... together ... to help one another grow."

My God, she's already beginning to push in that direction. Leave it to Juliette. My new friend continues: "Each of us have some sort of a gift, something unique about her."

"What do you mean?" Annie naively inquires.

"Well, Annie ... you are a gifted psychologist. Every day you help kids deal with their emotions and traumas. You work with them to discover what's wrong, where they're hurting, and then you devise a plan for them to get better. This makes you unique from the rest of us." Juliette sits up, proud and confident as she makes her point.

"Sophia's the doctor," Annie says, missing the point. "She's the one who heals people."

"True, but Sophia's expertise is medical. She deals with the physical symptoms of her patients. Although her gift is extremely critical, it's different from yours. Do you understand?" Juliette asks. Annie nods, acknowledging this clear-cut explanation.

"And your gift is how you help people find peace on their mat," Sophia says to Juliette. "However, I have a strong sense you do much more. I believe you also inspire others, through both your skills as a teacher and your ability to motivate your clients to follow their own path. And, from what you shared on the car ride here, I anticipate you will flourish as an energy healer."

Without speaking, Juliette brings her hands together at her chest and humbly bows toward Sophia.

"Marlee ... what's your gift?" Annie asks, breaking the serene moment of silence between Sophia and Juliette.

"I'm not so sure I have a gift," I say half-heartedly as I stand up and go to the kitchen to fill a pitcher with water.

"Of course you do," Juliette calls from the table. "Think ... What can you do or what knowledge do you possess that's unique to you?"

Pausing for a moment as I add cubes of ice to the pitcher, I then say, "Honestly, I don't believe I possess anything special."

"Come on, Marlee ... It's so obvious!" Juliette says in an encouraging tone. "We all see it, and I'm sure if you look deeply enough, you could too."

I remain silent, struggling to answer this uncomfortable, yet fair, question. I feel similarly to when Sabrina asked me what I needed.

Think! This is embarrassing. What's special about me? I write, but that's not a gift; it's a profession.

"My writing?" I ask tentatively.

"Yes," Sophia says in an encouraging tone, "though there is more to what you offer. We have all witnessed one of your greatest gifts ... twice." She lets out a small giggle.

Standing at the kitchen counter, I rack my brain but cannot see what the rest can.

"It's your cooking," Juliette says impatiently. "You're amazing in the kitchen. Your food brings joy and healing."

My cooking is my gift? It's healing to others? I return to the women, who are now transitioning from the dining table to sit by the fireplace. After placing the pitcher of water and four empty glasses on the coffee table, I settle back into the padded rocking chair next to the fireplace, contemplating this novel idea. Do I really weave loving kindness into my meals? Was it possible the foods I prepared not only nurtured the body but also replenished the soul? Could my careful measuring, precise chopping, and mindful mixing be making a difference?

Annie, who's been quiet, most likely feeling the effects of one and a half Old Fashioneds and wine, says, "Marlee, twice we've had dinners you've cooked. I can't explain it, but I feel satiated afterward, satisfied and content. I know the recipes you choose are delicious; however, there's something more to it. You have a special touch when it comes to food."

"I agree. When Jared and I first tasted your polenta and short ribs, a certain warmth settled over both of us. He mentioned it on the drive home. We attributed it to the beautiful table setting and the excellent company ... Now I know it is more. You infuse yourself and your loving energy into what you cook," says Sophia.

Humbled, I say, "Thank you for your kind words. And speaking of gifts"—I intentionally shift the conversation away from me—"I want to thank you each for connecting me with your alternative healers. I met with each a few weeks ago."

"What did you think of Roberto?" Annie asks as her eyes widen. "Was breathwork as scary as it sounds?"

"Out of all three sessions, I have to say breathwork was the wildest." I take a big sip of my water then set the glass on the table so I can stand up and demonstrate his technique. "He had me breathing in a bizarre way for close to thirty minutes." I then proceed to show them, from a side view, how I had to distend my stomach so I could breathe with my diaphragm and then exhale in a short breath. "But the strangest thing is my hands started to clench like claws and then, all of a sudden, I started crying."

"Marlee, I am so sorry. Had I known it would have made you sad, I wouldn't have recommended Roberto." Annie shrinks as she says this, her eyebrows furrowing.

"Don't be silly. I wasn't sad. The tears were a release, and apparently a big one for me. In fact, I felt amazing afterward." Having some distance between that session and now, I can better appreciate the effects induced breathing had on me.

"Well, Sabrina told me she enjoyed meeting you. She said you had great questions and appeared truly open to the idea of gemstone energy," Juliette, who's sitting on a chair facing the fire, says as she tucks her legs beneath her.

"Talking with Sabrina was incredibly interesting," I say, recalling the warmth and genuine goodness I felt from our time together. "I totally buy into the crystal healing effects. After all, gemstones are from this earth, so their energetic vibration seems natural. Sabrina introduced me to the basics, but I'd love to learn more. She gave me this piece of barite." I pull the stone from my front pocket and hand it to Juliette, who holds it for several moments before passing it to Sophia. "Sabrina said it will help me with my intuition and dreams." I leave out the part about friendships and negative thought patterns. "In fact, I asked Sabrina to come to our house and do what she called a crystal healing grid. It's supposed to balance the energy and provide protection inside of your home."

"Does Tom know you're doing this?" Annie, who now has the barite, asks, eyes wide with concern.

"Not exactly." I grin, admitting this aloud. "I don't think he'd notice any stones I placed around the house. He's been working long hours lately. Patrick and I barely see him." My inflection drops as I say these words, as I realize the truth in them. It's not something I've consciously complained about. Nevertheless, Tom's been ridiculously busy with work.

The room becomes silent. Hoping my comment didn't cross the line with any of these women, I'm quickly relieved when I see all three nod their heads.

"Jonathon's never home. And when he is, he spends most of his time in his study, reading up on the newest procedures and latest research."

"It is the same with Jared. I, too, am busy with my own work. Yet I am conscious about taking time for myself." Sophia pauses and a look of concern comes over her. "I worry about my husband. I am beginning to notice the stress on his face."

"Well, Michael and I don't live together," Juliette begins, causing me to momentarily wonder if their relationship might be headed in that direction. "However, it's obvious his hours are treacherous. Being he's one of the youngest surgeons, I get he has to take the worst call schedules. Guess it's all part of the profession." Juliette scrunches her shoulders toward her ears in a resigned fashion.

"What did you think of Elena, Marlee?" Sophia asks, shifting to a more pleasant subject.

Realizing I've discussed every healing session except for the one with Elena, I quickly smile before saying, "My session with Roberto was mind-blowing and caused a huge emotional release. And what Sabrina shared about crystals sounded logical, making it easier to comprehend the information. However, while I personally connected most with Elena, I can't begin to explain what Reiki is or how it works." I let out a small laugh as I shake my head, perhaps in disbelief of the concept of energetic healing. "It moved me, literally. I could feel currents flow through my body. Later, there was a lightness inside of me, one that certainly wasn't there when I arrived. It's hard to describe. It felt as if she took away some of the heavy muck … you know, the feelings that weigh you down." I'm having trouble finding the correct words to relay the experience.

"Elena is gifted. She possesses a unique ability to home in on your vulnerable areas and then begin to release the source of your blockages, layer by layer." Sophia's eyes drift toward the ceiling. Perhaps she's also at a loss to appropriately describe the sensations she receives when she is on Elena's table.

"I'm certified in Reiki, level 3, actually," Juliette says, as she stands to refill her wineglass.

Immediately, I'm reminded of Juliette's offer to "work on me," and I feel horribly I haven't followed up.

Juliette returns the half-empty bottle to the table, puts the glass to her lips, and takes a sip. "For me, doing Reiki on someone kinda feels like taking a strong vacuum and sucking out all of the yucky stuff inside, making everything clean and smooth again." Juliette grins.

"Is it possible to become free of the muck?" I ask as I tilt my head to the side, truly interested in the answer.

"Ultimately—at least that is the goal. But the layers are thick. Even after working on one issue for years, it doesn't mean you resolved the problem. Most likely, it will resurface, to test whether you are finally ready to fully release it. Occasionally, the process becomes two steps forward then one step back ... or possibly more at times." Juliette looks intently at me, as if trying to convey a deeper message.

Gathering my courage, I ask, "Does your offer still hold? I'd love to see what it's like ... you know ... what you do with your energy healings."

"Absolutely. We could do it this weekend—that is, if you're up for it."

Luckily, Annie chimes in, rescuing me. "Now that you've met with these healers, have you finished the article?" Her eyes beam as if ready to congratulate me on completing my assignment.

"No." I pause, wondering how much I want to share. "I've completed a version of the article, but it is not convincing." I exhale before continuing. "There's no true substance to it. Right now, it reads like I'm presenting ways to feel better without getting medical help. What I need is some sort of evidence that inspires readers to seek alternative healings. Don't misunderstand, I think what I've written will nicely promote Reiki, crystal healing, and breathwork ... and of course yoga and meditation practices." I look toward Juliette. "Plus, there's another component I'm including ... Ayurveda. My friend Natalie is in the process of receiving her certification," I say. Looking at the women across the table, it's evident Juliette and Sophia are familiar with the term. However, Annie looks perplexed.

"Ayurveda is an ancient Indian practice widely used in various parts of the world. It's based on *doshas*, or body types. For each *dosha*, there is a suggested way to eat, take care of your skin, even exercise. In fact, the practices also take into account the seasons of the year, physical locations, and the time of the day." I stop there. "It's hard to explain, and honestly, I'm trying to figure it all out myself. Nevertheless, the problem with the article is I'm stuck. But I've blocked off all of next week to figure out how to tie it together." I try to sound confident as I share this. However, I suspect the problem's bigger than I'm admitting.

"What do you normally do when you experience this? Surely you have had writer's block in the past?" Sophia asks as she leans toward me. I sense a mix of concern and compassion in her voice.

Appreciative Sophia appears to understand my dilemma, I say, "That's the strange thing. Normally, writing comes easily to me. Although something about this assignment is different. It's as though I have more to learn." I shake my head. "I don't feel ready to complete it."

"Well, then trust your instincts," Juliette chimes in. "This isn't your first rodeo. You're an experienced writer, Marlee. When you're ready, the words will come."

And with that comment, I pause, knowing Juliette's 100 percent correct. You can't force writing, for if you do, it ends up being utter crap.

Once again, Juliette surprises me, as she pulls a joint out of her shirt pocket and lights up, takes a hit, then turns toward me and asks, "You smoke?"

Totally caught off guard, I'm speechless. Then, after I realize the last time I smoked pot was during my senior year at University of Vermont, I say, "Why not?" I take the joint, inhale, then lean across the coffee table and pass it to Sophia.

Sophia looks unfazed. I watch her inhale, hold her breath, then slowly exhale white smoke. I turn and look at Annie, who is seated on the sofa to Sophia's right. Wide eyed, Annie appears stunned.

"Annie, this is totally your choice," Juliette says. "Seriously, don't do it if you're not comfortable."

Annie's eyes dart toward the braided rug beneath the plaid sofa. Slowly, she looks up and says, "I've never tried marijuana." Embarrassed, she shrugs her shoulders.

Sophia places her hand on Annie's shoulder. "I have recently started smoking for insomnia." She lets out a big sigh. "I find it helps me sleep. Actually, Jared suggested it. I had been experiencing too many restless nights, and it was beginning to interfere with my ability to function soundly during the day."

"I *do* have trouble sleeping some nights. Do you think it would help me?" Annie asks.

"Give it a try. It certainly won't hurt," Juliette says as she takes the joint from Sophia and takes another hit. She looks toward me, but I smile and shake my head no, so she offers it to Annie.

Hesitantly, Annie reaches her right hand toward the lit rolled paper, then with great caution, brings the joint to her lips and takes the slightest inhale.

"Try it again. I don't think you got anything," Juliette says, a tone of encouragement in her voice. "Take a slow inhale, hold it, then release."

Annie does as she's told, and as the smoke leaves her mouth, she coughs. Moments later, a calmness comes across her. The three of us do a sideways glance.

"That's it," Juliette says as she takes the joint from Annie.

Annie doesn't speak. In fact, she says little for the rest of the night. Instead, she watches, listens to our conversation, and occasionally nods in agreement.

Before long, we call it a night. After putting any remaining dishes and glasses in the sink, we each head to our bedrooms, declaring no wake-up calls tomorrow. Everyone wants to sleep in.

AN

UNEXPECTED VISITOR

February 13

Although I deliberately did not set an alarm, I'm wide awake by seven o'clock. It's funny, I get so hot at night, waking up multiple times to throw the covers completely off of me. But in the morning, I'm freezing—the joys of menopause, a way-too-early menopause caused by needing to take Tamoxifen.

After wrapping the fleece robe tightly around me, I head to the bathroom to brush my teeth and complete my now-daily Ayurvedic rituals. When I enter the family room ten minutes later, it's totally quiet. I smile, thankful the others are able to sleep in. Plus, this allows me time to prepare breakfast.

Peering out the front window, I note close to six inches of new snow has accumulated on top of the railing. It's the perfect amount for snowshoeing. Uncle Pete assured me there were six pairs, all in good shape, in the shed outside. In fact, prior to leaving for Florida this November, he'd taken inventory of everything in that shed. He told me he put a list on his laptop so he'd have access to it at all times. I shake my head, envisioning my aunt and uncle and their lists.

Doing my best to keep noise to a minimum, I make a pot of coffee as I sip a cup of hot water and lemon juice, which, surprisingly, tastes soothing this morning. Grabbing a ripe cantaloupe from the bowl of fruit sitting on the counter, I cut it into cubes, neatly arranging the fresh melon onto a beige stoneware platter I find stored in a cabinet below the oven. After retrieving a container of washed berries from the fridge, I add them to the plate before garnishing the platter of fruit with fresh mint.

It's then I remember Sophia brought croissants. Searching the pantry, I find a jar of Aunt Sue's homemade blackberry jam. It takes a bit of muscle to pry the lid open, but as soon as I do, I smell the sweet woodsy scent as it rises from the glass jar. I'd forgotten how much I loved her jam. This sensory recall returns me to one summer afternoon spent helping Aunt Sue with this exact recipe. I remember the huge pot on the stove filled with blackberries we had picked earlier that day. My job was to add the sugar while she stirred. And, despite her warnings, I burned my tongue, unable to resist licking the berry mixture from her wooden spoon when she wasn't looking.

A noise shakes me from my trip down memory lane. Turning toward the sound, I see Annie walk into the kitchen. She looks absolutely horrible—her eyes appear lifeless, and her face has a pale cast to it.

"Good morning, Annie. I started a pot of coffee. It should be ready in a moment." Hopefully, that will do the trick. We did drink a lot last night, and I'm guessing Annie's feeling the effects.

"Thank you, Marlee," Annie says, her voice strained. "I don't feel well. My stomach is really upset."

"Let me check if there is any Pepto Bismol in the bathroom closet. I believe my aunt keeps Tylenol there as well." I place the jar of jam on the counter and begin to walk toward the linen closet.

"That would be—" However, before Annie can finish her sentence, she runs into the hallway bathroom, quickly shutting the door behind her. It's then, despite the closed door, I hear her vomit. Immediately a wave of queasiness comes over me. Whenever anyone throws up, it makes me feel like I will as well.

Ten minutes later, Annie reemerges, looking paler than before. I hand her a bottle of Tylenol, a bottle of pink Pepto Bismol, and a glass of water.

"I know it doesn't look appetizing, but try it. I think it will help."

As Annie struggles to swallow the pink liquid, Sophia comes down the stairs.

"Good morning. I hope everyone slept well." Her cheery voice, accompanied by her beautiful, warm complexion, immediately brightens the room. Sophia's pulled her raven-black hair into a neat ponytail at the nape of her neck.

"Thank you, I did," I say.

Then Sophia sees Annie hunched over the island counter.

"Annie, what is wrong?" Sophia asks.

"Oh, I don't know … I think it was the Old Fashioneds … or the wine … or both. I'm not a big drinker. I feel horrible." Her hands go to her stomach. "And I threw up."

I'm beginning to wonder if Annie remembers smoking pot last night. Sophia approaches Annie, placing the back of her hand on Annie's forehead.

"You do not feel warm," Sophia says, closely examining Annie's face. "Let me make you some tea and toast. See how that settles before you try to take anything." Sophia quickly moves about the kitchen and, in minutes, places a plate with a dry piece of toast and a cup of warm peppermint tea in front of Annie.

Annie nibbles a corner of the toasted bread between sips of tea. Slowly, a tinge of color returns to her cheeks. However, it's Sophia I watch, not Annie. It's as though she knows something but is keeping it to herself.

Juliette, dressed in black yoga pants and a flowing embroidered tunic, joins us.

"Sleep well?" I ask as I pour myself a cup of coffee.

"Most definitely. I think I slept until six." She proudly announces this as she reaches inside the canister filled with tea bags.

I look at the clock. It's a bit after eight.

Juliette must have noticed my confused expression because she adds, "I meditate then do yoga every morning. Normally my day begins at four thirty. Having ninety extra minutes of sleep was amazing."

Never in my wildest dreams could I imagine rising daily, before the sun, to sit on a meditation cushion, silently, then practice yoga. Perhaps that explains why Juliette looks like she does, and I'm lucky to have breakfast and make it to a nine o'clock appointment.

Assembled around the counter, three of the four of us continue where we left off last night, sharing stories from our past. As Sophia, Juliette, and I slowly reveal more of our true selves to the group, Annie remains silent, leaning on the counter as she slowly drinks her tea. She must feel horribly.

Before we know it, it's ten thirty. By now, the sun's shining brightly, causing a sparkling effect on top of the fresh snow outside.

"Would anyone be interested in snowshoeing?" I ask.

"I would love to, though I have not snowshoed before." Sophia's eyes light up in anticipation.

"I'm game," Juliette says as she takes a banana from the fruit bowl, pulls back the peel, and takes a bite.

"Thank you, Marlee, but I am going to pass. I think I'll spend the rest of the morning on the sofa, resting." While Annie looks better, she continues to nurse her second cup of tea.

"That's probably a wise decision." I smile as I gently touch Annie's shoulder. "Before we leave, let me make a fire." Annie nods in response, no doubt appreciative of this offer.

Twenty-five minutes later, the kitchen's cleaned up, Annie's reading a book by the fireplace, and the three of us—dressed in jeans, warm puffy coats, hats, and gloves—head to the shed, ready to strap on snowshoes and explore the nearby area. I remember to put the blue barite in my back jeans pocket. I'm not sure why, but carrying it somehow makes me feel better.

"Uncle Pete said there are multiple pairs of snowshoes in the shed," I say as we make the three-minute walk from the front porch to the outdoor building. "They're made to fit any size shoe."

"This is no ordinary shed," Juliette says as we approach what must measure a forty-feet-long and twenty-feet-wide building.

I laugh before saying, "I know. Uncle Pete has so many toys ... boats, snowmobiles, cornhole ... and then there is all of his equipment and tools." Lightheartedly, I pull the key from my coat pocket to open the door to the shed, but it's not locked. And when I open the door, the overhead light is on.

"How odd the bulb did not burn out if your uncle forgot to turn off the light before he went to Florida," Sophia says, a confused expression on her face.

Knowing she's absolutely right, I freeze for a moment as my eyes dart from one corner of the shed to the other. It's then I notice the wet footprints on the wooden floor. They lead to the back right corner of the shed. However, there are none returning in the opposite direction. Suddenly, my throat tightens. Something is definitely wrong.

"Um, let's leave. It looks like someone may have been in here ... or still may be." I begin to walk backward, motioning for Juliette and Sophia to follow. "I'll call the police when we get back to the house."

First there's a rustle, and then we hear a shivering voice. "Wait. Don't call the police. I didn't mean any harm."

All three of us jump, startled by the female voice coming from the back of the shed. Slowly, a disheveled woman appears from behind an old tractor. She's clutching a tarp—what looks like a cover to one of the snowmobiles—around her, most likely for warmth. Her shoulder-length blonde hair hangs in clumps over her makeup-smeared face. Despite the winter weather, she does not appear to be wearing a jacket. Her body sways unsteadily, and her eyes are wide, causing me to think she may be disoriented, perhaps even in shock.

I look at Juliette, whose face does not exhibit fear. Instead, despite being a bit shorter than me, she stands tall, in a strong, assertive stance, as if ready to combat this intruder. Then I turn toward Sophia, who has a totally different demeanor, one of compassion and true concern.

"Have you been here all night?" Sophia softly asks as she begins to approach this deranged-looking woman.

The stranger, who appears to be in her thirties, slowly nods her head, tightly clinging to the ragged cover. Her red nails stand out against the dingy gray tarp. When Sophia is less than four feet from her, the stranger dissolves into tears. It's then I realize this woman is not dangerous—she's distraught. In less than a moment, Sophia takes the remaining steps and envelops the stranger in her arms.

"Come with us." Sophia's voice is calming as she strokes the woman's back. This unknown person seems to trust her, releasing the tarp to hold tightly onto Sophia as they walk toward the shed's entrance.

Juliette remains with them as I sprint to the house. Annie appears startled when I bolt through the front door and run toward my bedroom. Yelling in what must sound like disconnected phrases, I attempt to explain the situation. By the time the others are inside, I've retrieved three woolen blankets from the armoire in my bedroom. We wrap the blankets around the woman then lead her to sit on the rocking chair next to the fireplace.

"Clearly she is in shock," Sophia whispers, her eyes wide with concern.

"Do you think she spent the whole night in the shed?" Annie quietly asks, suddenly looking more alert and back to her old self.

"I think so. The snow from her boots had melted, but it's so damp outside, the footprints on the shed's plank floor were still wet." My statement seems logical enough. However, I am unsure how long she'd been there. Or how she'd gotten into the shed. Uncle Pete keeps it locked.

Sophia then kneels on the floor next to the woman, softly saying, "My name is Sophia, and this is Marlee, Juliette, and Annie. I believe we should take you to the hospital. Although I am a doctor, I would feel better if the hospital staff examined you."

I'm amazed at the ease with which Sophia interacts with this stranger. Although I believe this unknown woman is harmless, we know nothing about her or why she was in Uncle Pete's shed. After all, she could have gone to the house and knocked on the door if she needed help.

Tears stream down the woman's face as she whispers, "No, I can't. No one can know. They'll think I did it." Her voice is soft, but the fear on her face cannot be disguised.

The four of us freeze, quickly glancing at each other. All I can think is … *Did what?* Unable to remain quiet, these words fly out of my mouth. "Did what?" I ask as I move toward the panic-stricken woman. Clearly, something is terribly wrong.

It's when I sit down on the hearth next to her and gently touch her arm that her tears turn into sobs. Unsure how to handle this stranger's behavior—after all, she appears confused and apparently spent the night sequestered in our shed—I sense compassion may be the best response, so I put my arm around her shoulder, pull her toward me, and allow her to cry.

Eventually, her sobbing subsides. After clearing her throat, she wipes her wet cheeks with the back of her hand. Sophia momentarily leaves her side, only to soon return with a box of tissues. She hands several to the woman.

"My name is Nicki Keating." She speaks the words softly. Immediately, I am startled by the last name. Could this be Travis's wife? I distinctly remember him having a younger brother, but I know he did not have a sister.

"Last night, someone close to me ..." Nicki pauses, looking intently at each of us before continuing: "The man I was having an affair with ... was murdered." She stops, stares at the floor, and gulps a few times before looking up.

I fall into a bit of a shock. *Murdered? Here? In Hawley Falls? And she was having an affair?*

"How do you know this, Nicki? Were you there?" I force the words out of my mouth, not wanting to hear the answer.

Nicki only nods, returning her gaze to the rug beneath her. "Not when it happened ... afterward."

"Did you call the police?" Juliette asks in a somewhat author- itative tone. This question definitely rattles Nicki.

"No. They would have thought I did it." Nicki freezes as she stares at her hands. Finally, she speaks: "I didn't. I would never do anything to hurt Wyatt. I love him ... loved him." More tears fall.

"You said having an affair with him." Juliette is not letting up. I'm somewhat surprised with her aggressive tone.

"Yes, I'm married." She fiddles with her naked left ring finger. No doubt she removed her wedding ring before she went to meet her lover.

That's when I gulp. Unable to resist, I ask, "Does your husband know about the affair?" I take in a deep breath, waiting for her answer before I exhale. If this is Travis's wife, could he have killed Wyatt?

Her hands rub her forehead as she shakes her head. "Billy has no idea about Wyatt. Wyatt lives in New York City. He comes here ... would come here ... once or twice a month ... just for the weekend ... to get away from the city ... and to see me." She starts to sob again.

Then I remember—Travis's little brother's name is Billy. Nicki is Travis's sister-in-law, not his wife. I let out a sigh of relief.

"And he has an older brother, Travis?" I ask in confirmation.

"Yes," her face momentarily brightens, but then she looks confused. "Do you know Travis?"

"Yes." I pause for a moment before continuing. "I spent summers here growing up. He and I were, um, friends," I say, noticing Juliette's eyebrows raise a bit when she hears this.

"Travis and I became close after his wife died," Nicki says in a matter-of-fact fashion. "He's like a brother to me." It's then her face softens, and her thoughts appear elsewhere.

However, my heart is plunging into my stomach as I contemplate what this man has been through. *His wife died.* How tragic. When did this happen? Did they have children? Why hadn't Uncle Pete or Aunt Sue told me?

My brain's scrambling, trying to comprehend Travis's loss while I also attempt to figure out how to help Nicki without going to the police. If there's been a murder, we must contact the authorities. Not doing so would be reckless and illegal. But wait, how do I know she's telling the truth? She could be the murderer.

While my mind's desperately searching for a plan, Sophia, who remains sitting on the other side of Nicki, begins to examine the young woman. I watch as she takes Nicki's pulse, checks her reflexes, and carefully scans her extremities for frostbite.

"Nicki, I want you to think back to last night and tell me exactly what happened," Sophia says in a soothing voice as she continues to check Nicki's vitals.

Biting her lip as she takes in a big breath, Nicki hesitantly begins speaking: "I arrived at Wyatt's home around seven thirty. I have a key for the kitchen door ... It's on the side of the house." A look of shame comes across her face. But she continues: "When I walked into the kitchen, I could see he had dinner ready to be cooked ...

like we talked about … We were going to celebrate Valentine's Day early." Her eyes linger on the edge of the wooden coffee table. "I didn't see or hear Wyatt, so I figured he was in his office, finishing up work." She hesitates. "I left the kitchen and headed toward the stairs." Nicki stops, and her body begins to shake as she looks down at the braided rug beneath the coffee table.

Sophia places her hand on top of Nicki's shoulder. "What happened next?"

"There was blood … everywhere … and Wyatt was lying on the floor." Her voice is barely audible.

I inhale deeply. Grief surges through me as I envision the horrid scene she encountered. "Where, exactly, was Wyatt?" I ask, worried I may push her over her edge.

"In the hallway … near the front door." Her words are now robotic, as if she's somewhere else.

"Was there a murder weapon, Nicki? Did you see anything on the floor near him?" Juliette asks.

Nicki shakes her head no. "It looked like he was stabbed … There were slashes on his chest … and blood … everywhere … on the floor … the walls," Nicki repeats herself, then retreats inward as she clenches her knees to her chest and begins to rock back and forth.

"Nicki, what did *you* do?" Sophia asks, her voice soft and soothing.

"I felt the cold … the front door … It was partially open." Nicki's body shivers as if she's reliving the experience. "I touched Wyatt's face … His skin was still warm." She gulps hard. "It must have just happened … and the killer probably left through the front door … without shutting it." She buries her head in her knees. "I didn't want the police questioning why I had a key … or thinking I did it." And then she goes silent, burying her head in the blankets, which muffle her cries.

"So you ran outside?" Juliette asks as she stands up and begins to pace around the seating area.

"Yes ... I panicked," Nicki says after she lifts her head. "I ran out the front door, but then I remembered my coat and purse were inside ... in the kitchen. But I couldn't go back ... I couldn't bear to see him lying there. So I kept running," she says then freezes before looking straight into our eyes. "It was so cold ... and dark. I didn't know where to go."

"How did you end up in Pete and Sue's shed? I know he keeps it locked," I say, wondering if she even knows my aunt and uncle.

"Pete and Sue have always been so kind to me." Nicki's shoulders drop a bit. "Pete knows how much I love to pick blueberries each July. He often tells me to borrow his paddleboat so I can get close to the blueberry bushes that line the lake's shore. They usually have the sweetest berries." Nicki's face softens as her mind drifts to another time. Then she returns to the present, looking directly at me. "He showed me where he keeps the spare key he tucks behind the rocks. That way, I would have access to the paddleboat, or whatever else I needed."

Annie, who has been taking it all in, is unusually quiet. I wonder if she still feels lousy. However, something tells me otherwise.

No longer pacing, Juliette, now sitting on the sofa next to Annie, states exactly what's on my mind: "We have to call the police. Your coat and purse are at the crime scene. Nicki, there's no way you won't be linked to this." Though her words appear harsh, the compassion on her face is anything but. "So we need you to be honest with us, not hold anything back, OK?"

Nicki nods as she says, "I promise, I'm telling you the truth."

Believing Nicki's innocence, I gently prod her, hoping she'll recall more from last night. "Was there anything that seemed off about Wyatt's house? Anything out of place?"

Without lifting her head, Nicki responds: "Yes ... there were wineglasses on the coffee table by the fireplace ... two of them ... One had lipstick on it." She pauses. "I thought Wyatt was cheating on me." Her head falls lower.

I'm struck by the irony of someone who's cheating on her husband fearing her lover's cheating on her. Knowing I'm being judgy, I let go of this critical thought.

"Did Wyatt have friends in the area? Anyone who would have stopped by?" Juliette asks, avoiding the cheating part.

"No, he didn't know anyone in Hawley Falls but me. This was his getaway place. He loved the solitude, the anonymity." Nicki bites her lip. "He's kind of a big deal in Manhattan ... heads a recording agency ... Musicians are constantly trying to get his attention."

"Nicki, perhaps someone followed Wyatt here from Manhattan. It could have been anyone." Juliette then softens her voice. "I know you don't want to get the police involved, but someone murdered Wyatt, and we need to contact the authorities. Not doing so only makes you look guilty." Juliette tilts her head as if to say, *What are you going to do?*

"Can I call Travis? He'll know what to do." Nicki's voice remains meek, yet she speaks quickly. And for the first time, I hear a glimmer of hope coming from this shaken woman.

"You can use my phone," Juliette says as she whips out her cell from her back jeans pocket, unlocks it, and hands it to Nicki.

In less than a minute, we watch Nicki huddle over Juliette's cell, speaking quietly into the phone as tears roll down her cheeks. It appears her words continue to come out in broken sentences, accentuated by moments of sobbing. Then she hands the phone back to Juliette.

"He said he'll be here in twenty minutes." Nicki pulls the woolen blanket tightly around her as she lets out a shiver. By the color on her cheeks, I don't think this reaction is from the cold. No,

Nicki's been caught. Not only did she cheat on her husband, but she's also tangled up in the murder of her lover.

Sophia stands up and takes Nicki's hand. "Come with me. I want you to take a warm shower before Travis gets here. Surely someone has extra clothing you can borrow. Yours must be damp from being out in the snow." Sophia refrains from mentioning how dirty Nicki is.

"You should fit into my clothes, Nicki," Juliette says as she rises from the sofa and heads upstairs.

Annie and I remain in the main room while Sophia leads Nicki upstairs to one of the unused guest bathrooms. Despite everything that's happening, I'm well aware of Annie's most unusual behavior. She appears to be feeling much better than she did earlier today. Why was she so quiet around Nicki? I'd think she would have had more to say, especially from the perspective of a psychologist. Yet Annie appears frightened. Does she think the murderer is nearby, looking for Nicki? Or could Annie feel we are in danger? However, as soon as the others are gone, Annie answers my unasked questions.

"Marlee ... I ... I think I may know what happened." Annie's eyes brim with trepidation as she clenches her jaw, as if she's holding in something she does not want to share.

"What do you mean?"

"As Nicki relayed what happened last night"—she pauses for several seconds before continuing—"I could see the whole thing in my mind. Every bit of it ... what his house looked like ... what Nicki did ... I even saw Wyatt and can describe him in detail." Annie's eyes are wide, almost catatonic.

I gasp, unable to digest what Annie's saying.

"That's not all... I saw *her* ... I know who killed Wyatt."

ANNIE'S GIFT
February 13

My jaw drops with Annie's pronouncement. This weekend is certainly not the girls' getaway I expected. Yesterday I bumped into Travis, last night I smoked pot with my *new girlfriends*, and this morning we find a stranger huddled behind a tractor in the shed—a stranger who, by the way, had witnessed the aftermath of her lover's murder. But then I discover Nicki's not a total stranger—she knows Sue and Pete. And it only gets weirder. She's also Travis's sister-in-law, who could soon be his ex-sister-in-law when his brother, Billy, finds out about Nicki's affair with some record mogul from Manhattan. I shake my head, trying to keep the players and the plot straight.

However, Annie's statement surpasses everything. She claims to *have seen* exactly what Nicki described: the house, the wineglasses on the table, Wyatt, *and* Wyatt's murderer.

Annie must be gauging my reaction because she quickly says, "This hasn't happened to me before, Marlee. Sure, there are times I could figure things out when I didn't know all of the information. But nothing like this." Her hands are trembling, and her eyes stare wildly at me.

Juliette returns and sits down on the braided rug, leaning her back onto the sofa. "What did I miss? You two look like you've seen a ghost."

"Well, not exactly, but close," I say, then proceed to tell Juliette what Annie shared with me. Annie remains silent, frozen on the sofa, as if she cannot believe what happened.

"Annie, tell me about your experience." Surprisingly, Juliette does not appear to be startled, not in the least.

"When Nicki started to tell her story ...," Annie begins then pauses. Her eyes dart to me then back to Juliette before continuing. "I saw frames of it occurring in my mind ... simultaneously ... like a silent movie. It started with Nicki walking into the kitchen. I remember seeing a vase of beautiful pink peonies on the counter, next to a decanter of red wine," Annie says as she shuts her eyes and appears to drift into a different state of mind.

I look at Juliette. "Nicki didn't tell us that."

Juliette only nods at me then refocuses on Annie, placing her hand on Annie's arm, as if to comfort her during this anything-but-normal experience.

"Then Nicki takes off her coat and places it on a metal coat rack before she walks toward this large room. The house is gorgeous—modern and rustic at the same time. There is a spectacular stone fireplace. A fire is lit. I see a large mocha-colored leather sofa ... It's shaped like an L ... with deep-green textured pillows. A huge chandelier ... made from deer antlers ... hangs overhead. Between the sofa and the fireplace is a square glass coffee table, with two wineglasses on top of it. One is empty; the other has a bit of white wine, but it's the red lipstick on the empty glass that stands out."

"Yes, Nicki said that." I confirm what Annie's recalling.

Juliette turns to me and puts a finger to her lips before saying, "Look around the room, Annie. Can you see anything else?"

Suddenly, Annie begins to tremble. "Yes ... there's a man ... on the floor. He looks to be in his midfifties ... His hair has streaks of gray ... and bright red ... There's blood everywhere." Annie's shaking increases. Juliette immediately wraps her arm around Annie.

"OK. That's good, Annie. You're doing a great job describing everything. You can stop for a moment. Clear your mind."

Annie listens to Juliette's instructions, keeping her eyes tightly shut.

"Now I want you to go back ... to earlier that evening ... before Nicki arrived at the house ... around the time it started snowing. What do you see?"

"I see the same man. He's extremely handsome, in a sophisticated way. His facial features are pronounced ... and he's tall, lean, moves with confidence and ease. The man is in the kitchen. He's opening a bottle of wine, then pours it into the decanter. He reaches into the refrigerator, removes a package ... it's meat ... unwraps it, then puts steaks on a plate, seasons them." Annie stops. Her face scrunches a bit.

"What's going on?" Juliette asks.

"The doorbell rings. This confuses the man. He looks out the side window ... He looks to see if anyone is in the driveway, but it's dark outside. The sun set a while ago. He doesn't look happy. He washes his hands, dries them with a dish towel hanging on the dishwasher handle, and walks out of the kitchen toward the front door. When he answers the door, a woman is standing there ... She is smiling ... as if she is trying to be nice. She looks about Nicki's age, but it's not Nicki. He's surprised—not a good surprise, more taken aback. There are words. After a bit, he invites her in. She hands him her black parka, and he hangs it on the banister of the nearby staircase. It doesn't feel like he wants her there. I can tell by the change in the way he moves ... He's more cautious around her."

I glance at Juliette. She raises her eyes and nods, as if she is saying, *Now watch what happens next.*

"The woman walks around the first floor, like she's been there before, knows the place. She appears nosy. The man doesn't approve. Then the woman pulls a bottle of white wine from the large handbag on her shoulder. She gives it to him. She wants him to open it. The man goes into the kitchen and uncorks the bottle, pouring two small glasses. He returns, gives one to the woman, and she goes and sits down on the sofa. He follows, reluctantly, like he senses something's not right."

"You are doing really well, Annie. Keep going." Juliette's tone is encouraging, yet she is not letting up. She's on a mission.

"After several minutes, the man looks at his watch, saying something, like he's excusing himself. The woman finishes her wine and puts her glass back on the table. He walks her to the door, turns to retrieve her coat from the banister. But before he can get there, the woman pulls something from her bag and moves toward him and ..." Annie freezes midsentence.

"What does the woman do?" Juliette's voice is soft, mystical.

Annie continues: "She stabs him in the back with a large butcher knife." Annie's shaking returns, though her voice remains monotone. "The man staggers as he turns around to face the woman ... He looks shocked ... but she doesn't stop. She keeps plunging and plunging the knife into his chest ... again and again. His mouth stops moving ... He crumples to the ground." Annie's voice fades into nothingness.

"I want you to look at the woman, Annie. Tell me what she looks like, what she does next."

In a childlike tone, Annie answers: "She has auburn hair ... in a bob ... and she's wearing black pants, a crisp white button-down shirt, and a deep lavender jacket—all splattered with the man's blood. She's wearing a lot of makeup ... has fake eyelashes ... and red lipstick, dark red. Her lips are smiling, but her eyes ... they're evil."

I look at Juliette, amazed with how she is coaxing this information from Annie, who's in some sort of trance.

"What does the woman do with the knife?"

"She takes a plastic bag from her handbag and places the knife in it ... then puts it back inside of her bag."

"And how does she leave?" Juliette's questioning is calm, steadfast.

"The way she came ... out the front door. First, she walks over to the banister, picks up her coat, and leisurely puts it on. She looks around, surveying the room. Then she jumps ... A door's opening. It's Nicki. The woman runs out the front door."

"That was perfect, Annie. You can relax now," Juliette soothingly says as she places her hands on Annie's shoulders. "Imagine your feet reaching past this floor, into the earth ... Feel the dirt below." Immediately I'm brought back to the grounding at the end of my Reiki and breathwork experiences. This must be necessary to bring Annie back from wherever she is.

I closely observe Annie's expression, wondering what kind of impact this remembering will have on her. After several long moments, she opens her eyes.

"How are you feeling?" Juliette asks, leaning closely to Annie.

"Strange ... but OK." Annie gulps. "Juliette, was that ... what I saw ... was it real?"

"I think so." Juliette stands up and begins to walk around the room as she attempts to explain what occurred. "It seems you have a gift, Annie—you are clairvoyant. This means you can see things others cannot. Of course, we'll confirm some of the details about the house and Wyatt's appearance with Nicki when she comes downstairs. Still, from my experience, your recall sounded incredibly accurate. And this hasn't happened before?"

"I don't think so," Annie says as she pulls her knees toward her chest, readjusting herself on the sofa. "Wait, I kind of remember something." She sits up straighter. "Once, when I was about eight, I remember my dad couldn't find his wallet. He was angry because he had recently been to the bank where he cashed a large check, placing the cash inside of his brown leather wallet. My father became frantic ... and started to yell. I remember looking at him and saying,

'Daddy, you left it in your car, in the little box across from where Mommy always sits.' I meant the glove compartment, but I didn't know the words for it. I had not been with him in the car. There was no way I could have known this. My dad looked at me, shook his head, then disappeared into the garage. Moments later, he returned … with his wallet in his hand."

"Did he thank you or acknowledge you knew where it was?" I ask, intrigued with this story.

"No … the opposite. He wouldn't look at me. Later that night, I asked my mom if I helped Dad find his wallet. She sat me down and told me that was silly and to never think about it again."

Juliette stops pacing then looks directly at Annie. "This means you've been clairvoyant for some time and have been suppressing it. Since you didn't think your parents believed you, you told yourself it wasn't true." Juliette pauses and shakes her head. "In reality, this happens all the time. We fuck up our kids by making them think they're crazy, either hearing or seeing things that don't exist. But they're not. What they undergo is real. Yet, as adults, we deny their experiences, shutting down their special gifts."

I clear my throat and tilt my head to the right, wanting to alert the others that Sophia and Nicki are coming down the stairs.

Juliette doesn't note my warning, or she chooses to ignore it, saying, "Nicki, Annie told us some things that may help us figure out who killed Wyatt."

Nicki stops, and her eyebrows furrow as she asks, "How would Annie know anything?"

Sophia remains silent, shifting her focus from Nicki—who she's been watching like a hawk—to Annie.

As Juliette's about to explain Annie's newly discovered psychic ability, we hear a knock on the door.

After looking at my watch, I realize twenty minutes have passed since Nicki called Travis. I pop up from my chair to answer the door, suddenly conscious of how I look. Yet, considering the circumstances, does it matter?

Apparently, I'm not the only one whose physical appearance is affected by today's trauma. When I open the door, Travis is standing there, his face bearing the burden of worry. This man, who only yesterday appeared so youthful, now has creases in his forehead and a heaviness in his eyes.

"Hey," I say. "Thanks for coming. We could use your help. We're going to have to contact the police, but Nicki's terrified she'll be accused." That's all I say, as I find it hard to finish the sentence with *of killing her lover.*

Travis offers me a half smile as I take his coat. However, I can tell this is weighing heavily on his soul. After all, he has an allegiance to his brother. But from what Nicki shared, he is close to her as well. When Nicki sees her brother-in-law, she jumps up and runs to Travis. I give them a few moments before I introduce him to Juliette, Sophia, and Annie.

"Would anyone like a cup of coffee?" I ask. Five heads nod yes.

As I make a fresh pot, I observe the interaction between Travis and Nicki. The two go to the side of the room and talk quietly. Travis shakes his head, then says a few words, which causes Nicki to begin crying again. Gently, he puts his arm around her shoulder, then draws her into his chest as she visibly melts right into his red plaid flannel shirt.

Ten minutes later, I place a tray filled with mugs, sugar, and cream on the dining table, then return with a large carafe of coffee and a plate of oatmeal raisin cookies. In time, everyone moves to the dining table and takes a seat. Coffee is poured and cookies are passed. No one says much. I guess it's up to me to get things started.

"We have some decisions to make, and we don't have a lot of time. If we wait much longer, we could be accused of detaining a witness or interfering with a crime." I inhale deeply, momentarily considering the consequences of not contacting the authorities as soon as Nicki divulged Wyatt had been murdered.

"I don't want anyone to get in trouble." Nicki's voice is clear and direct. Travis, seated to Nicki's right, places his hand on top of hers.

"That's not going to happen. We're going to get this sorted out, right away," he says in a firm yet caring tone.

Juliette speaks up. "Before we call the police, I want everyone to hear what Annie saw, what she *knows*."

In a slow and deliberate manner, Sophia shifts her body to face Annie. "Annie, did you have a vision?"

Both Nicki and Travis stare at Sophia, as if trying to comprehend her question.

"I think so," Annie says before clearing her throat and turning toward Nicki. "When you were telling us what happened last night, I could *see* everything … in my head. But that's not all." Annie pauses, looking intently into Nicki's eyes. "I know what happened before you arrived at Wyatt's house. I saw what the murderer looks like."

I'm astounded with the confidence in Annie's voice. Silence fills the room as Nicki's and Travis's expressions range from shock to disbelief. It's only after Annie shares her vision, aided by Juliette's explanation of how clairvoyance works, that both begin to ask clarifying questions. Sophia is silent. However, she remains intently focused on Annie.

"How did you know what Wyatt's house looks like? You described it to a T." Nicki's brow wrinkles in wonderment.

"I can't explain. Pictures kept popping up in my mind, correlating to your description. I could see you move through the house … and I saw things you didn't mention." Annie then tells Nicki about the peonies and the decanter of wine.

Juliette interjects: "What's most important is Annie can identify the woman who killed Wyatt."

My eyes shift to Nicki, watching her body sink into the chair. By the distress on her face, I imagine she's mentally rehashing discovering Wyatt's body. She's drifting, as if stuck in time. It's only when Travis touches her arm that she returns to the present.

It's Travis, not Nicki, who then asks, "What did she look like, Annie?" I wonder if Nicki is afraid to know.

Annie shuts her eyes. "She was Nicki's age ... but a bit shorter. And her hair was dark ... auburn ... cut above the shoulders ... with bangs. She had deep-green eyes, not the intriguing kind of green eyes like Sophia's. There was a wickedness to them. Oh, and she wore red lipstick ... the same shade as what was on the wineglass." Annie takes in a big breath then lets out a sigh. "I wish I could tell you a name. Unfortunately, all I can do is see. I couldn't hear anything either. However, I could sense Wyatt didn't want her there. She seemed familiar with the home, as if she had been there before. But there was a strangeness between them. He definitely didn't like her."

Nicki lets out an exhale with Annie's last statement. Perhaps she truly believed Wyatt was seeing someone else.

"Annie, I am not an artist, but I have taken drawing classes. Together, we might be able to create a picture to help Nicki and Travis identify who this woman is," Sophia says. "I have a sketch pad upstairs. I will be right back." Sophia gracefully rises then walks quickly, yet regally, toward the stairs.

"I hope I can provide enough details," Annie says as she rests her forehead into the palms of both hands, elbows propped on the table.

"OK, now we're getting somewhere." Juliette stands up when Sophia returns with a sketch pad and pencil. "Sophia, while you and Annie try to come up with a sketch, I am going to see if I can pick up anything, energetically, with Nicki."

Nicki's eyes shift from Juliette to me.

"Don't worry," I say. "Juliette does energy work. She may be able to help you remember more of what you saw last night. Trust her, OK?" As the words exit my mouth, I can't believe I'm actually saying this. Haven't I been terrified to do a session with her?

As Annie and Sophia move to the kitchen counter, Juliette tells Nicki to lie down on the sofa, then sits on the floor next to her. I look up at Travis then reach for a cookie before taking a small bite.

Softly, I ask, "Did you know Nicki was having an affair?"

Travis shakes his head no. "Billy is going to be devastated. He's crazy about Nicki. They started dating in high school. In fact, got married when they were eighteen. Nicki was pregnant … then she lost the baby shortly after the wedding." Travis's eyes glance at the floor.

It's then I remember Travis lost his wife. "Nicki said you were married … and your wife passed away." I pause, wanting to say more—to show I care—but conscious I may be crossing boundaries.

"Yes," he begins, then clears his throat. "Connie and I were married the summer of '96. We met two years earlier. Connie wasn't from here. She grew up in New Jersey … She and her family moved here during her sophomore year at Rutgers … where she was getting her nursing degree." He runs his fingers through his hair. "It all happened pretty quickly … We just kind of knew. I figured, why wait, so I proposed, and she said yes." He turns toward me, and a sweet smile comes across his face.

Remembering how drop-dead gorgeous Travis was at that age, I may have said yes to him too, had he asked.

"We had five amazing years together." He pauses, and I can see his eyes well up. Instinctively, I take his hand in mine and give it a squeeze. His eyes return to the floor as he shares the ending to their story. "She was ice skating on the lake. Everyone thought it was fully frozen. She must have gone over a spring. One minute I saw her, skating backward in a circle, laughing, without a care in the world … then I heard the crack … but I was too far away to reach her in time." A tear falls down his cheek. "I dove into the hole, but I couldn't find her. Kept coming up for air then diving back down. Someone pulled me out of the water. I don't remember much after that." Another tear rolls down his cheek. "They found her body the following spring after the lake thawed."

"Oh my God … I am so sorry." I wish I had a better response. Nevertheless, I doubt any words could soothe the pain Travis has endured.

"Yeah, well, as I said, we had five amazing years together." Travis reaches over to the carafe and pours himself another cup of coffee.

As he does this, it hits me I haven't told Tom what's been going on. We talked last night and early this morning. However, that was before we discovered Nicki in the shed. Tom's on call all weekend, and it may be difficult to reach him.

Returning to the inevitable dilemma, Travis says, "We can't wait much longer to call the police. The chief and I go way back; we've spent many Saturday nights playing poker and drinking whiskey." Travis gives me a look, as if to say, *Trust me.* "If I tell him what happened, and Nicki is innocent, I think he'll believe me. The hard part will be to convince him Annie had some kind of psychic vision of who the murderer is." From the tone of his voice, I'm not so sure he believes what Annie saw was real.

"I know. What about fingerprints on the wineglass? And from what Annie said, the murderer was looking around the room when she heard Nicki come in the kitchen door. Maybe she was looking for any evidence that could be linked to her. Then when she heard the back door open, she took off. *If* we can identify the person, and *if* the police chief trusts you, he may check if the prints match."

"Assuming we can figure out who the woman is from the sketch, the chief will need cause to fingerprint her. There's no way he'll get a warrant because some clairvoyant lady from Philadelphia had a vision." He lets out a loud sigh.

Travis has a point.

I bite my lower lip in frustration. "There has to be a way to clear Nicki. Unfortunately, she has no alibi. From what Nicki told Sophia, she was alone most of the afternoon and hadn't seen your brother since he left for work that morning, so Billy can't confirm her whereabouts."

"Yeah, and I can only imagine his reaction when he finds out what's been going on."

"Wasn't he concerned when Nicki didn't come home last night?" I ask, realizing that is a missing piece.

"Nicki shared she had told Billy she was spending the night at a friend's house ... She used the excuse her friend was upset about being single on Valentine's Day weekend ... I guess Nicki told all sorts of lies to be with Wyatt." Travis hangs his head.

"You seem to be pretty tolerant of her cheating on your brother," I say. "Can I ask why?" Again, I hope I haven't gone too far, but considering how close Travis and I were in the past, it feels natural to ask.

"Nicki's faced a lot of challenges, beginning with a bad home life. She's a survivor." Travis pauses then looks into my eyes. "I love my brother, but I know he's held her back. Nicki wants more. She tried to convince Billy to move out of Hawley Falls, go someplace new to live. I guess he's pretty set in his ways. He likes his routine." Travis shifts his eyes to the half-empty cup of coffee in front of him. "Honestly, Billy and Nicki have grown apart. I know it's no excuse. He still loves her. And something tells me Nicki never stopped loving him ... I hope they can work it out."

Surprised with Travis's pragmatic response, I smile, acknowledging each relationship is unique, and it's not our right to judge another's.

I look up as Sophia and Annie sit down at the table, directly across from us. Sophia hands a sketch of a woman to Travis. I watch as he intently scrutinizes the drawing, only to shake his head.

"I'm not certain, but this kind of resembles the photo of one of the realtors in town. You know how they put their faces on those fliers you see everywhere? Actually"—Travis pauses as he scratches his head—"I think this person went to high school with Nicki and Billy. Nicki should be able to tell you her name." Travis then glances over to the sofa, observing Juliette holding both hands over Nicki's forehead.

"What *is* she doing?" he asks, squinting his eyes, as if seeing more clearly will provide an explanation.

"Juliette is studying to become an urban shaman," Sophia says. "She shared this with us during yesterday's drive. Juliette is learning how to tap into others' thoughts, both conscious and subconscious."

"Yes, she doesn't *see* things like I seemingly do," Annie adds. "Nor does she hear things like people who are clairaudient. Juliette *knows*, or feels what happens, without visual or audial confirmation. It's called claircognizant."

Travis appears totally confused. "I've read some stuff about this, but I don't know anyone who has these powers," he says, shaking his head.

"Perhaps it is easier to grasp if you do not view them as powers. Consider them gifts … that each one of us possesses," Sophia says as she places her hands on top of the table. "We can all access these abilities. However, to do so, we must trust in the unknown."

Travis repeats her last words: "Trust in the unknown?"

"Yes." Sophia's voice is kind and serene. "My grandmother was psychic. Unfortunately, my mother forbade her to discuss it with me." A big grin comes across Sophia's face, and I now realize why Sophia accepted what Annie said without any reservation. "But my nonna used to tell me things when we were alone. It was she who taught me to believe." Sophia gives Travis a knowing wink.

It's then Juliette and Nicki join us at the table.

"Well, that was productive," Juliette says. "Even though Nicki's not aware, for the past several months, she's been subconsciously worried about Wyatt. It's not that he said anything to her. She noticed a shift in his personality. He appeared distracted, concerned. I think that's what scared her when she saw the two wineglasses on the table. Deep inside, she felt something was wrong, but she couldn't place her finger on it. So she assumed Wyatt was seeing someone else."

I look to Nicki, who appears shell-shocked, unable to comprehend Juliette's tapping into her mind.

"Wyatt wasn't cheating on Nicki. Something else had him concerned," Juliette confidently announces before her voice drops. "However, I could not discover what was troubling him."

"How do you know this?" Travis's voice sounds baffled.

"I just do. I'm able to tap into people's heads ... both the living and those who have passed." Juliette is a bit curt in her response. I suspect she doesn't appreciate people doubting her abilities.

Nicki looks at the drawing in front of Travis, then picks up the paper, studying it closely. "That's Caroline ... Caroline Rhimes. What's going on?"

"Wasn't she in your class in high school?" Travis asks.

"Yes. She moved here in fifth grade ... never left town. Now she's a realtor for RE/MAX."

"Was Wyatt interested in selling the house? If so, that would explain why the woman walked around the house like Annie described. But it sounded like Wyatt was surprised when the doorbell rang. And it doesn't make sense that a realtor looking to acquire a new client would bring a bottle of wine with her," Travis says, as if doing his best to believe Annie actually saw the murder and the actions that led to it.

"Nicki, did Wyatt build that house, or did he buy it from someone else? Could she have been *his* realtor?" I ask, trying to connect these random dots.

"The house was brand new, although he didn't build it. A local contractor built it as a spec home. Wyatt bought it directly from the builder." Nicki's voice is solid. She seems calmer and perhaps more centered since Juliette worked on her. "I remember him telling me this when he first walked into my store."

"What would be her motive? Why would a realtor from Hawley Falls murder Wyatt?" Sophia asks the question we're all wondering.

"Because she hates me." It's Nicki who speaks.

"That makes no sense. Why would she hate you? Everyone in town loves you, Nicki. And didn't you guys know each other in high school?" Travis's mouth curls a bit as he questions his sister-in-law, a habit I remember from earlier years.

"Yes ... we *were* friends ... good friends ... at least for a few years. Caroline and I were both on the cheer squad together. Then everything blew up. She stopped speaking to me."

"Why?" I ask.

"Caroline had the biggest crush on Billy. Apparently, he didn't feel the same way about her. I remember her hinting to him that she wanted them to go to prom. Instead, Billy asked me. Caroline was furious." Nicki's baby-blue eyes dim. "Six months later, I found out I was pregnant. Billy thought we should get married, and so we did. I don't think she spoke to me after that."

The pieces are beginning to fall into place, but there are too many holes. "OK. She didn't like you. What does this have to do with Wyatt?" I ask, confused. "Why would Caroline want to kill him?"

"Caroline knew about Nicki and Wyatt. She wanted to punish Nicki." Juliette then speaks, her voice having shifted. It's now monotone, similar to the tone she used when she taught the meditation class.

Everyone in the room becomes silent as Juliette slowly explains her statement.

Finally, Nicki speaks up. "I thought she saw us together." Nicki pauses, scrunching her forehead as she looks down at her lap. "This past August, when Wyatt was in town, he and I were walking outside, holding hands. We didn't think anyone was around. I remember someone unexpectedly drove by. I thought the car looked familiar. Later, I realized it looked like the car parked outside of the RE/MAX office downtown, a powder-blue Subaru wagon." Nicki heaves out a sigh. "But her hating me is not enough of a reason to kill anyone." As Nicki's voice inflects, she rises from her chair, hands moving to her hips. It's as though she's taking a stand, perhaps in her defense or, more likely, in anger at Wyatt's death.

"Jealousy does strange things to people," I say, thinking this may be deeper than Nicki suspects, especially if this Caroline Rhimes is emotionally unbalanced. There has to be more.

"Friday night was a full moon," Sophia says. "I know many patients behave differently whenever the moon is full."

"Sophia, you're absolutely correct," Annie says. "My clients' issues also appear to escalate around the moon's cycle."

Yes, full moons could make Patrick a bit more antsy when he was little. Still, I doubt its gravitational pull would prompt someone to commit murder. We're definitely missing something.

I look at Travis, who is now rubbing his temples. Clearly, he's having difficulty grasping this conversation.

"Let's say all of this is true," Travis begins. "What do we do? I told Marlee I'm friends with the chief of police, but I need facts, not intuitive assumptions," he says, then looks at Annie and Juliette. "Sorry, no offense meant." Travis lets out a sigh. "How can we protect Nicki *and* solve the murder?"

"Call the chief," Juliette says. "Ask him to come to the house. We can explain everything to him. He can then go to Wyatt's house and collect the evidence. If the crime scene correlates to what we're saying, then he'll have to believe us."

"I know it sounds risky, but what else can we do?" I rest my chin on top of my clenched fist, staring down at the dining table, searching for a better solution. However, no brilliant ideas come to me.

I lift my head and watch Nicki as tears fall down her face once more. "Do you think he'll believe us. Why would I hurt Wyatt? I have no reason ... I loved him." Nicki pauses when she sees Travis flinch. "I'll come clean, Travis. I swear I'll tell Billy about the affair." Nicki hangs her head. "He's probably wondering why I'm not back yet."

Suspecting this necessary confession to her husband may destroy whatever is left of their marriage, I speak up: "What if Travis were to speak with Billy after we call the chief? I don't think we can wait any longer to make the call, Nicki."

There's a ping, and everyone reflexively checks their cell.

It's Travis's phone. "It's Billy. He's worried ... hasn't heard from you. What do you want me to say, Nicki?" Right then, looking at Travis's expression, I'd wager to say Nicki's got a fifty-fifty chance of saving her marriage.

"Tell Billy to come here," I interject, unable to refrain. "Billy and Nicki need to sort things out. He shouldn't be hearing about this after we contact the police." I look pleadingly at Travis as I contradict my earlier statement.

Travis inhales deeply, rubs his forehead. "OK, I'll tell him Nicki's with me." He looks at Nicki and she nods. "What great plan do you have once he gets here, Marlee?"

"I'm not sure. But we can't let Billy be blindsided."

"Don't you think I want to protect my baby brother?" Travis's tone becomes defensive. "You can't fix everything, Marlee, make it what you want it to be. You realize that, don't you?"

God damn him. He had to say that ... the exact words he used when we broke up close to thirty years ago. He called me out then, same as he is now.

"I'm not trying to fix anything." My response is harsh. Then I soften my voice. "Tell him to meet you here. Say I bumped into you and Nicki at the store, and I wanted you to meet my friends, or something like that." I'm grasping at straws, but what else is there to do?

Travis doesn't respond. He's glued to his cell as he sends a text to Billy.

Several moments later, he looks up at me, grimaces, and says, "He'll be here shortly."

THE CONFESSION
February 13

No one speaks as we wait for Billy to arrive. Rather, each one of us remains silent, lost in our thoughts, consumed by the uncertainty of what is about to occur.

My stomach rumbles. Although I'm not the slightest bit hungry, I need *to do* something, so I go to the kitchen and begin preparing lunch. I'd brought rotisserie chicken and fresh baguettes for today, anticipating four hungry women after a morning of snowshoeing. Instead, there are now six people, distraught, fearful, frustrated, angry, confused, or newly dumbfounded by unanticipated abilities to see what others cannot.

In situations such as these, I resort to what I know. I cook so I can feed others. Perhaps it is my gift, my own way to heal people's emotions.

After heating the oven, I remove two cardboard boxes containing flatbreads and put them onto parchment lined cookie sheets before placing the pans into the oven. As the flatbreads warm, I busily cut up the rotisserie chicken, slice the baguettes, and quarter several Fuji apples, arranging everything on platters on the kitchen counter. While I doubt anyone is thinking about lunch, it's probably best we all eat. Who knows, this day could become even longer than it already has.

Moments after I pull the crispy flatbreads from the oven, there's a knock on the door. My heart falls into my stomach, knowing what's about to occur. As difficult as this morning has been, I suspect this afternoon will only become worse. I move toward the entrance, but Travis is one step in front of me, his expression stoic, protective. I watch as he slowly opens the front door.

There, on the other side, is a man who closely resembles Travis, but shorter and somewhat stocky. The last time I saw Billy, he must have been eight years old. Now he's all grown up. His sandy-brown hair is several shades lighter than his brother's, and his eyes are crystal blue. Dressed in jeans and a canvas-colored shirt, Billy is handsome in his own right, but he can't compete with Travis's looks.

"So Nicki's here?" Billy asks, a confused expression on his innocent-looking face.

"Yeah … come on in," Travis says as he puts his arm around Billy's shoulder, guiding him into the house.

"Marlee, I know it's been some time, but you remember Billy, don't you?" Travis speaks as if he's taking charge of the situation. I do my best to smile as I nod, taking several steps toward him to shake his hand. "And these are Marlee's friends from Philadelphia … Sophia, Annie, and Juliette." As Travis speaks each woman's name, my friends offer a quick wave, but the room remains somber.

Nicki stays frozen in her chair. Her eyes slowly look to me, not her husband.

"Hey, Nicki, I've been looking all over for you," Billy says, a tone of relief in his voice as he walks toward his wife.

Instead of getting up and greeting Billy, Nicki remains seated, shrinking into the rocking chair. As if on cue, Annie, Juliette, and Sophia stand up and move into the kitchen area, excusing themselves, saying they are going to grab a bite to eat. As they busy themselves getting plates of food, they speak in hushed whispers. We all watch as Billy pulls up a chair next to Nicki. I look at Travis, motioning with my head for him to join us.

Two minutes, three minutes, five minutes pass. Finally, I turn my head to face the couple, if I can call them that, sitting by the fireplace. Clearly Billy knows something. His head hangs, and his large hands massage his temples. Nicki leans in closely to him. I can see the strain on her face and her lips moving, but I hear nothing.

Then, Billy stands abruptly, and I hear him mutter, "This is bullshit," as he storms toward the door.

Travis drops his chicken sandwich on the plate as he heads after his brother. "Billy, wait," he says.

"For what? Why? She's been fucking some guy and lying to me … for over two years? I'm out of here." Billy reaches for the doorknob. However, Travis intervenes, placing his hand firmly on Billy's shoulder.

"I know you're pissed … and I don't blame you. But there's a bigger issue here. Nicki could be accused of homicide."

I watch as Billy attempts to compute the gravity of the situation. Finally, he takes a step back from the door. Turning toward his brother, he asks, "What do you want me to do?"

Travis, who is gripping Billy's shoulder, pulls his brother into him as he says, "I don't know, Billy. I can't tell you what to do. You and Nicki have a lot to talk about, and I'm guessin' you've got some tough decisions to make. But right now, we've got to call Dennis and let him and his guys begin their investigation."

Billy nods, then turns and looks at me, his blue eyes bloodshot and brimming with tears. "Marlee, I don't understand how you're involved." It's at that moment I see the little boy I remember so well staring directly at me.

I flinch as I try to put myself in Billy's shoes. His marriage is crumbling in front of him, yet Travis wants Billy to help Nicki, the woman who has been cheating on him for the past two years.

"We found Nicki in Pete's shed this morning. She'd been there all night." I refrain from sharing more—her disoriented state, the freezing temperature in the shed, or the terror in her eyes when she heard we were calling the police. Instead, filled with compassion for the little boy who used to spy on Travis and me watching television in their basement, I move toward Billy, wrap my arms around him, and whisper, "I'm so sorry," into his ear. The maternal instincts within ignite, as I sense his deep pain of feeling betrayed by the woman he adores.

"How 'bout I make that call to Dennis?" Travis asks.

I nod as I pull back from Billy. "Are you OK?" I ask. "This is going to get messy."

Billy exhales before saying, "I'll do what you need me to do." He looks toward Travis, as if his older brother is the source of his strength.

But its Nicki who surprises me. She leaves the rocking chair and walks toward the three of us standing by the front door. "Please, let me make the call. It's better that way. Plus, Dennis and I go way back. We used to be neighbors growing up."

Travis, apparently unaware of this fact, hands his phone to Nicki. That's the thing about Hawley Falls. Everyone is connected in some way.

After several moments, which seems like forever, Dennis answers.

"Dennis ... this is Nicki Keating. I need you to come out to Pete and Sue Connelly's house." There's a pause. "No, they're in Florida. Their niece Marlee is here with some friends." Silence. "No, Marlee and her friends are fine. It's me. I need to speak with you ... tell you what I saw last night." Pause. "I'll tell you when you get here ... Thanks, Dennis." She hands the phone back to Travis.

"He said he'd be here shortly," Nicki announces, refraining from looking at either Travis or Billy. Instead, she turns to Sophia, who has returned to watching Nicki's every move, as if gauging how close she may be to her breaking point. Sophia, who's by the counter making a cup of tea, offers one to Nicki. Several moments later, Sophia and Nicki take their tea and sit down at the dining table.

Annie, Juliette, and I join them. However, Travis remains in the kitchen with Billy.

The grandfather clock chimes. It's now two o'clock. I look out the window. The sun's still shining, but ominous clouds hover over the lake, no doubt an accurate parallel to what's occurring inside this house. Sophia, who is sitting to the left of Nicki, gently places her hand on Nicki's trembling arm. I watch as Nicki's arm stops shaking. However soothing Sophia's presence is to Nicki, it cannot erase the fact that within minutes, Hawley Falls' chief of police will be grilling her about last night, as well as her connection to the victim.

We hear a car on the gravel driveway. Even though I know it's coming, I flinch when the door to the police car shuts. The thump of boots on the two porch stairs reverberates throughout the silent house. Travis moves to the door, opening it before the chief has an opportunity to knock.

Younger than I imagined, Hawley Falls' chief of police stands over six feet tall and looks to weigh around two-fifty. His mere size causes me to gasp, though I've done nothing wrong. Yet his face looks kind, and his light hazel eyes show concern, not suspicion. I watch the familiar interaction between Travis and the chief. Then I turn to Nicki, who remains huddled close to Sophia.

Travis introduces the four of us to Dennis. Nicki remains seated, giving Dennis a slow nod of her head.

"Nicki, what's going on?" Dennis asks as he sits down on a kitchen stool.

Slowly, Nicki leaves Sophia's side and moves toward the men and me.

"Dennis." Nicki's voice cracks when she says his name. But I'm watching Billy as he turns away, facing the window, and clenches his hands into tight fists. "There was a murder ... over on Sparrow Road."

With this pronouncement, Dennis stands up, instantly trans-forming from Dennis who plays poker with Travis on Saturday nights to Hawley Falls' chief of police. "Sparrow Road, why there's only two houses on that street. And I saw the Burgers this morning when I stopped at the Wawa for some coffee."

"Yes." Nicki's voice becomes weak. "It was the other house. The one belonging to Wyatt Bixby." Nicki hangs her head.

"How do you know this, Nicki? As I recall, that guy is from New York City. He's a loner, only comes here now and then. His house is mostly unoccupied, which, if you ask me, is stupid, as it had to cost him a bundle."

"I know Wyatt." Nicki pauses.

I look at Billy. His face is turning bright red as he glares at his wife. Travis stands next to him, placing his hand on his back, as if to calm his younger brother.

"How do you know Wyatt, Nicki?" The chief is succinct with his words.

"I ... we ... we were having an affair." Nicki looks at Dennis, then Billy, then back to Dennis. Despite her trembling hands, she holds her head high, owning these words as well as her actions.

"I see," Dennis says, pausing for a moment as he glances at Billy from the corner of his eyes. "You say he was murdered ... How do you know that?"

"Because I found him ... stabbed ... last night."

"Last night? And you *just* called me this afternoon? What the hell were you thinking?" Dennis's voice booms throughout the first floor of the house. Reflexively, I recoil, as if I'm the one being scolded.

"I was scared ... I didn't know what to do ...." Nicki's face contorts, eyes darting between Billy and Travis, but neither comes to her aid.

It's Sophia who stands up and moves next to Nicki, recount-ing what Nicki had shared. "Nicki and Wyatt had planned to have dinner on Friday. Nicki had a key to the side door. The house was quiet when she walked into the kitchen. She thought Wyatt was in his office working. As she began to make her way upstairs to his office, she saw him … lying on the floor … He had been stabbed to death." Sophia speaks in a smooth and confident way. Though the words describe a violent crime scene, her tone remains strangely calming.

"Well, what did you do?" Dennis's eyes pop out of his head as he confronts Nicki.

"I got scared … I ran. I'd never seen anyone dead before … let alone someone I'd been … well, close to." Nicki lowers her head, avoiding the chief's looks. "It was clear someone had been there before me… There were two wineglasses on the table … one had lipstick on it … and the front door was slightly ajar. I didn't know if the killer was outside or what. Plus, I didn't want anyone to know about us." Her head droops even lower.

Dennis takes in a deep breath then asks, "Have you been back to the house, Nicki?"

She shakes her head no.

"Well, at least you've made one good decision." Dennis runs his fingers through his cropped ash-brown hair. "Who else knows about this?" he asks as he glances around the room.

"Only us, Dennis," Travis says. "Marlee and her friends found Nicki in the shed this morning. Pete had told Nicki where he kept the key. She went inside to try to escape the snowstorm." Travis pauses for a moment before continuing: "After Marlee and her friends found Nicki this morning, Nicki called me. And well, later, I had Billy come out so Nicki could tell him for herself." Travis bites his lip, perhaps to prevent himself from saying more.

"So only the seven of you know about the murder? And no one's been back to the house?"

We all nod yes.

"OK, then I need to go to Sparrow Road." Dennis stands and begins to turn toward the door.

Juliette looks at me, tilting her head toward Annie.

"Wait," I say, getting up and moving toward the chief, my mind searching for the words that need to be said. "There's more." I place my hand on the kitchen counter, as if the granite will help support me.

This catches Dennis's attention, as he stops, turns, and faces me. "What haven't you told me?" His tone is direct, and those kind hazel eyes seem anything but.

"You should sit down," Juliette adds as she joins me at the kitchen counter.

Dennis pulls out a stool and takes a seat. His face becomes stern, and his eyes pierce into mine. Remaining standing, I say, "I know this is going to be difficult to believe but … we … um, my friends and I … think we know who committed the murder."

Dennis's eyes become immense as he asks, in a drawn-out manner, "You do?"

"Yes," I stammer, unsure how to explain Annie's clairvoyance. "You see … my friend, Annie"—I motion to Annie who is seated at the table—"has this ability, a gift of sorts." I watch as Dennis stares directly at me, clenching his jaw as he hangs on to each of my words.

"She, well, she can see things," I blurt out.

"What kind of things can she see?" His tone is sarcastic and somewhat impatient.

It's Juliette who rescues me. "Annie is clairvoyant, meaning she's capable of seeing things others cannot." Juliette pauses, as if allowing time for Dennis to digest this information. "When Nicki told us what occurred last night, Annie had flashes of those exact scenes roll through her mind. Then, she was able to see what happened *before* Nicki arrived at Wyatt's. She was able to describe the killer." Juliette walks over to the table where Sophia's drawing is sitting. "Here, this is who killed Wyatt." Juliette lifts up the picture so Dennis can see the sketch.

"Your friend drew this?" Dennis asks as he scrutinizes the picture.

"Annie didn't. Sophia did," Juliette says.

"Yes, Annie described the woman in her vision, and I did my best to capture the description." Sophia's serene tone appears to settle Dennis a bit.

"Dennis," Travis says, "Nicki identified the woman in the drawing. It's a picture of Caroline Rhimes."

"Caroline? The RE/MAX realtor? Why would she be involved?" Dennis walks over to Juliette and takes the picture. He holds the paper close to his face as he studies it.

"We asked the same thing," I say, finally pushing myself away from the counter. Tucking my hair behind my ear, which I'm now realizing is a nervous habit, I continue: "Caroline was in Nicki and Billy's high school class. Apparently, she liked Billy … a lot. But he chose Nicki, and his decision destroyed the girls' friendship." I pause, unsure if I should mention the rest, yet I do, as it's all we have. "Nicki told us that several months ago, when she was outside the house with Wyatt"—I take a deep breath as I glance sadly at Billy—"she saw Caroline's car drive by. Caroline had seen them together."

"So what? Caroline saw something going on between Nicki and the guy from New York? That's no cause for murder." Dennis shrugs his shoulders as he dismisses this fact.

"No, it's not. While Caroline may have harbored jealousy from high school, it doesn't provide the motive to kill Wyatt. We believe she was at the house earlier that day. Also, we think she could have been one of the realtors when Wyatt bought the house. And, if you look at the fingerprints on the wineglass … the one with the red lipstick … I bet you'll find they match Caroline's." I stop talking, unsure of what is left to say.

Dennis rests his elbows on the countertop, and I watch as he slumps forward. "So," he speaks into the granite, as if gathering his own thoughts, "a man's murdered ... most likely stabbed to death ... and you're telling me Caroline Rhimes is the murderer because her lipstick and fingerprints match those on a wineglass? How do you know he wasn't sleeping with her too?" Dennis pauses. "No offense, Nicki."

Now Nicki's head is in her hands, Billy's pacing up and down the entryway, and the rest of us are looking bewildered, unsure how to answer the police chief.

"I saw what happened." It's Annie who speaks. She then meticulously describes the chain of events.

Dennis listens, refraining from commenting until Annie stops talking.

"If what you're saying is true, then not only will Caroline's prints match those, but she'll also have the murder weapon." Dennis rolls his eyes then stares directly at Annie, as if he thinks she's batshit crazy.

"Dennis, there might be other DNA matches at the house," Travis adds, tilting his head toward his friend as if to suggest, *You should listen to her.*

"Why would she keep the knife?" Nicki asks as she scrunches her nose.

"Killers do strange things. She could view it as a trophy of sorts. Or she could have gotten rid of it," I say, disgusted anyone would hold onto a murder weapon. "There has to be more to this." I slowly shake my head, remembering what Juliette said, how Nicki was concerned about Wyatt. My journalistic instinct tells me we're missing something big.

"Travis, I want you to come with me to the house," Dennis says in an authoritative tone before adding, "You too, Marlee. The rest of you, stay here. I'm serious ... don't anybody move."

Everyone freezes with the chief of police's commanding directive. I'm shocked Dennis would want me to accompany him to the crime scene.

"How could I possibly help?" I do my best to project a positive voice, though I'm terrified at the thought of entering that house and seeing Wyatt's dead body. Plus, I can't fathom what propelled Dennis to ask me to come with them.

"I'm not sure you can. The way I see it, this is anything but a clear-cut murder." Dennis pauses as he clears his throat before looking directly into my eyes. "Let's just say I have a hunch *you* could prove useful." With that pronouncement, he stands up, as if to state the matter is settled.

Quickly, I go to my bedroom and grab my purse before returning to the others. "Are you OK if I leave?" I ask, hoping someone will come to my aid and request I stay here.

"Don't worry about us, Marlee. Go figure out Caroline's motive. Because without it, who knows what's going to happen," Juliette says then glances to Nicki, who's sitting on a stool, hunched over the kitchen counter.

"I'll be back soon," I say as I remove my coat from the wooden peg by the front door. "At least, I hope so." I offer my friends a halfhearted smile.

As I leave the warmth and safety of Eagle's Landing to accompany the chief and Travis to the murder scene, all I can think is this is some horrible dream. My perfectly planned weekend in the Poconos has turned into a nightmare, and a woman—most likely an innocent woman—may be charged with murder unless we can discover a motive.

"Ready?" Dennis asks as he holds the door open for me. Travis is seated in the front of the police car. I climb into the back and fasten the seatbelt.

During the short drive to Sparrow Road, I realize this will be the first time I will have seen a dead body, let alone a murdered one. We didn't have viewings for my parents, and I had not been with them when they passed. Suddenly, I miss my husband terribly. I pull out my phone to text Tom. As I'm about to hit *Send,* Dennis turns toward me.

"Do not be texting or calling anyone. This is official police business."

I stop, put the phone back into my purse, and say, "I understand." I'm afraid, and I want to talk to Tom, but I can't. He's always been there for me, beside me. I guess this time I have to do it alone.

HIDDEN CLUES
February 13

After calling for backup, Dennis, who's clenching a forensic kit in his left hand, pulls a gun from his holster with his right. He motions with his head for the two of us to remain behind.

Slowly, Dennis opens the heavy front door, yelling inside, "Anyone here? Police."

Against Dennis's orders, Travis slides out of the passenger door and moves toward the house. "I can't stay here," he says as he walks across the hardpacked snow. "What if Dennis needs help?"

I want to follow Dennis's orders and remain safely inside of the car, but I'm terrified to be alone, in case the murderer is lurking outside the house. Of course, I know this thought is illogical. Against my better judgment, I exit the police car and follow Travis down the walkway, staying close by his side.

As soon as we're within five feet of the doorway, I see Wyatt's body. His skin has turned a horrid shade of gray, and dried blood covers everything, exactly as Nicki, and Annie, described. I let out a gasp, and my hand flies to my face, as if pushing the bile back into my stomach. Travis turns back toward me.

"You OK?" he asks, offering me his hand.

Unable to speak, I take his hand, holding tightly as we enter, careful not to get too close to the body. Yet I find myself staring at this man. How can one go from a vibrant, sought-after recording exec who has the world at his fingertips to a lifeless corpse, dead in its own pool of blood?

"House is empty. Come on in," Dennis loudly yells from the top of the stairs, but we're already inside. "Remember, don't touch a thing. If you see something suspicious, let *me* know. I'm calling the coroner."

As soon as we pass the body, I release Travis's hand. Cautiously and with purpose, we begin to search the house, yet I'm not sure for what. Dennis has opened his kit and is dusting the wineglasses for prints. I head toward the kitchen. Travis follows.

"What about the bottle of wine Caroline brought? Annie didn't say anything about her taking it with her, only the knife. Wouldn't that have her prints as well? I wonder where it could be." I begin to search the countertops for an opened bottle of white wine.

"This decanter is filled with the wine Wyatt brought, right?" Travis asks, to which I nod my head yes.

"I'm guessing Wyatt knew his wines. Unless Caroline gave him a good bottle, he could have tossed it out, especially knowing he had no plans of offering her another glass," I say as I move toward the tall metal trash can. Pressing my foot on the pedal—stepping is not touching—I see a partially full bottle when the lid pops open.

"Dennis," I yell. "I think I've found something." I look up at Travis, whose eyebrows arch, perhaps impressed I've discovered possible evidence.

"Way to go. Didn't know you had the detective gene." For a brief moment, his eyes gaze into mine, the way he used to look at me when we were younger.

Reflexively, I blush, quickly responding, "I keep replaying the scene in my mind. I may not be able to visualize it like Annie, but I did note the facts." I have yet to tell Travis I'm a journalist and rely on observations in order to write.

"What did you find?" Dennis's voice has a slight echo in the empty house.

"I think it's the bottle of wine she brought. The wine inside should match what is in the glass."

Dennis puts on a clean rubber glove before reaching into the trash can to retrieve the amber bottle. After he sets it on the counter, I look carefully at the label. I am not familiar with this brand.

"It's a fairly cheap bottle," Travis says as Dennis goes to work, taking samples of wine and dusting the bottle for prints.

"Of course, the liquor store. I forgot you worked there."

"Yeah, I've been managing it for a few years. Took over the place after my uncle retired. It only requires about twenty-five hours a week. Which is perfect … lets me keep my business running."

Confused, I ask, "What's that?"

"I have a studio, outside of town."

"You're sculpting?" I ask, remembering how talented he was when we dated.

"Yep. I went to RISD. Learned a lot from some really great professors."

Rhode Island Institute of Design—that's impressive. Amazed with how little I know about this man, the one I left because I thought we wanted such different things, I cannot help but smile. I'd underestimated him, thought he didn't have vision. I was so wrong.

We hear the car doors shut outside. "Backup's here," Dennis says as an older male and young female officer hurry into the house.

"What's going on, Chief?" the man asks as the woman looks suspiciously at Travis and me.

Dennis briefs the officers, omitting the part about Annie's vision.

"Do you want us to officially question Nicki Keating?" the woman offers, a bit too eagerly. Immediately, I see the strain form in Travis's face as he struggles to remain silent.

"No, I need you here. At some point we'll question Nicki, 'cause she discovered the body. She's pretty shook up, being she and this guy were involved and such." Dennis pauses, looking toward Travis. "I think it's best to wait."

"Yes, sir." The female officer heaves out a sigh, perhaps in disappointment, causing me to wonder why she's so anxious to question Nicki.

"The prints on the wineglass out in the main room appear to match the prints on this bottle." Dennis motions with his head to the half-empty bottle of pinot gris on the counter. "We need to find who stopped by for a drink with the vic. If she's not the killer—and I'm suggesting it's a female because of the lipstick—then she was the last person to see the victim alive. Comb the place to see if anything looks unusual."

Both officers give a brief nod then disperse and begin to search the house.

"So what's your next move?" Travis asks Dennis.

Dennis runs his hand through his short ash-brown hair. "I can only delay things for so long. I'm gonna have to pick up Nicki and take her in for questioning."

Travis sighs as he places his hand on Dennis's shoulder. "I know. And I appreciate your waiting. There's gotta be something here that will point to a motive."

"Dennis, would it be all right if I went into Wyatt's office and looked through his files?" I ask as I tuck a loose strand of hair behind my ear. Yep, I'm definitely nervous.

"Where are you going with this, Marlee?" the chief asks as a frown forms on his face.

"I'm not sure. Something tells me we may find answers there." I cannot explain the feeling I have—it's as though an inner voice, definitely not Margaret's, is leading me upstairs.

"OK, but you gotta wear these," Dennis says, handing me a pair of blue rubber gloves. "We don't want your prints all over the place."

After putting on the gloves, I head up the staircase. Wyatt's office is located off of the second-floor landing.

"Chief ...," the policewoman says loudly as she sees me enter the upstairs room.

"It's OK, Alice. I told Marlee she could look in there."

The woman glares in my direction, then turns her back and walks into the master bedroom.

There is a filing cabinet encased in a mahogany credenza behind Wyatt's desk. It's unlocked. I pull open the top drawer, only to find it's filled with perfectly labeled files, all containing warranty booklets. Quickly, I flip through them, although there's nothing out of the ordinary. The lower drawer houses information on the sale of the home, notes from the builder, and legal documents. My heart rate quickens. Caroline's a realtor, and from what Annie saw, Caroline acted familiar with this home. If this was a spec home, then she could have represented either the builder or Wyatt.

My fingers meticulously move through the files. Bingo! I see the label, "Purchase," and pull the thick folder from the drawer, placing it on top of the desk. After sitting down in the ribbed leather swivel chair, I page through the file's contents, looking for anything that could possibly have Caroline's name on it. As I flip through a stapled official-looking packet that seems to be a Sale of Agreement, I see Caroline's signature with her name printed below. She represented the buyer, Wyatt, not the builder. Why did Wyatt choose Caroline as his realtor? Was it random, or could there have been a connection of sorts?

"Travis," I call.

"What did you find?" he asks, somewhat out of breath after running up the stairs.

"Caroline was Wyatt's realtor. She knew him ... for more than two years. The date on this sale was October 29, 2018."

Travis stands up and moves out into the hallway by the stairs. "Dennis, Marlee's got something."

I hear the thuds of Dennis's boots as he bolts upstairs.

"Caroline Rhimes was Wyatt's realtor. They'd known each other for close to two and a half years." My words are clear and precise.

"You don't say." Dennis pauses, and then a small smile appears on his face as he asks, "Marlee, can I have that document?"

"Of course," I say, handing the stapled contract to him.

Without saying another word, Dennis goes downstairs. Travis follows him. I keep looking through the file folders, hoping to find something else, anything, that might shine some light on Wyatt and Caroline's relationship.

Everything appears to be normal transactional information—title documentation, insurance papers, a certificate showing the down payment for the property. Yet I keep looking. I know I'm missing something.

After thoroughly combing through the file, I replace it in the drawer and examine the remaining folders. Nothing appears out of the ordinary. There are only utility bills, property taxes, and receipts for furniture, appliances, and household items. Wyatt was certainly organized. I sigh as I resign to the fact there are no hidden secrets in the filing cabinet. Frustrated and knowing I'm missing something obvious, I lean onto the mahogany desk and place my head into my hands.

There's nothing on top of this desk except for a small box. The lid is a replica of a Rolling Stones album cover. Looking closely, I see writing and what appears to be a signature. Doing my best to decipher the scribble, I laugh as I read the words aloud: "To my buddy, Wyatt—Mick Jagger." There are three *x*'s underneath his signature. Wyatt must have been a big deal.

Carefully, I lift the lid. Inside are several photographs of Wyatt with famous musicians including David Bowie, Bob Dylan,

Pete Townshend, and Michael Jackson. I shake my head, trying to grasp the enormity of this man. As I remove the final picture, I see a small key at the bottom of the box. Wondering if this is to the filing cabinet, I check, but it doesn't fit inside of the lock.

Confused, I scrutinize the office, wondering if there are other locked cabinets anywhere. After combing the entire room, I realize there are none in obvious places, so I get down on my hands and knees and begin to look under furniture. Perhaps he had a hidden storage space built into the credenza. A safe of some kind would make sense. After all, he wasn't here that often.

However, I see nothing. As I sit down on the hardwood floor, the barite gemstone pokes into my left glute. Pausing, I reach into my back pocket and pull out the blue stone. Holding it tightly in my left hand, I shut my eyes, wondering if this stone could possibly help my intuition. I say a silent prayer, though I am not sure anyone is listening.

Frustrated when no brilliant idea appears in my head, I turn and begin to stand, once again placing the stone in my back pocket. That's when my eyes catch an irregularity underneath Wyatt's desk. Crouching back down, I discover a small compartment, barely an inch deep. Using my phone as a flashlight, I see there's a lock. After reaching for the small key still sitting atop the desk, I carefully insert it into the opening. It fits perfectly.

Slowly, I pull open the tiny drawer. Inside are several folded papers. I remove them then sit back in the chair and begin to read what Wyatt had so carefully hidden. I pick up the first piece of paper. Actually, it looks more like a note card.

September 15, 2020

Wyatt,

I expect the payment to be made to me by Friday. If not, I am going to call Billy and tell him. It's your choice. Make the wise decision.

Caroline

What is this? Quickly, I pick up the second card, which appears to be identical in shape and size to the first.

November 5, 2020

Wyatt,

I haven't received the money. Your little tryst with Nicki is about to end.

While not signed, it's written in the same handwriting on matching stationary. So Caroline was blackmailing Wyatt about his affair. None of this makes sense. If she was blackmailing him, why would she kill him?

As I reach for the last piece of paper, I feel its texture is different from the others. This is more of a formal letter, written on standard sheet paper. Carefully, I unfold it, noting there's a New York address at the top, and the letter's addressed to Wyatt.

December 17, 2020

Mr. Bixby,

After conducting a thorough investigation on a Ms. Caroline Rhimes—2634 Foxgrove Lane, Hawley Falls, PA—I have found the following information:

- Ms. Rhimes was convicted of shoplifting from the Hawley Falls Walmart in January of 2002.

- Ms. Rhimes was convicted of prostitution in Atlantic City in July of 2012.
- Ms. Rhimes has had three formal complaints to RE/MAX regarding professional conduct and, as a result, has been placed on probation until March of 2021.

The invoice for my services has been included in this mailing.

Sincerely,
Roger Evans
PI #5253364

"Dennis, Travis … you've got to see this," I yell, unable to move from the desk chair. This is it, what Juliette picked up on when she was feeling Nicki's energy.

Within seconds, both appear.

Handing them the papers, I say, "Well, we've got motive. Apparently, Caroline was trying to blackmail Wyatt. She threatened to tell Billy about Nicki and Wyatt's affair. Wyatt must have hired a private investigator who found some not-so-nice things about Caroline, including a prostitution charge. My guess is Wyatt wasn't going to be swindled, so he did his own background check and then confronted Caroline, refusing to play her game. The date on Caroline's last letter is before the date on the investigator's correspondence to Wyatt."

"Wyatt probably thought the whole thing was over. Then, unexpectedly, Caroline shows up at his place on Friday evening," Travis says. "Reluctantly, he lets her in, never expecting she'd be violent."

"Especially if she brought him a bottle of wine … perhaps as a peace offering, to call a truce?" I say as I lean back in the chair.

"What you're both saying makes sense." Dennis scratches his head before continuing: "I think we've got plenty of cause to bring

Caroline in. I checked prints from the Sale of Agreement, and there are prints on the signature page that match the prints on the wineglass and the bottle." Dennis gives me a quick wink.

"Alice, Mike," he calls to the other officers. "Marlee's found strong evidence against Caroline Rhimes. I want the two of you to go pick her up and bring her down to the station. I'll meet you there. First, I have to take these two back to the Connelly place."

Both officers nod and turn to leave. However, I can't help but notice when Alice turns back, looks me in the eye, and gives me a quirky smile. Might she approve?

"I think we're done here ... at least for now," Dennis says as he leads us down the stairway. The coroner must have arrived while I was upstairs. I somberly watch as he covers Wyatt's body. As we walk outside, we see a van pull up. Two men get out, go to the back, and pull a folded gurney from the rear doors.

The three of us remain silent during the ride back to the house, even after the car stops in our driveway. However, as I shift to open the car door, Dennis turns to me and says, "Marlee, you probably don't remember me, but I recall you as a kid. You and your family were only here during the summers. We lived by the lake too ... full-timers. I used to think there was something different about you. You didn't play with the older kids. You kept to yourself. Every time I went past your dock in my fishing boat, you were reading on one of those big Adirondack chairs. Seems to have done you good." Dennis nods his head at me. "Thank you," he says, his eyes projecting the kindness I had seen earlier today.

"I *do* remember you." The image of a little towheaded kid, close to my age, comes to mind. "You were quiet and shy, right? And your mom used to make the best sugar cookies," I say, reminiscing about the time I saw Dennis and his family having a picnic by the lake. His mom offered me a sugar cookie. It was absolutely delicious.

"She still does," Dennis says. A big smile beams on his face.

"See you soon, Dennis," Travis says before following me out of the car. "I think I'm due to get some money off of you tonight."

"Then you had better draw some good cards." Both men laugh, a relief of sorts after all we've been through.

Before we walk inside to let the others know what happened, Travis turns to me and says, "I always hoped I'd see you again, but I didn't think it would be like this." He sighs as he gazes into my eyes.

"Yeah, it's been a pretty strange day," I say.

"Do you ever wonder *what if*?"

Seemingly impossible, this day is becoming even stranger. Although it's Tom who is on my mind, not Travis. I want to know what my husband and son are doing. While I've never doubted how much they mean to me, my love for Tom could not be stronger than what I feel at this moment. I want to tell him everything that's happened, how we helped solve a murder.

"Things happen the way they're supposed to. The older I become, the more I believe this." I take his hand and give it a gentle squeeze before letting go. "Let's go inside. There's a lot to share."

INNOCENT,
BUT STILL GUILTY
February 13

"I'm cleared?" Nicki's voice is timid yet hopeful.

"Yes, Nicki. The police are probably questioning Caroline right now. Dennis got a set of her prints off of the contract she had signed when Wyatt bought the house. That set matched the prints from the glass and the wine bottle, so they have enough evidence to prove she was there. Plus, the letters in Wyatt's secret under-the-desk storage suggest motive. If they can find the knife at her place, well, that will seal it." Travis's voice is confident, assured.

"Still, I'm struggling with how Wyatt met Caroline in the first place. Did he randomly pick a realtor to represent him?" There's something about this mere coincidence that doesn't sit well with me.

Nicki responds, "I've been thinking about that too, Marlee. There are at least twelve realtors in the area. I guess he saw her name somewhere and contacted her."

I nod, still acknowledging something doesn't add up.

"It's been a long day," Travis says to Billy and Nicki, who are now sitting next to one another on the sofa. "I'm sure you'd like some privacy to sort through things." He raises his eyebrows at his sister-in-law.

Nicki nods, but Billy, who has remained quiet the entire time, stands and looks to us and says, "Thank you ... for helping to clear Nicki."

Billy puts on his coat and heads out the door, leaving Travis and Nicki behind. Before following Billy, an emotional Nicki embraces each of us, expressing heartfelt thanks, especially to Sophia, who now has tears running down her own cheeks.

Travis lingers for a bit. "If you guys need anything, call me. Here is my number," he says as he gives me a business card, the one for his studio, not the liquor store.

I give Travis a quick hug. "It's been good seeing you, really good." I refrain from saying more.

Travis then gives me that smile, the one that would make me melt inside. Although it still warms my core, I now have a different appreciation for this man. He is a good soul, definitely someone I'd be proud to call my friend. Regardless, he's not Tom.

As I watch my first love walk out the door, I am not lost in what was or might have been. Instead, I am in the present. Thinking of my husband, I feel a spark begin to flicker. No doubt it's been a bit dormant for some time. However, I now know the light for Tom hasn't gone out; it has only been waiting to be stoked.

"What the fuck just happened?" Juliette speaks first. "I've been through a lot of shit, but I don't think I've *ever* had a day like this before."

"You're right," I say. "So much for our relaxing girls' weekend." I joke, but not really.

"We still have tonight, and most of tomorrow." Sophia's optimistic tone brings a bit of normalcy to the afternoon.

Annie chimes in: "I'm not ready to go home. I need more time to unwind."

"I think we all need to relax a bit, at least I need to," I admit, as I collapse onto the sofa.

"Amen to that, sister." Juliette smiles as she heads to the kitchen and returns with a freshly uncorked bottle of chardonnay and four wineglasses.

"There's no way I'm drinking tonight," Annie says with wide eyes, causing me to giggle.

"Best remedy for a hangover." Juliette offers Annie a glass, but she declines.

The rest of us empty our glasses in no time. Juliette's quick to refill them. It's then I decide to come clean to everyone regarding my past with Travis.

"Guys, I'm curious. None of you asked how Travis and I knew one another."

"Oh, we knew," Annie says as a mischievous grin evolves on her face.

"Was that something you could see?" I ask, eyes popping from my head as I wonder what else Annie might know about me.

"No, Nicki told us, when you went to Wyatt's house," Annie says. A small snort escapes as she tries to hide her laughter. "Apparently, you left a definite mark on Travis," Annie teases.

"Yeah," Juliette says, grinning. "I think a part of him will always love you."

"That could be why he believed you, Marlee … believed us. I doubt many people would accept Annie's vision, unless they trusted the person telling them." Sophia looks deeply at me as she takes a sip of wine. "You must have meant a great deal to him."

"We fell hard for each other—at least I did." I pause, taking a big inhale before continuing the story. "It began after my senior year of high school. I worked as a lifeguard at The Birch Lodge." I point out the window toward the building by the western side of the lake. "I met Travis within the first week of arriving that summer. Aunt Sue and Uncle Pete held a family barbecue at Eagle's Landing. Travis came with his parents and Billy," I add. "I was standing by the fire we'd built near the dock. This hot guy … Travis … came up to me, offering me a Solo cup … filled with root beer." I pause, beginning to blush.

"Ha," Juliette laughs. "What a nice guy."

I nod. "Before long, we were inseparable. In fact, I thought about not going to college so I could stay here, with him."

"But you went to school, right?" Juliette asks.

"Yes ... I tried to talk Travis into coming with me to Burlington ... I went to the University of Vermont," I explain. "Thought he could take a few classes, work part-time, and then apply to be a full-time student for second semester." I hesitate before continuing. "I told him I knew what was best for us ... for him. I was trying to help, but he took it as me trying to fix him, like he wasn't good enough. I didn't think that," I say, and my shoulders slump as I lean back into the rocking chair and wrap my arms around my knees. "I hadn't seen him since the day we broke up ... not during any of our family reunions." I shake my head. "Then this Friday, before you got here ... we bumped into each other at the liquor store."

"Think about it, Marlee. It wasn't a mere coincidence, was it?" Juliette asks. "You needed to be comfortable being around each other ... after so much time ... or otherwise, it would have been strange, and he might not have believed you. And, for all we know, Nicki could be the one in custody, not Caroline."

She has a point. I smile, looking outside toward the lake, momentarily returning to that summer. But tonight is not seventy degrees, there are no sailboats making their final lap around the lake, nor is there a gentle breeze blowing through the pine trees. There's most likely eighteen inches of ice on the lake, and we can hear the howling wind through the glass. Plus, I'm now forty-six, not eighteen.

"Was it strange," Sophia asks, "seeing him after so much time has passed?"

"At first," I say, admitting how I'd knocked over the cardboard vodka display. "Bumping into Travis was the last thing I expected." I pause, remembering how it felt seeing him yesterday. "Then, being around him today ... with all that was going on ...

everything became sort of natural ... like time hadn't passed, but we had moved on."

Sophia nods as a grin emerges on her delicate lips.

However, it's Juliette who asks what they all are most likely wondering. "Did you have *any* feelings?"

Appreciating Juliette's direct nature, I inhale deeply, consider her question, then confidently shake my head no.

"Actually, it was good to see Travis, to know he's OK, especially after hearing he lost his wife at such a young age. But I don't understand why Aunt Sue or Uncle Pete didn't tell me."

"Nicki talked about that too." Annie's head tilts to the side as she softly says, "I can't imagine what that poor man went through. Nicki told us Travis specifically asked your aunt and uncle not to tell you ... He didn't want you to feel sorry for him."

I nod in acceptance, realizing how proud Travis is. Funny, I guess we're kind of alike—I never wanted anyone to feel sorry for me when I had cancer and lost my hair. "He seems to be somewhat happy now." I pause, reflecting on how he appeared when I first saw him on Friday. "This afternoon, he told me about his business and how he received training at RISD. Travis sculpts. I remember how talented he was." I recall the beautiful bird he'd made for me, one I kept for ages. It broke during my move to Philadelphia. "But back to Juliette's question. Those feelings are long gone, replaced by warm memories."

"Perhaps this weekend offered a bit of closure for you?" Sophia asks as she leans back into the sofa.

It has. That was then, and this is now. Suddenly, I have an urge to call Tom.

"I'll be right back. There's something I want to do," I say, smiling as I head to my bedroom, shut the door, and settle onto the bed to call my husband. Tom answers.

"Hey, I miss you." I must sound wobbly, off balance.

When I hear Tom's voice, I begin to dissolve. All day, I remained strong, positive, and helpful—exactly how Margaret would have wanted me to be. However, as soon as I connect with my husband, I fall apart. Clearly, Tom is my pillar.

I pull myself together, to first tell him how much I miss him, then to share what's occurred these past nine hours. Tom offers comforting words, praising my intuition, showing concern. Though 120 miles apart, it is as if he's sitting by my side.

Then I tell him about bumping into Travis yesterday at the liquor store. Tom knows about Travis, as we've shared all past relationships. My husband's quiet, but I don't sense jealousy. He's not that way.

Ten minutes later, feeling more myself, I say goodbye to Tom and return to the others. Before long, the clock chimes eighteen times. After we all agree we're hungry for dinner, I head to the kitchen. First, I set the oven to 350 degrees then pull from the freezer a Pyrex dish of chicken enchiladas I'd made earlier in the week. As I wait for the oven to heat, I plop down on the sofa, between Sophia and Annie. Juliette's sitting lotus style on the braided rug.

"Marlee," Juliette begins, "we were talking." She turns to face me. "You know how you said your article lacked substance, like you were merely telling people about the benefits of holistic practices?"

"Yes," I murmur, wondering where she's going.

"What if you wrote about this weekend, you know the murder … include how Annie saw what happened … and how your intuition led you to discover the letters, which provided the motive? You could then write about your sessions … and how those experiences may have opened you up to knowing. What do you think?"

I don't need to think. My body suddenly feels warm, satiated, and sure. This may be the exact piece I've been missing.

"I'll do it," I say, fully acknowledging some readers will think I'm out of my mind, brainwashed with woo-woo ideas. But I'm not.

Annie's clairvoyance and Juliette's ability to know Wyatt was under stress are what saved Nicki from being accused of the murder. "Of course, I won't be able to discuss too many of the details. Nevertheless, it may be exactly what I need to pull this article together." Instantly, I feel a surge of energy course through my body.

There's a knock at the door.

"Who could that be?" Annie asks, sitting up a bit straighter.

Curious, yet cautious, I slowly walk toward the front door. Before opening it, I look out the side window, only to see Dennis's car in the driveway.

"It's Dennis. Wonder what he wants."

When I answer the door, Dennis is standing there, looking bewildered. "Can I come in and speak with you and your friends?"

"Sure. Let me take your coat," I say as he shuffles toward an empty chair by the fireplace. I see him eye the bottle of wine.

"Would you like something to drink?" I ask, wondering if he's on duty or if this is more of a friendly visit.

"Do you have anything stronger?" he asks. A hint of stress in his voice answers my question.

"Sure." I go to the cabinet, pull out the bottle of Jack Daniel's, and pour some into a short glass. "Ice?"

Dennis shakes his head no.

After handing him the glass of whiskey, straight up, I return to the sofa, wondering what's going on.

"So I have to ask." He pauses to take a swig. "How did you *really* figure out the case? Sure, I know what you told me ... about Annie seeing things ...but it makes no sense. None of you are from this area. And even though Marlee visits in the summer, I doubt she'd have any idea of who Caroline Rhimes is. You said her prints would be on the glass ... and they were. And Marlee, that lockbox was hidden beneath the desk. I'm not so sure Alice or Mike would have found it."

"It must sound pretty unbelievable," I say as I look into my own glass. "I'm not sure I understand it."

"The guys at the station kept asking me how we connected the dots. I told them the letter you found made me think Caroline was our prime suspect. They acted like they believed me. So how do you see things in your head?" he asks Annie, looking absolutely confused.

Annie remains quiet, most likely because she's grappling with accepting her visions.

Finally, it's Juliette who speaks: "Some things cannot be logically explained. Annie's ability to see … which, by the way, she just discovered and is trying to accept … is something that merely *is*. We all have access to information that is not easily known. But it won't come to us unless we have faith and trust. And then, when it happens, well, we have to believe."

Dennis stares at Juliette, perhaps hoping to see something deep within her. After a few moments, he shakes his head and leans back into the chair.

"You've charged Caroline Rhimes with murder?" I ask, wanting to confirm she's behind bars and we're all safe from any potential danger.

"Yes, we did. And we found the knife. It was in the trunk of her car. I guess she didn't have time to dispose of it."

I nod, grateful this case appears to be solved. "Dennis," I begin, "there's still one thing bothering me."

"What's that?"

"Why was Caroline Wyatt's realtor? How did he pick her? Was it merely a coincidence?" As the words come out of my mouth, I'm reminded there are few coincidences in life. "Do you think they knew each other beforehand?"

I carefully watch Dennis, hoping he will provide an answer. Instead, he lets out a huge sigh, takes another swig of his drink, and says, "Whatever the reason, having her as his realtor ended up being the biggest mistake of his life."

I nod, aware I may never know the answer to this question.

Dennis drains the rest of his drink, clears his throat, and says, "Thank you, ladies." He stands as if to leave, only to turn and add, "This was the most unusual case I've *ever* handled." The tense muscles in his face soften as he continues. "I certainly can't explain it … and hope I don't have to … but I couldn't have done it without the four of you." He does a quick bow with his head then gives me a wink. "Now I have a poker game to get to," he says as he retrieves his coat. I walk toward the door to say goodbye.

"And don't worry, Marlee, I'll take good care of Travis." His tone is caring, as if he understands our history.

Of course he knows. This is Hawley Falls. I doubt there are many things that actually remain secrets in this town.

***

After inhaling copious amounts of chicken enchiladas, we return to the fireplace to settle in for the evening. It's been a long, exhausting, and emotional day. Still, I don't want it to end. But we leave tomorrow afternoon so everyone can be back for Valentine's Day dinner.

"Thank you," Annie says as she wraps the throw around her shoulders. "I *really* needed this trip. Of course, I didn't expect to be involved in a murder investigation."

"Or be the one to solve it?" Juliette teases.

"Yeah, that too," Annie responds a bit hesitantly. "I'm having trouble believing this whole thing. It could have been a once-and-done vision. Do you think I saw the crime in order to help Dennis arrest Caroline?"

"Or you can accept the fact you're clairvoyant and can see things," Juliette says with a big smirk.

"Annie, look at this as a true gift. Perhaps it could help you with your practice, in a healing way. If you can see what your patients cannot, then you may be able to help them realize what is causing their pain." As Sophia speaks, Annie seems to settle.

I distinctly remember Annie mentioning in my kitchen how she often knew what troubled her patients before they shared that information with her. Maybe Juliette's correct—Annie could have been clairvoyant for some time, but unaware, suppressing it for years.

These thoughts quickly fade as my attention moves from Annie to Sophia. Sophia's closely watching Annie, similar to how she kept an eye on Annie earlier this morning when Annie wasn't feeling well. Juliette, however, appears oblivious to this subtle interaction. It's as though she's on a mission to convince Annie of her gift.

"During my time in India, when I was learning Reiki and more advanced energetic healing methods, my intuition exploded. Suddenly, I started to know things, predict what would happen. It totally rocked my world, started to scare the shit out of me. And then, once I realized I could sense things in advance, I wanted to know *everything*. I studied tarot cards, used pendulums, dove into astrology ... whatever might help me see into the future. Then it started to mess with my mind, so I had to take a step back, unplug a bit." Juliette tucks her legs beneath her as she shakes her head. "Now I've learned balance. I can tap in, and I can remove myself. You'll learn that too, Annie."

Despite Juliette's enthusiastic assurance, Annie looks unsure.

"What about your intuition, Marlee? How did you know about the box under the desk?" Annie asks in a tone more concerned than curious.

"I have no idea." I pause, thinking back to earlier this afternoon when I felt a need to search Wyatt's office. "I guess something inside told me he'd have information in his files. Not a voice or anything like that. I kind of remember a strange sensation in my core, a confirmation of sorts, suggesting there was information hidden somewhere. Plus, I also remembered what Juliette said … Wyatt was concerned about something. I figured any important documents would be somewhere in his office."

"Did your mind tell you to go upstairs, or did your body?" Juliette asks.

I inhale as I try to return to earlier this afternoon, asking myself what propelled me to want to go to the second-floor office. Rubbing my eyes, perhaps in hopes for a clear vision of what truly occurred, I distinctly remember being downstairs with Dennis and Travis. Then I felt a pull of sorts, directing me upstairs. "It wasn't my thoughts that told me to go there; it was an unfamiliar sensation in my body." Suddenly the spot between my eyebrows begins to throb. Instinctively, my fingertips begin to massage the area.

"Do you feel pressure between your eyes?" Juliette asks as she swings her legs out from beneath her so she can sit on the edge of the chair.

"Yes, like a sinus headache is suddenly coming on." The pain practically causes me to wince.

She lets out a quirky laugh. "That's your third eye, Marlee. It's where our sixth chakra is located. Our third eye helps us see … not physically, but energetically."

Swallowing hard, I try to comprehend what Juliette's saying. Did something unknown inside of me guide me upstairs to Wyatt's office and to the hidden drawer beneath his desk? Or was it me, putting two and two together, using deductive reasoning I've honed through years of writing? My hands move through my hair as I stare at the floor.

Juliette stands up then moves to sit on the floor next to me. "This is awesome. You're learning how to *know* by trusting your intuition. Few people are able to do this."

Could she be right? Can I tap into my intuition? Or was it all only a coincidence?

It's only a headache, Marlee. Don't pretend you have some sort of special ability.

Then I remember the blue barite, which remains in my back jeans pocket. Maybe Margaret is wrong. Perhaps the crystal did have something to do with it. Or could I have possibly *known* on my own? I look toward Sophia, hoping she may share some insight. After all, her grandmother was intuitive.

"Believe." That's all she says. Yet that one word holds so much—requiring *faith, trust, surrender*—all of the elements I struggle to embrace.

TRUE MEANINGS

February 13

Annie's been quiet all evening. She lets out a big yawn. "Do you mind if I call it a night? I know it's only eight thirty, but I'm exhausted."

"Of course. Go get some rest," I say as I stand up and give Annie a gentle hug before she heads upstairs to bed. I return to the floor with my back against the cushioned chair. Sophia and Juliette, seated on the sofa across from me, appear totally relaxed.

After we hear the door to Annie's room close, Sophia speaks up. "Have you noticed anything different about Annie? I know her vision today most definitely upset her, but I sense there is something more."

"Kind of … Discovering you're a clairvoyant is a pretty big deal," Juliette says as she kicks off her shoes then pulls her knees into her chest.

I look at Sophia. "What are you thinking?" I ask as I rise and head to the kitchen to put some of the remaining cookies on a plate. Sophia is silent, gathering her thoughts.

As I place dessert on the table, I wait for Sophia to explain her observations. Finally, she speaks.

"I have read several studies showing how women can be open to visions … a *knowing* of sorts … when their hormones shift … when they are pregnant."

I pause, remembering Annie's behavior earlier in the day. "Annie threw up this morning. And she was totally exhausted tonight."

"She thought she was hungover," Juliette says, and a slight scowl comes across her face.

"She most definitely drank a great deal more than she normally would." Sophia pauses before continuing. "But I do not think alcohol was the only reason for her feeling poorly. I *felt* something else," she explains as she leans over to take a cookie from the plate.

"So you sense things too?" I ask, eyes wide open as I stare at the woman in front of me. Recalling the first impression she made on me this past December—exotic, graceful, stunning—I now add *intuitive* and *knowing* to the list of words to describe Sophia.

"Yes, since I was little. And it is usually tied to the body, connected in a medical sort of way." Sophia delicately takes a small nibble of the oatmeal cookie.

"Of course," Juliette says, slowly nodding her head. "That's why you're a doctor. Your intuition allows you to better diagnose your patients. You sensed this ability when you were younger, and it led you to follow your life's path … your journey … to be a healer." The corners of Juliette's mouth turn up into an *I've figured you out* smile.

Sophia blushes. "I would not call myself a *healer*, perhaps an enlightened physician."

"No, Juliette's right. I saw how you watched Annie this morning. And then, when we brought Nicki inside, you became glued to her, as if you were sensing whether Nicki was physically OK," I say. "Had you thought she required medical attention, you would have insisted we take her to the hospital. You realized her body was fine … and it was something deeper causing her pain."

Sophia only smiles.

"You think Annie's pregnant?" I ask, knowing how being so would rock Annie's world. "She'd told me she wanted children. However, it sounded as though she and Jonathon weren't able to."

"I believe she is capable of becoming pregnant … and that she is." Sophia's tone has shifted to her doctor voice. "If Annie feels poorly tomorrow, I will suggest she take a pregnancy test as soon as she gets home." With this statement, she sits up a bit straighter before propping a pillow behind her back.

"That is fuckin' awesome." Juliette smiles broadly as she shifts into a cross-legged position on the sofa. Suddenly her joyful look becomes inquisitive. "You're both moms, so what's it like?" Juliette's eyes beam brightly with curiosity.

This question, which seemingly comes from nowhere, causes me to wonder why Juliette's so interested. Motherhood is not something I'd predict Juliette would care much about. However, I do my best to answer honestly.

"Well, Patrick's an only child. He's been super easy, even as a baby." I reflexively cross my fingers, a habit I hope will prevent him from poor decision-making or lapses in judgment, both common occurrences among boys his age. "Besides, I was ready ... we were ready when I became pregnant. And I loved all the stages: infant, toddler, elementary school. Don't get me wrong—being a mom can be hard," I say before emitting a sigh as I think about Patrick in goal. "Still, I wouldn't trade any of it." As the words exit my mouth, I have absolutely no doubt regarding their truth. There is true peace in my heart.

"I agree with Marlee," Sophia says as her eyes begin to narrow, suggesting she's elsewhere. "Max and Lizzy have been the highlights of our life. Now that they are grown and no longer living with us ... I miss them greatly." Part of the light that naturally surrounds Sophia dims when she acknowledges her children's absence.

Witnessing Sophia's reaction only intensifies the concerns I've been struggling to address. "That's what scares me," I blurt out before pausing, hoping to properly explain my fears. "When Patrick leaves ... and it's only Tom and me ... what's it like? It's been so long. What if ..." I stop, as if unable to finish my question. *What if he doesn't love me like he used to?*

But Sophia does not need me to say the remaining words. Without hesitation, she moves to sit next to me on the hardwood floor, taking my hands in hers. Looking straight into my eyes, she says with the utmost certainty, "You will definitely miss Patrick. How could you not?" She pauses, then gently wipes a tear falling down my cheek. "You and Tom will discover a new life, one no longer centered on your son, but built around the two of you … and it will be beautiful … trust me." She gently kisses my forehead in a tender fashion.

"I'm sorry," I say, suddenly self-conscious of my emotional reaction. I let go of her hands and sit up straighter. "I guess today's catching up with me."

"Never be embarrassed about expressing your feelings. It's natural to want to know what is next in life. The unknown can be stressful. You must trust, Marlee. Remember what I said earlier … *believe*."

It's then I begin to melt. Not only do I let go of today's stress, but also pent-up pain—which I've held so tightly and suppressed deep inside with all of my might. Yet perhaps it is more. Maybe I don't *believe*, am incapable of doing so. I pull my knees toward my chest as I dissolve into a pool of tears. Trusting and believing do not come easy for me. I require certainty. I want to know what's next.

"Marlee, what is it?" Juliette's voice bears concern. She comes and sits to my left, wedging herself against the sofa, perhaps sensing there is more to my reaction.

Flanked between Sophia and Juliette, I stare at my lap, which is quickly becoming dotted with wet tears. What is happening? I don't break down—and certainly not like this—in front of others.

"Let it go." Sophia's soothing voice encourages me to release the years of sadness I've kept inside. "You are safe with us." Tenderly, she rubs my back.

"What is causing you so much pain?" Juliette delicately asks as she hands me a tissue from the box sitting on the coffee table.

Her question only causes me to fall deeper into the reservoir of despair that is apparently at the center of this issue.

After several minutes, knowing I cannot continue like this forever, I do my best to answer her question. "I'm scared ... that after Patrick goes to college ..." I pause, unsure whether or not I can verbalize my fear.

"Yes?" Sophia encourages me to continue.

"That Tom and I ... that ... we've grown apart. That I'll feel alone ... by myself ... without Patrick." After I spit the words out, a wave of relief rushes over me. It actually feels good to share this.

"First of all, Tom adores you," Juliette says as she raises her perfectly formed eyebrows. "Michael tells me this all of the time. In fact, the two of you are role models for the type of relationship he wants." I lift my head to look at Juliette. Her eyes shine brightly, confirming they've had more serious discussions than I had assumed.

"And remember, soon it is time for Patrick to discover his own life journey," Sophia adds, of course knowing this from experience. "Our job as parents is to help guide our children, not keep them by our side. And do not worry. You will not lose your connection when he goes to college," she says in an assuring tone. "He will always love his mother." It's then a most knowing expression comes over her face. Sophia's wise eyes appear miles deep, as if she's dealt with this exact issue many times, perhaps in previous lifetimes.

"Besides, why would you feel alone? Sure, things will be different when Patrick goes to college, but then you'll have more time for your friends."

As Juliette says this, I flinch, causing both of them to look at one another.

"Marlee?"

"I guess that's one of the areas in my life where I'm not so gifted." I let out a big sigh as I wipe my eyes.

"What are you saying?" Sophia asks.

"Well, there aren't a lot of people who I'd call my friends. Sure, I have lots of acquaintances … the moms from Patrick's school, neighbors … but those are all women who live in my world … They are not part of it. There's no real connection." My confession fills me with fear of losing these two, my new friends, the ones I've now bared my soul to.

"I don't believe that," Juliette says. "You're one of the most friendly and welcoming women I know."

It's Sophia who remains silent, looking intently at me. She knows I'm being truthful.

"Well, it's not like I have a ton of girlfriends," Juliette admits then bites her lip. "I usually don't trust women … except, of course, both of you … and Annie … The three of you seem different." She quickly offers a quirky smile before continuing. "All day long, I watch the interactions in my studio. So many of the women appear sweet to one another. But once class starts, you should see their glares. They are constantly judging and comparing themselves … from how they look in their yoga clothes to how they move on the mat. And instead of supporting one another, I usually only witness eye rolls when one of the participants nails a pose … It makes me nuts." Juliette frowns then asks, "Sophia, what about you? Do you find women difficult?"

Sophia remains quiet for several moments before answering Juliette's question.

"Throughout the years, I have learned a great deal about interacting with other women. Surely, I do not have the answers, though my observations have assisted me in forming healthy friendships."

I sit attentively, hoping Sophia will share her sage advice, perhaps allowing me to understand what I've been missing.

"Whenever I have experienced trouble with a friend, it was because one of us crossed a boundary or made an inaccurate assumption." Sophia's neck lengthens in a regal fashion as she speaks.

Juliette runs her fingers through her long, flaxen hair, as if captivated by this woman who is twice her age.

"Often we fail to set boundaries, so it is natural for us to be unaware when we have crossed another's line." Sophia pauses, as if recalling a difficult situation. "When my friends and I understand what is and is not acceptable ... and do not assume how another *should* behave, then our relationships flourish. However, if one of us is not clear about our boundaries, inevitably someone will say or do something that is taken as too personal, too critical, or perhaps too insightful." Her eyebrows arch as if to make this point. "Does this make sense?" Sophia asks as her emerald eyes narrow.

My thoughts first go to high school. I'd shared too much about myself, become vulnerable to girls I had no reason to trust. I had failed to establish boundaries. Instead, I immediately assumed they were my friends, implicitly trusting them before a solid connection could naturally form. And then, later in life, when I overheard my two "friends" talk about my implants—insinuating I wanted them, not needed them due to my mastectomy—I'd realized I set myself up again. I guess I craved female interaction so badly I was not discerning about who I called my friend. My need to belong and feel accepted overrode my ability to clearly see those in front of me, whether or not we were a good match, natural candidates for a solid friendship.

Sophia's simple yet accurate explanation is correct. It wasn't them. All this time it was me—I had failed to set appropriate boundaries, and I most definitely made inaccurate assumptions. I overshared my truth.

"It makes perfect sense. Perhaps more than you may realize." I take in a big breath and let out a hearty sigh. After using the back of my hand to wipe my face, I say, "My entire life, I've wanted to feel as if I belonged." I swallow, as though I am finally accepting this truth. "Growing up, my older brothers and sister pretty much ignored me. I spent a lot of time alone. I guess I've been a bit too eager to make friends ... so I'd feel included."

Sophia listens intently; her compassionate expression doesn't waver. However, it's Juliette who seems truly unsettled by my confession. I wonder if at times she doesn't see things as clearly as she thinks she does.

Sophia then offers more wisdom. "True friendships require work. We can certainly be friendly with many, enjoy their company, and share wonderful memories. However, when we assume those around us think as we do and want similar things from life, we may find ourselves disappointed. Likewise, if we stop being true to ourselves so we fit in, we will ultimately encounter difficulties. Wearing masks and pretending to be who we are not hurts us in so many ways. Still, we do it to feel safe, valued, special." Sophia looks straight into my eyes, as if to confirm I understand her words.

I take a moment to sit quietly, mentally rehashing how past friendships fell apart or, more accurately, exploded. In each case, someone crossed a boundary, made an assumption, or pretended to be who they weren't—and most of the time it was me.

"I think I've been the one wearing masks." As I admit this sad truth, my shoulders droop and my head hangs.

"We all have," Juliette says, biting her lip. In an instant, she transforms from a confident woman to a young, unsure girl. "So many of my friendships ended badly because of this exact thing." Juliette then looks up at Sophia. "How do we find the right women to be our friends ... the ones we can be vulnerable around and take off our masks? It's hard to set those healthy boundaries and not assume others should and do think like we do."

"Juliette, is that not what the four of us have done since we have met?" Sophia asks this in the simplest of manners.

Once again, Sophia's clearly stated the truth. This is exactly what's been happening this weekend. Annie, Sophia, Juliette, and I have shown up as our true selves, respected one another's space, and spoken with kind and compassionate words. We haven't judged, made assumptions, or crossed boundaries. Instead, we've openly accepted our differences, listened to understand, and held space for one another. We've been true friends.

My eyes brighten, and suddenly the weight I've unknowingly carried effortlessly lifts. My entire body feels lighter, perhaps freer. And then two dots, so far apart from one another, have finally been connected. There is nothing *wrong* with me. My only fault is I didn't know how to be a true friend.

"Thank you, Sophia," I say as I lean toward my friend to embrace her. Tears of joy now silently trickle down my cheeks. "For so long, I've been lost in my own world and caught up in past dramas that I've not been aware of my own behavior or properly understood the reactions of others. Instead, I've created what I've wanted to see instead of accepting what is. And when things became difficult, I either compromised who I was or disregarded others for being different than I'd assumed they should be."

Sophia slowly nods her head as she listens to my big aha moment.

"To be authentic friends, we don't have to see things the same way. We can be our true selves ... have our own views, perceptions, ways of doing things. The important part is that we show up as we are without expecting others to be like us ... and we value them for who they are, not try to change or fix anything we don't like about them." I spit these words out in rapid phrases.

"Exactly." The space around Sophia's body appears to be glowing in a mystical way. She seems to be outlined in a soothing green light.

Then Juliette confirms what I see. "Holy shit, Sophia. I see your aura. It's green ... Why, of course ... you're a healer ... and right now your words are healing Marlee."

"Are you certain?" Sophia's voice emits a bit of confusion. "I only deal with the physical."

"Not anymore." Juliette's smirk reappears. "I think you are expanding, helping people understand, healing through sharing your knowledge."

Sophia's demure nature appears, and I notice a slight blush come across her cheeks as she says, "Perhaps the four of us were meant to be friends so we could help each other see our gifts."

Juliette nods as she holds her glass up in a toast. "To women ... may we all learn to accept our true selves, honor our differences, celebrate our successes, and hold space for one another without trying to fix, solve, or improve."

"To my friends ..." I clink Sophia's and Juliette's glasses before taking a sip, fully embracing this uncanny bond, one which I've never experienced before. Suddenly, I realize I've been myself this entire time, and they've accepted me as I am.

After placing her glass on the table, Juliette stands and runs upstairs. Several moments later, she returns, holding a deck of cards in her hands.

"I recently bought these animal spirit cards. Let's see what they say," Juliette says as she places a small box covered in pictures of wild animals on the table.

"Are these similar to tarot cards?" Sophia asks as she leans closer to examine the unopened box.

"No, they're oracle cards. Instead of predicting the future, these cards offer insight ... They guide you in decisions and help you see opportunities. Want to pick one?" Juliette opens the box and begins to shuffle the ornate laminated cards.

After Juliette spreads the cards on the coffee table, she looks up at me, motioning for me to choose a card. All have a beautiful geometric drawing on the side facing up. Somewhat apprehensive, I lean forward and examine the deck spread out in front of me. I have no idea which one to pick.

"Trust your instinct, Marlee. Which card calls to you?"

Listening to Juliette, I allow my left hand to guide me. I place it down on top of a card. When I turn it over, I see a mystical picture of a strange-looking animal, its unusual face surrounded in a glow of gold.

"You pulled the armadillo card," Juliette says as she reaches for the small book that accompanies the deck. I watch as she quickly pages through the tiny guide. Juliette becomes quiet as she reads the page with an illustration of an armadillo at the top of it.

After a moment, Juliette laughs. "This is perfect," she says as she looks up at me. The message here is to better understand boundaries. For you to live your best life, it's important for you to be conscious of your limits as well as others'. It says, 'Be honest with yourself and those around you. If something doesn't feel right, then say so. Listen to your body.'" Juliette picks up the card then mixes it back in with the others.

"Seriously," I say as I shake my head, "could I have pulled a better card? Now it's Sophia's turn." I think back to how my body told me to go upstairs into Wyatt's office.

On cue, Sophia leans forward, looking intently into the pile scattered across the table. She appears to deliberately choose a particular buried card beneath several others. Slowly, she turns it over, revealing a picture of a spider.

Without hesitation, Juliette quickly leafs through the booklet. "A spider spirit shows you that you are ready to create. It serves as inspiration for you to begin a new project or go in a new direction. Spirit will support you with your endeavors."

Sophia is visibly taken aback. Her eyes widen and her normally cool and confident expression transforms to one of uncertainty. What could she be thinking?

"Is there anything you've been considering doing ... a home improvement project or something like that?" I ask, though I have a feeling this may be something more significant than redoing her kitchen.

Sophia casts her eyes down toward the rug. After several moments of silence, she speaks: "I have been considering taking my practice in a new direction. Although I am unsure what my partners will think."

"What do you want to do?" Juliette asks as she tilts her head and her eyes become glued on Sophia.

After lifting her gaze back to us, Sophia says, "I have been considering expanding how I practice medicine. Traditional methods work some of the time, but not always." She pauses to sigh. "I believe there are better ways, less intrusive ways, to help my patients. I want to explore certain healing modalities that are not fully recognized by my peers."

"You're talking about holistic medicine?" I ask, shocked Sophia's been considering this avenue all along. She didn't mention this when I discussed writing the article. However, I do remember her strong interest in the area when we had dinner together at our home.

Sophia clears her throat. "Actually ... yes ... I have my Reiki certifications ... but that is only the beginning. There are more advanced practices I plan to learn. And I have spoken with Elena. She is eager to join me, offering Reiki sessions to my patients." Sophia becomes quiet.

"This is brilliant." Juliette's reaction doesn't show surprise. Instead, it reveals admiration. "You'd be creating a healing center of sorts. And what if we could work together in some way? I would love to expand my energy work."

"Yes, that would be amazing." Sophia smiles at Juliette before she exhales loudly. "Nevertheless, I must sell the concept to my partners. I am a bit concerned about their reaction."

"Well, if they don't like it, then you can go out on your own," Juliette says, her voice intense with conviction. "Besides, I'm sure your patients adore you. And if this new direction isn't for them, they'll find another doctor. And those who believe will find you."

Sophia softly sighs, once again looking down at the floor. "I hope so."

"What are Jared's thoughts?" I ask, hoping I'm not crossing one of those boundaries that could impact our friendship.

"He is encouraging, though he is worried some in our profession will dismiss me." With that, the glimmer in her eyes dulls a bit.

"But if you're following your true path, do you care what others think?" Juliette asks as she gathers the cards, placing them and the booklet back into the box.

"No," Sophia says as she bites her lower lip.

"What is it?" I ask.

"I have not shared this with my parents. I am unsure how they would react."

It's then I remember Sophia telling us her nonna was intuitive ... and Sophia's mother did not want Sophia to know about her grandmother's ability.

"They don't believe, do they?" I ask, again, hoping I'm not crossing a line.

"Not at all," Sophia says, then becomes quiet as she plays with the cross she so often wears. "My parents are extremely Catholic. In fact, my uncle is a priest, and my aunt spent fifteen years in the convent before she decided to leave." Sophia releases her necklace then interlaces her fingers in a gripping sort of way.

"And you're a practicing Catholic?" I ask.

"Perhaps not by others' definition. However, my religion is most definitely part of who I am."

"And you have been able to combine it with your spiritual side?" Juliette's nose scrunches a bit as she asks this. No doubt she's struggled with this. In fact, I remember her sharing she is anything but religious.

"I grew up with both worlds. My parents, devout Catholics, sent me to a strict Catholic school. However, I was incredibly close to my nonna. It was she who taught me to question and think independently." Sophia exhales, and the slight lines in her face seem to disappear. "Despite my parents ridiculing her in front of me, I knew Nonna told the truth." Sophia releases her hands then takes in a big breath. "Even as a child, it saddened me how my parents dismissed her. Against their warnings, I would visit Nonna … so I could learn her ways. They called her a witch, an atheist. They were wrong. Nonna shared with me how to honor both my Catholic upbringing as well as my connection to the Universe. I was only thirteen when she passed." I watch Sophia's eyes momentarily shut, as if in respect for her grandmother.

"This explains so much," I say, rubbing the spot between my eyes, what Juliette called the third eye. "The two of you had a special connection. Perhaps you inherited her gift."

Quietly, Sophia nods. "And I am honored to continue her ways."

We sit in silence. The sound of the crackling fire fills the void of spoken words. The grandfather clock strikes ten o'clock, but none of us seem tired.

Sensing we're going to be up for some time, I go to the kitchen, open a bag of tortilla chips, grab some salsa from the fridge, and pour it into a bowl. "Would anyone like more wine?"

"Please." It's Sophia who answers, which makes me giggle under my breath. She then says to Juliette, "I assume you have seen quite a bit on your travels and learned from masters. Did you open your yoga studio as soon as you returned from India?"

"Shortly afterward," Juliette says as I place the bowls of chips and salsa on the coffee table. I return to the kitchen and grab another bottle of wine. "My father was wealthy, and after he died, I inherited a fair amount of money. It was only me … I don't have any brothers or sisters," she states without saying more. "I used part of it to buy a vacant property near Rittenhouse Square. Then I made the necessary changes to the space and bought what I needed to open a yoga studio."

"I'm so sorry you lost your father," Sophia says. "You must miss him."

"Every day. My father raised me … all by himself." There's a distinct note of pride in her statement. However, it only emphasizes the hatred she must harbor for her mother.

"Then how lucky you are to have had such a loving father."

Amazed at the ease with which words come from Sophia's lips, I wish I, too, could find the perfect response in these situations. Despite a pure intention, I too often say something that could be taken the wrong way, only to shove my foot farther down my throat as I try to explain my awkward comment. I admire this beautiful trait Sophia possesses. It's as though everything about her flows with grace and elegance.

"I lost my parents at a young age too," I say, though I'm unsure whether or not Juliette's mom is alive.

She looks at me with knowing eyes then answers my unspoken question. "Supposedly, my mother is living. We haven't spoken since she left my father." She shrugs as if she does not care; however, the look in her eyes tells me she carries a great deal of anger.

"I'm so sorry." I can't imagine choosing to disengage from a parent. I sense this is a sensitive subject for Juliette, so I refrain from questioning her more about their relationship. Instead, I ask, "Did you incorporate some of what you learned in India into your studio?"

"Yes, from both India and my time at Yale."

I remember Juliette mentioning a degree from this Ivy League school when we first met at the holiday party. However, Sophia was not there at the time and looks confused.

"I have a doctorate in philosophy." Juliette shrugs her shoulders. "I know, I'm a bit young to have done this. I began my undergraduate degree at NYU when I was sixteen. I grew up in Manhattan, so I didn't need to live on campus. Then my dad died, during my senior year." Juliette pauses for a moment. A sadness comes across her face when she mentions her father. "I graduated right after my twentieth birthday. Let's just say India was a graduation present to myself." She laughs as she runs her fingers through her golden hair.

"When I traveled in India, I learned so much information about life, spirituality, the unknown … but I didn't have any foundational beliefs to attach to this knowledge. We never went to synagogue— both my parents grew up Jewish." Juliette adds this information as she shrugs her shoulders as if to dismiss this part of her heritage. "Then, when I returned to New York a year later, I decided to apply to grad school. Yale had two programs leading to doctoral degrees, of course incorporating all prerequisite courses. One track emphasized the classics—you know, Greek and Roman philosophy—and another focused more on psychology. At that time, I was ready to leave New York for New Haven, in fact I looked forward to the change."

"Which path did you choose?" I ask, betting she'll say psychology.

"I opted for the degree with an emphasis on psychology. My dissertation dealt with the aesthetics of Indian art and its impact on the followers of Hinduism."

"How fascinating. This must explain the amazing artwork I saw in your studio."

"Yes. I love pictures of Ganesh … mostly because of how he is believed to remove obstacles. After all, who doesn't face challenges in their life, and how cool would it be to have help to get rid of them?" Her attention appears to float elsewhere, making me wonder what she's had to deal with in her past.

We spend the rest of the evening sharing stories from our childhoods, some of which fill in blanks about Juliette's obstacles. I learn her mother is an alcoholic and, despite her father's wishes, would not seek treatment. Finally, Juliette's mother left, choosing gin over her daughter. Her dad, a respected lawyer at one of the oldest and most prestigious firms in Manhattan, died of a stroke when Juliette was on spring break during her senior year at NYU. I could not help but note the look in Juliette's eyes when she shares this. The normal turquoise sparkle subsides and is instead replaced by a dull sheen.

Sophia then tells us of how she first met Jared. It was during her internship at Penn. Apparently, one of Sophia's former professors from medical school was recruited to teach at University of Pennsylvania. He wrote to her, offering a summer internship as his research assistant. She accepted and moved to Philadelphia where she remained for her residency. Of course, this was against her family's wishes. Her parents sound controlling, even if their behavior was based on love and a fear of Sophia forever leaving Italy. Despite their efforts to keep her with them in Florence, she chose Philadelphia, a city halfway across the globe. Meeting Jared only confirmed her decision to stay.

Learning about Sophia's and Juliette's pasts cements how different our lives and experiences have been. However, each of us has faced adversity at some point and, as a result, has become a stronger woman. Finally, I'm unable to suppress a yawn.

"Should we call it a night?" I ask as I look at my watch, noting it's now 12:20.

"Sleep sounds delightful," Sophia responds.

"The alarm's going to go off sooner than I'd like," Juliette says, though I suspect she'll be up early to meditate and practice yoga.

After putting our glasses and the empty chip and salsa dishes in the sink, we say goodnight and head to our respective rooms.

As my head hits the pillow, I say my prayers then begin to take in all that happened this day. What started out as an innocent snowshoeing excursion evolved into a murder mystery, discovering Annie's clairvoyant, and realizing I have an intuitive ability. But there's more. I finally had full closure with Travis. And this led to understanding how strong my love is for Tom. I learned what's important in maintaining friendships, and I opened up to two incredibly special friends. With that thought, my breathing softens, and my thoughts begin to fade.

PRETTY IN PINK
February 14

This morning, I'm not the first up. When I walk into the kitchen, Annie's sitting at the kitchen counter, wearing a baggy Pitt sweatshirt and sipping on a glass filled with ice and what appears to be ginger ale.

"Good morning, Annie. How did you sleep?" I try to be cautiously optimistic. Still, I'm curious about what Sophia said last night and whether it could be true.

"I slept well, but when I woke up, I felt lousy again." Annie leans her elbows on the counter. "I'm not sure what's going on." Her skin's pale, and her eyes look like they're buried deep in their sockets.

"When did this start?" I ask her, wondering if she could be pregnant as Sophia suggested.

Annie scrunches her nose. "Come to think of it, I felt off on both Thursday and Friday morning. Then, as soon as I had a bagel for breakfast, I felt better." Annie rubs the back of her head. "I hope you don't mind I took a bottle of ginger ale from the pantry.

"You know you are welcome to anything," I say with a warm smile. Unable to resist inquiring what's on my mind, I pause, move closer to Annie, and then gently ask, "Is there any chance you could be pregnant?" I inhale, hoping I didn't cross a line. Perhaps I should have waited for Sophia to broach this subject.

"Pregnant? I wish that were the case." She lets out a sarcastic laugh. "Jonathon and I tried to conceive for five years … in vitro … We did everything. I was on all sorts of medicines. Nothing worked." She hunches, leaning deeper onto her elbow.

"I know several people who didn't get pregnant until they stopped trying." My voice inflects as I look closely at her. Then I glance at the glass of ginger ale before raising my eyebrows.

Juliette comes in, dressed in yoga pants and an oversize long sleeve tee. "Hey, how are you today, Annie?"

Annie only lets out a big sigh.

"Have you considered you might be pregnant?" Juliette asks, as if this were totally her idea.

Annie looks from Juliette to me. "OK, you two. So you were talking after I went to bed last night?" she asks, a scowl coming over her face.

"Actually, it was my thought." It's Sophia who is now walking into the kitchen. "Annie, I think you should take a pregnancy test when you get home. You are showing all of the signs."

"Oh, and Sophia said she'd read clairvoyance can be enhanced by pregnancy," Juliette quickly adds. "Probably something to do with hormones."

Annie slowly sits up straighter. "You all think I'm pregnant and that's why I saw what I did." Her eyes widen in a state of panic.

I look at Sophia and then Juliette. One by one, we begin to nod.

"Perhaps it did not cause you to become clairvoyant, but it may have reminded you *how to see.*" Sophia speaks in a calm and assured manner.

"You said you and Jonathon tried to have children." My tone is enthusiastic, as I want her to see how wonderful this would be if true.

"I'd given up all hope. It's one of the reasons I put all of my time and energy into my practice."

"You can do both. Of course, it may require you to cut back on your hours." Sophia then pauses when she sees Annie's reaction. "Or consider not taking new patients." Sophia's assuring tone and encouraging smile make it sound simple.

"I'm forty-four. Isn't that old to become a mom?"

"Not anymore," I say, remembering the age of some of the mothers whose kids are in Patrick's class.

"Why wait till you get home?" Juliette's eyes widen as she moves toward her purse she had put on the bench next to the front door. "Marlee and I will drive downtown and pick up a kit for you."

Before Annie can object, Juliette grabs her coat and walks outside toward my car. Unable to suppress a giggle, one which is not well received by Annie, I head to my bedroom, quickly throw on sweats, and grab my purse. I then return to the kitchen and fill a travel mug with coffee before pulling my jacket from the peg.

"We'll be back," I nonchalantly say as I shut the door behind me and head to my car. It's as though the Universe is actually laughing at me thinking I had any control over this weekend.

***

Thirty minutes later, we return. Juliette forcefully hands a brown paper bag to Annie.

"OK, go pee on the stick." Putting her right hand on her hip, Juliette directs Annie upstairs. "Now."

Annie pushes herself off of the stool, takes one more sip of ginger ale, then, paper bag in tow, goes upstairs and shuts the bathroom door.

"I can't stand the suspense," Juliette says as she runs up the steps.

Knocking loudly on the bathroom door, we hear Juliette say, "Annie, let me in. I want to see if it changes colors."

"She is certainly a force," Sophia says then gently laughs as she takes a sip of her coffee.

I refill my cup, then say, "I've known Michael since he's been at Jefferson. He was quite the ladies' man, but none of the women he dated seemed to last. Juliette may be exactly who and what he needs." I grin at the idea of Michael having a serious relationship.

Small talk ensues as we wait patiently. Finally, after what feels like forever, Juliette comes prancing down the stairs, followed by a somewhat catatonic Annie.

"Are you going to tell them?" Juliette impatiently asks as she turns toward Annie.

Annie moves closer to both of us, and in a voice that's practically a whisper, she speaks: "It says I'm pregnant." Slowly, her face begins to beam.

After rounds of hugs and congratulations, the rest of the morning is spent talking about the various stages of pregnancy, childbirth, and infants. Annie asks Sophia and me lots of questions—about what to expect, what she must buy to be prepared for the baby, and how to share this unexpected news with Jonathon. No doubt Annie has concerns about something going wrong with the pregnancy. Nevertheless, overall, she's positive. Perhaps she *knows* it's all going to work out.

But what might be the most interesting aspect of this morning's conversation is observing Juliette. For once, she is quiet, obviously clueless about these topics. Yet she remains as attentive, if not more so, as Annie when we attempt to answer Annie's questions. This makes me wonder—might Juliette be interested in becoming a mother sometime soon? And if so, is Michael on board?

Before we know it, the grandfather clock strikes twelve times. Sadly, we acknowledge our weekend away is nearly over. Deciding to pack before we finish up the remaining food in the fridge for lunch, we each leave the kitchen counter and head toward our respective rooms to gather our belongings. Luckily, Aunt Sue gave me the name of a cleaning service, so we don't need to worry about tidying up the place before we leave.

Before I join everyone in the kitchen for lunch, I send a quick text to Travis, thanking him for his help and letting him know we're leaving. Within several minutes, he replies.

Travis: *It was great to see you. If you ever need to solve another murder mystery, give me a call.*

I respond with a smiley face. However, it's with the next text I use a heart. Knowing Tom's working all day, I send him a quick message, letting him know I'll be back before six.

I toss my phone into my purse, grab my bags, then join the others, who are gathered around the counter. I place my weekend bag and tote by the front door, throwing my puffy and purse on top. Then I go into the kitchen and open the fridge, eyeing the leftovers. It's definitely enough for lunch, but that's all. Thankfully, I'll be bringing an empty cooler home.

After the remaining salads, chili, croissants, and enchiladas are consumed, we put our dishes in the dishwasher, resigned there's nothing left to do. Though no one seems eager to depart, we all know it's time. While on our way to the drugstore earlier this morning, Juliette offered to ride home with me so I wouldn't have to drive alone. She said if Annie is pregnant, she would be bound to have endless medical questions for Sophia. However, I think Juliette wants some alone time with me, perhaps to talk about Michael.

Before leaving, the four of us agree to meet next Saturday for lunch at Parc downtown. Patrick has a soccer game that morning, but it's at eight o'clock, so I'll be back in time. Surprisingly, Annie does not hesitate to commit. In fact, I watch as she takes out her appointment book from her purse and writes in our lunch date, in pen.

As we pull down the gravel driveway to the main road, I pause, turning back for one last look. The midday sun sparkles off of the snow still remaining on the home's roof. A warmth within confirms this place will forever hold a special spot in my heart. It's then I make a commitment to visit more often—next time, I'll come with Tom and Patrick or, better yet, only Tom.

Eagle's Landing is not merely a vacation home meant for weekend getaways. No, I realize this place is part of me and has impacted who I've become. Summers spent trying to tag along with my siblings taught me resilience. Mornings exploring the woods invoked my curious spirit. And the quiet afternoons by myself introduced me to journaling, permitting me endless time to write about my feelings and aspirations.

Juliette remains quiet, as if allowing me this time to reflect. It's not until we are on the main highway that she finally speaks, asking the question I anticipated she would have for me.

"Marlee ... you've known Michael longer than I have." She clears her throat. "He and I are pretty open. He's told me all about the women he dated. And I've been totally honest about my past." She waits a few moments, then says, "Do you think he's capable of committing? He says he wants to have kids someday, and you know, the big house ... Is he telling me the truth ... or only what he thinks I want to hear?"

My body settles into the car's leather seat as I think about Juliette's question. Gorgeous, bright, flirtatious, and most definitely talented, Michael usually gets exactly what he wants. At least, that's been my assessment from the many conversations we've had over the past few years. Yet I remember how he acted around Juliette, both during December's holiday party and at our home. It was different from how he's behaved around the other women. Unsure whether it was the way he looked at Juliette or the amount of attention he gave to her, I saw another side of Michael emerge both nights. Could it be because Juliette's the first woman who hasn't pursued him? Instead, I sensed their attraction was balanced, authentic, mutual. And most certainly, no one in their presence could deny the sizzling passion existing between them. Yes, I believe Michael may be ready to commit.

Staring straight ahead at the road, I say, "The night I met you at the holiday party, Michael seemed different. Sure, he had all of his typically charming traits, that's not what I'm talking about." I pause, searching for the exact words to describe what I noticed. "Of course, Michael's dated a lot of gorgeous women." Out of the corner of my eye, I can see Juliette flinch when I say this. "But it was the way he looked at *you*. I'd never seen him do that before."

I momentarily turn my head to my right. Now it's Juliette who's gazing at the road ahead.

"And you are certainly not like any of the other women he's dated," I add, then laugh aloud.

"Yeah, he told me about the model who only ate hard-boiled eggs and kale." A snort comes from her mouth, causing me to giggle.

"Oh yeah, I remember her. We met them for dinner, and I remember her being, um, interesting." I laugh aloud as I recall her tiny skintight dress, ridiculously high heels, and enhanced lips nibbling on a plate of sautéed kale.

"Michael's also dated a lawyer, a pediatrician, and someone who ran her own hedge fund." Juliette turns to look at me. "Why me? What makes *me* different from the others?"

Knowing her question is valid, I think about Tom and why I knew he was the one. "I can't answer that. All I know is how it was for me …. when I met Tom." I become silent, returning to the early days of our relationship.

"Did you fall for him right away?"

Shaking my head, I say, "No. I didn't." I let out a brief laugh. "Of course, that had been my pattern with former boyfriends." I pause, attempting to explain the situation in simple terms. "I'd lose myself, become enraptured with them. It felt like a whirlwind.

Inevitably, it would end when I'd finally begin to see who they were, not who I wanted them to be."

"And it wasn't like that with Tom?"

"Not at all." I can't help but roll my eyes and sigh. "It started slowly, and I remember being frustrated, unsure whether or not he liked me. I guess we were both pretty guarded, scarred from past relationships." I let out another sigh. "However, once we both surrendered to what was, well, everything fell into place. We didn't try to please the other or change who we were to make our relationship work. It just did … and it was amazing." There's a calmness within. I don't think I've verbalized these sentiments before. Although it's true. That's what made Tom unlike the other guys I dated. I could be myself around him, and since the beginning, I've accepted him as he is. I didn't try to fix or change anything.

"When Michael and I first met, I wasn't sure what I felt," Juliette says as she glances out the side window. "Sure, he was totally hot … and successful—not so easy to find both in a guy. I guess it took me some time to emotionally commit. Plus, he's constantly surprising me, showing me unexpected aspects of his personality. Michael keeps me guessing. When I least expect it, he becomes vulnerable … and he's so damn cute." She exhales.

"Most things come easy for Michael. He tends to get what he wants when he wants it. Perhaps the fact you didn't fall for him right away shifted his perspective."

"What do you mean?" Juliette's voice sounds confused.

"I'm not suggesting it's about the chase, but what if, for the first time, Michael had to think about whether or not he cared about someone else? Before, everything landed on his lap." I bite my tongue when I realize my poor choice of words. "Of course, not you," I pause, trying to offer an example to my point. "Instead of your relationship happening because you readily reacted to him and his advances, this time *he* had to pursue *you*. Maybe it's given him time to consider what he wants."

"I hope you're right," Juliette says, "because I am falling ... fast."

***

It's a bit after four by the time we arrive at Juliette's apartment in the Northern Liberty section of Philadelphia. She gives me a heartfelt embrace as we say goodbye.

"Thank you for everything." She laughs aloud, and that familiar smirk forms on her mouth. "That was certainly one wild weekend. Can you believe the whole Nicki/Wyatt thing? And Annie realizing she's clairvoyant ... and pregnant?" Juliette shakes her head. "But being with you ... and Annie and Sophia ... was amazing." She exhales, and a sincere look appears on her face. "And I appreciate you sharing your insight about Michael. It helps me to see him through your eyes."

I get out of the car to hug her goodbye. Surprisingly, she holds on a bit longer than I would expect, then begins to climb the stairs to her apartment. Before leaving, I lower the window. "I forgot to ask, what are you guys doing for Valentine's Day?"

"He hasn't told me. All he said was to be ready by seven." Her turquoise eyes light up, and her cheeks begin to glow. Knowing Michael, he has something fabulous planned.

Juliette waves one last goodbye then heads up the remaining stairs to the door of her apartment building. This wild, Ivy League–educated yogi has fallen head over heels for Michael Sutton. I hope he realizes how incredible she is. I call out, telling her to have fun, then close the window and head toward the Schuylkill Expressway, back to Radnor, to my husband and son.

MY

VALENTINE SURPRISE

February 14

There's a beautiful glow of pink, purple, and orange streaks in the sky, what often precedes a Pennsylvanian sunset on a clear winter's day. Pulling into the driveway, I spot Tom's car when I open the garage door. This makes me happy, as I wasn't sure how long he'd be at the hospital.

When I walk into the house, music's playing, causing me to wonder why Patrick's using the Sonos in the house. He doesn't do this. Patrick streams music from his phone with AirPods. And I doubt he'd be playing Van Morrison, Tom's favorite artist.

Roxie comes running toward me, jumping up on my legs to say hello. I lean down and scratch behind her ears. After dropping my bags by the staircase, I notice the light's on in the kitchen. However, it's the aroma that captures my attention—my nose tells me there are mushrooms and onions sautéing. Confused, I move toward the kitchen, only to find Tom—dressed in jeans, a white button-down shirt, and a black fleece vest—standing by the stove with a wooden spoon in his hand, stirring some unknown contents in a large pot.

"Hey," I say as I move closer, wrapping my arms around my husband. "I missed you."

"And I missed you," he says, setting the spoon on the ceramic spoon holder then putting a lid on the pot before pulling me into him for a long and delicious kiss.

"What's all this?"

"Well, it is Valentine's Day, in case you've forgotten," he teases.

"You *never* cook …"

Tom interrupts me. "Because you *never* let anyone into your kitchen." He kisses me again, this time in a teasing manner, pulling away when I try to kiss him back.

"What are you making?" I ask as I begin to lift the lid of the large pot sitting on the back burner. Tom picks up his wooden spoon and playfully smacks the back of my hand with it. *Who is this man, and what has he done with my husband?*

"Beef bourguignon," he announces, looking extremely proud of himself.

"I didn't know you could do this."

"How do you think I fed myself before I met you?" There's a crafty grin on his face.

"The hospital cafeteria?" I ask, using my coy voice.

"Most days." He laughs. "I figured you'd be tired after the weekend … and with everything the four of you went through, I thought you might enjoy a home-cooked meal. That's why I canceled the reservations I'd made and went to the store instead."

It's then I see the vase of gorgeous calla lilies on the kitchen table. There's no way Tom remembered those were the flowers in my wedding bouquet. I dismiss the thought from my head. Noting the table's set for two, I ask, "Where's Patrick?"

"At Matt's house. Since tomorrow is a holiday and there's no school, I told him he could sleep over."

"So we're all alone," I say, demurely casting my eyes suggestively in my husband's direction.

"Yes, we are." Tom walks toward me, his eyes locked on mine. "I've been so busy at work. I'm sorry we haven't taken time just for us." He then steps closer, pulling me into his arms. Slowly, we dance to Van Morrison.

"It must have been tough ... going to that house and seeing that guy, lying there, murdered," Tom whispers, his voice sympathetic, as we sway to the music.

"My first dead body," I say, perhaps a bit sarcastically. "There were so many levels of tragedy. I hope Nicki and Billy can figure things out."

"Does Travis think they will?" I note a bit of uneasiness in Tom's voice when he mentions Travis's name. Obviously, it's not his concern for a couple he doesn't know.

"I don't know what Travis thinks." I look deeply into Tom's eyes. "My relationship with Travis ended close to thirty years ago. Sure, it was nice to see him, to know he's doing OK. You know I don't have any feelings for him." I watch as Tom's face softens.

"Well, it's not every day you bump into an old boyfriend and then he helps you solve a murder," Tom says in a joking manner, but I wonder if there is a bit more behind this statement.

"Actually, it wasn't Travis who figured things out. It was Annie."

"Annie?"

"Yes ... Annie had visions of what actually occurred that night ... She described Nicki walking in and finding Wyatt. Then, with Juliette's help, Annie was able to see what had happened right before Nicki arrived at Wyatt's house ... when Wyatt was murdered." While I had shared most of the facts with Tom last night, I'd left out the part about Annie.

"You think Annie's clairvoyant?" he asks as he stops dancing and pulls back to look me in the eyes.

"At first, it seemed implausible, but when she was able to accurately describe Wyatt's house ... and the murderer ... without having any way of knowing what either looked like, I had to believe she is."

"So how was Travis involved?" Tom's eyebrows furrow.

"Nicki is married to Travis's younger brother, Billy. And she and Travis have a close relationship. Nicki didn't want us to call the police. Instead, she asked us to call Travis. So we did. Of course, when we told him what Annie saw, he had trouble believing her visions were real. Then Annie worked with Sophia to come up with a drawing of the person who killed Wyatt, and Nicki recognized the woman … Caroline Rhimes."

"You know this all sounds ludicrous, right?" Tom lets out a big breath.

"Yes, I realize it does. But somehow … maybe because Dennis, the police chief, trusts Travis … Dennis believed us, or at least part of what we told him. Then when we were at Wyatt's house, my intuition told me to look in Wyatt's office. That's where I found the real estate contract with Caroline's signature … and fingerprints … as well as the secret drawer containing her blackmail letters."

"Damn, girl. I didn't know you were so, um, intuitive." He smiles slyly at me, though I'm not sure if he truly believes my story.

"It's probably the strangest weekend I've had in my entire life," I say, nestling my head into my husband's warm chest. It's then I can feel his heartbeat. "It's good to be home … with you."

"So, when you weren't playing Nancy Drew with Joe Hardy, did you have fun with the girls?"

I laugh at his attempted joke. "Yes, they're awesome. I think … no, I *know* we will remain friends, close friends."

"Now that makes me happy." Tom holds me a bit tighter, and I inhale the musky scent of his cologne I so love. "I know how hard it's been for you … not having true friends." It's then he takes a step back so he can look directly into my eyes. "The others, well, they seemed fun, but not the type of friends you needed." Tom's eyes narrow as he says, "Sophia, Juliette, and Annie … they're different. And you seem happy being around them."

"They're real people, genuine and caring. And I trust them. Oh, and here's the best part." I'm so excited I stop dancing. "Annie's pregnant!"

"What ... Jonathon said they couldn't have kids," Tom stammers.

"Well, apparently they can. It's Sophia who figured it out."

"I find parts of this hard to believe," Tom says, shaking his head. "But I guess it all ended well." He pulls me back into his arms, giving me a quick twirl. "Then, despite seeing your old boyfriend and becoming embroiled in a murder mystery, it was a successful weekend?"

"Most definitely." I pull Tom closer to me. The song changes to "Moondance," our wedding song. "Tom, the music, the flowers, are you aware of their significance?"

"November 25, 2002 ... a good year." He leans closer, slowly kissing me.

When the song ends, we move upstairs, but only after Tom turns off the stove. He's worked too hard on dinner to have it overcook.

Sex with Tom has always been good, but tonight's incredible. There's no rush, no Patrick about to wake up or walk into the house, and no reason to be anywhere else. The world outside becomes irrelevant. Right now, it's only Tom and me. Maybe that's the way it's always been. Perhaps I've been asleep, immersed in matters that aren't so important, concerned with issues I've created in my own mind. However, there's none of that tonight. Instead, I surrender, completely.

When we finally come downstairs, Tom adds the final touches to dinner. I light the candles as he opens a bottle of cabernet. He insists I sit down so he can serve me.

As we savor the delicious beef bourguignon, we discuss the future—our future. I share my concerns about what life will be like when Patrick goes to college. Tom listens, holding my hand. When I'm done, tears fall down my cheeks. He comforts me, assuring his love for me is stronger than it's ever been. Tom talks about work, how long he sees himself at Jefferson, sharing he'd like to make a shift and teach the last few years before fully retiring. Amazed he hasn't before revealed this desire, I'm captivated, fully attentive. My mind does not wander to tomorrow, next week, or what household chores need to happen. No, I'm solely focused on my husband.

I then tell him about the article, the sessions I went to last month, and how I'm incorporating elements from this weekend into my assignment. Tom's encouraging, showing signs he's becoming more open to nontraditional healing methods. He asks questions about Reiki and the breathwork session, appearing genuinely curious as to how I felt during both.

Later that night, when we crawl into our unmade bed and turn on the television, I cuddle next to Tom, holding him tight, knowing we are fine—no, better than fine. We are stronger, closer, and more in love than we've ever been. And with this internal realization, I note there's no argument from Margaret. While I doubt her voice is gone forever, she's quiet, at least for now. My breathing falls into a steady rhythm as I sense an unfamiliar yet comforting peace. For once, no heavy thoughts weigh on my mind. My body feels light, free.

SUBMITTED

February 19

Finally, it's complete. I hit *Send*. Unlike the typical jitters I experience whenever I submit an article to my editor, today a vibrant energy surges through my core. Regardless of what Brad or my readers think about this story, *I know* it's true.

The Invitation

Have a headache? Take an aspirin. Feel a bit of indigestion brewing? Here is a bottle of antacids. Can't sleep at night—perhaps a sedative will provide relief.

Reliant on over-the-counter and prescription medicine to feel better, our society flocks to diagnosis, prescriptions, treatments, and procedures whenever something feels "off." Group think suggests swallowing a capsule will lighten our load, take away the pain, and allow us to function as we once did or believe we should.

When did we become so dependent on pills and other forms of medicines to make us feel whole? Why are more and more people suffering, despite a huge increase in pharmaceutical sales? Are we becoming a nation of individuals incapable of healing without a chemical intervention?

What if there were another way, perhaps a more natural method to calm the common physical ailments we all experience? Let's take this one step further—how amazing would it be if we were able to nurture our bodies, promoting wellness instead of treating sickness? What if we could rid ourselves of the toxins inside, creating vibrant, healthy, and resilient bodies and minds? Would this make you consider alternative approaches?

In no way am I suggesting we disregard traditional medicine. Doing so would be foolish. However, I do ask you to consider a new way of healing, one that does not require pills or surgical procedures. Instead, there are other options available to cleanse the body so it can heal from within. These preventative and prescriptive methods are not new—they've been practiced for hundreds of years throughout numerous countries and cultures. Although they may not satisfy our traditional medical protocols, a great amount of research validates their effectiveness. And they do not need to be practiced in isolation. They most certainly can be a complement to traditional medicine.

Please accept my invitation to explore the world of holistic healing.

However, before you type me as a New Age groupie, let me assure you I'm anything but. I am a suburban woman in her midforties who freelances for the Inquirer, spends weekend mornings watching her son play soccer, and enjoys cooking. Having grown up in an Irish Catholic family, I viewed God as an omnipotent being, one resembling man, who sits in the clouds, looking down at us. While he most definitely loves the children he created in his image, the nuns taught me God judges our every wrong, requiring a penance to erase our humanly sins. Let me assure you holistic healing has never been a part of my life. But this is certainly going to change.

During the past six weeks, I've experimented in this unknown world, dipping my toe into several healing practices. I'm certainly not proclaiming myself an expert—my only goal

*was to explore a few methods to determine whether any va-
lidity existed for this hype. Honestly, I had great doubts about
the entire assignment. In fact, I suspected I'd become cynical
of these practices.*

*This article challenged me in many ways. At first, it felt
burdensome and unsettling. I had no idea where to begin.
I'd promised my editor I'd write a piece addressing holistic
practices available in the Philadelphia area. So I put on my
big girl pants and committed to opening my mind, considering ways I can neither understand nor explain. Never did
I imagine this adventure would shift my limiting beliefs,
freeing my spirit as it strengthened my body. No doubt I'm
changing and beginning to view various aspects of life from
a new perspective. However, the biggest impact remains how
amazing I feel.*

*While I've only dabbled in six practices, there are many
more available. It's as though there is a holistic art for each of
us. This philosophy to wellness is anything but limiting. Still,
I needed to start somewhere, so I began by asking a good
friend to introduce me to Ayurveda.*

*First, let me explain that my friend is in the process
of receiving her certification in Ayurveda, an ancient Indian practice focused on longevity and well-being. She and I
spend many Saturday mornings together at our sons' soccer
games, and she's extremely aware of how anxious I become
when my son is in goal, especially whenever direct kicks of
any kind are involved.*

*Claiming daily Ayurvedic habits would help calm my
nerves as well as improve my overall health, she introduced
me to various practices, such as oil pulling, tongue scraping,
body brushing, and beginning my day with a cup of lemon
water—all meant to help detoxify the body. Ayurveda also*

considers one's body type—Vata, Pitta, or Kappa—when planning the best types of foods and exercises. For me, that meant altering my workouts to add lifting weights, as well as eating three balanced meals a day, incorporating foods that are bitter, sweet, and astringent.

Of course, I merely learned the "Ayurveda for Dummies" version. However, I've noticed small shifts even though I've only been following these daily habits for less than two months. I feel calmer, especially in high-stress situations. Though it's my body that seems to reap the most benefits. My skin is clearer, and my digestion has improved. Plus, so far, I've avoided my annual winter cold. I'll happily alter my diet and workout routine, as well as use a body brush, scrape my tongue, swish some oil, and drink lemon water before I hit the coffee if I can sustain these noticeable changes.

Although the benefits of Ayurveda sound promising, I could not feel a specific impact, you know, like a zing of sorts. Instead, its effects are more subtle. However, that changed when I experienced Reiki, as I could not help but detect the immediate potency of the practice. Reiki, an ancient Eastern healing art, focuses on unblocking energy stuck in our seven main energy centers, or chakras, by the movement of energy through the practitioner's hands. While I lack the understanding to fully explain what occurred during my Reiki session, all I know is afterward I felt physically lighter, mentally focused, and sensed an ease within. I learned these energetic releases can result in physical sensations as the toxins clear. For example, you may feel tingling, pops, or muscle pulls and releases as energy shifts within your body. However, this is only temporary and is not harmful. In fact, clearing blockages is said to help prevent illnesses, which can form due to stagnant energy.

My next step into the energetic healing world involved beautiful rocks. I met with a practitioner to learn about the impact these crystals can have on us. When I held various stones, I felt energetic pulses coming from them. Some were faint; others caused surges of electricity to flow through my hand. The practitioner shared how certain crystals correlate with the various energy centers in our body, the chakras, promoting specific benefits of well-being. Some gemstones can be worn or carried for aspirations such as prosperity, health, and confidence, and others are used for protection, to attract love, or enhancing intuition. I also learned there are ways to place gemstones in various areas of your home to help promote a positive and loving environment. Finally, certain crystals can be used for physical as well as emotional healing.

During my third session, I discovered the benefits of breathwork. This extremely powerful practice exceeded all of my expectations. Lying on a mat with only the sounds of specifically chosen music playing in the background, I followed a repetitive breathing technique. Halfway through the class, I found myself floating, as if high above my body. Then a huge wave of emotions began to crash over me, like a release of something stored inside. Although I shed many tears during these moments, I was not frightened; in fact, I felt quite the opposite. This unleashing of suppressed emotions provided me with a sense of peace. Again, I cannot fully explain what occurred; all I know is the impact it left on me.

My next exposure involved a more mainstream form of holistic practices—I tried my first yoga and meditation class. Certainly not a novel method of healing, both are incredible for calming the body and mind. Though some consider yoga a form of exercise—and it certainly can be—I found it a coming home of sorts, an entrance into my own body without the *need to be anywhere else. No doubt the physical movement has multiple benefits, including increased flexibility and balance. Yet, for me, the experience was more mental. And don't let meditation intimidate you. While sitting motionless for thirty minutes may sound horrid, it's not. When you can relax and release the self-imposed expectations of having a vacant mind, you can surrender to allowing your thoughts to come and go, without judgment. Only then do the true benefits occur.*

As a growing portion of our population realizes the advantages of alternate healing methods, more of these practices will become available, ultimately melding into our medical community. The benefits are immeasurable, and the cost of these sessions is much lower than most medications and traditional medical procedures.

Admittedly, I've only begun my journey down the path of holistic healing, and I lack a comprehensive understanding of its long-term impact on improved physical and mental health, which comes with consistent practice. However, a mere glimpse of these healers in action taught me to no longer question their methods. I am now hooked.

This is not the end of this story, for learning about something is rarely as impactful as witnessing it in action. And that is what happened this past weekend, cementing my belief in what can be.

Three friends and I planned a short trip to the Poconos, a getaway of sorts. What began as a "girls' weekend" quickly turned into three days of learning about hidden gifts that allow us to know, become open, and see.

Perhaps it's a voice inside that directs us in a certain way, or maybe it's a vision in our mind that shows us something others are unable to detect. Often, a person's intuition is in-

volved. Nevertheless, it can be more, a knowing of what is or what was. This past weekend, we experienced all of the above—some of us for the first time.

In this particular case, a friend's newly discovered clairvoyance provided the missing information to a police investigation, ultimately preventing an innocent woman from being accused of murder. Yes, I know it sounds far-fetched. And had I not been present and experienced another's ability to envision what three others and I could not, I most likely would have doubted clairvoyance exists. Yet, as there was no logical explanation for what occurred, I accept it to be true.

Surprisingly, this happens more frequently than we realize. People provide missing information based on hunches, often not questioning how this particular knowledge came to be. After all, we've been taught to suppress our gifts, our knowings, as we are made to think we've imagined them. Still, for us to become aware of and open to our hidden abilities—ones that we all possess—we must believe in the possibility they do indeed exist.

Doing so asks a great deal of us—we must trust in the unknown. This is difficult. Few of us embrace uncertainty. Instead, we want to connect the dots and see the evidence to prove an event. However, to experience life's unexpected miracles, we must have faith in what cannot be explained. Holistic practices open our mind and body to these possibilities. By clearing stuck energies, most likely created from years of fear and feelings of inadequacy, we create greater flow, permitting perspectives to shift and limiting beliefs to alter. This is how we grow into more aware versions of ourselves.

Despite more and more studies suggesting these unconventional practices lead to better health, clearer minds, stronger relationships, and overall wellness, they have yet to *receive a rubber stamp confirming they "work." Perhaps this is why so many of us continue to rely on pharmaceuticals to feel better.*

After my experiences, I do not need endless research to document how these methods can heal. Slowly, I'm learning it's not only the voice inside our head that speaks to us, judging our actions and thoughts. We can also listen to a different voice—the beautiful whispers that resonate from our heart and soul. These are the messages that can release our fears, anger, sorrow, and insecurities as well as support us in making decisions that can lead to a life filled with love, joy, and happiness.

This voice is our intuition. It helps us to know, to understand, and to see what can be. Discovering my intuition was the biggest gift from the past six weeks. I am learning to listen to my inner voice, to trust myself. For it is when we pause and take the time to hear that we begin to believe. We do not require others' proof, research papers, and confirmations to know what is true. Nothing can be stronger than embracing our internal knowing, trusting the quiet voice whose purpose is to guide us throughout our journey here on earth.

Although I'm thrilled to have finally submitted this assignment, one thing continues to weigh heavily on my mind. I cannot identify the connection between Caroline Rhimes and Wyatt—being his realtor is more than a mere coincidence. There must be something deeper to have prompted her to murder him. I feel there's a connection between these two. In fact, I *know* it exists. But I'm unable to determine what *it* is. Perhaps I never will.

WAIT,

THERE'S MORE

February 20

Natalie turns toward me. "Do you think you'll be OK?" she asks. "I'm ready." I take three deep breaths, clench my eyes shut, then reopen them, focusing on the far side of the indoor soccer field.

A tall blond boy wearing a navy shirt bearing the number 17 stretches his long legs in front of our goal. The ref paces off the required distance between the goal line and where the player may stand, prompting the kid to step back several feet. I look at Patrick. He shifts his weight from side to side, preparing for the penalty kick. He appears particularly agile and light on his feet today. But it's the serene look on his face, a mixture of calm and confidence, that catches my attention. He so resembles Tom. I can't believe I haven't witnessed this side of him. Of course not. I've been hiding, eyes tightly shut whenever my son's facing a direct kick.

The shrill sound of the ref's whistle reverberates through the indoor field house. The boy from the opposing team lunges left, though it's a fake. He quickly moves in the opposite direction, using his right foot to kick the ball into the upper ninety of the net.

I want to escape, retreat inside the safety of a dark and sheltered sanctum so I do not have to watch my son leap toward the corner of the net as he attempts to block the goal. However, I don't. Instead, I take a big breath and remain present. I watch.

Natalie jumps out of her seat then begins clapping her hands.

Tears stream from the corner of my eyes as I slowly exhale. Once the breath leaves my body, so does the tightness in my neck and shoulders. I'm happy for Patrick … for his team. But I'm also proud of myself. And so is Natalie.

"Look at you! You didn't cover your eyes. This is huge, Marlee." She leans down and gives me a hug.

"I guess I didn't." I look around at the crowd.

No one appears to be sheltering their vision like I did. Those in the stands and on the field express either enthusiasm or frustration on their face. There's no denying the feelings from both players and spectators.

Only then do I realize how much I've missed. By refusing to watch my son during direct kicks, I've been numbing my feelings, keeping myself from experiencing the emotions attached to the glory of victory as well as the disappointment of defeat. Lost in the dread of Patrick hurting himself or failing his team, I empowered my fears instead of witnessing what is and then releasing the natural joy or disappointment in a healthy manner. It's then I see Patrick searching for me. My heart fills with pure love for my only child. Once he spots where I am standing, a gigantic smile emerges on his face. He knows I've finally watched him prevent a goal.

***

During the drive back to Radnor, Natalie and I discuss Ayurvedic practices. She shares more about the three doshas, telling me she's convinced I am mostly Pitta with a touch of Vata.

"You know, it would be beneficial for you to consider how you're exercising. I think it might be good for you to try something new … What about a kickboxing or spin class? And balance these high-energy workouts with some yoga."

"Funny you should say this." I pause, looking in the rearview mirror at Patrick and Matt, who are both engrossed in playing electronic games. "I recently went to my first yoga class. It was a combination of yoga and meditation," I proudly announce, glancing sideways at Natalie.

"*Fabulous!*" From her level of enthusiasm, I'd bet she was a cheerleader in high school. "Yoga will make you stronger, help you with your balance. The Vata in you can be seen in your build and smaller bone structure. If you only run and fail to strengthen your muscles, you could be prone to injury." I take note of her cautionary tone.

I cannot help but chuckle as I now fully embrace the woman who once annoyed me. I focus on driving as Natalie continues to spew facts. At one point, she shares how she's hoping to connect with local doctors who are open to alternative methods.

"I may know the perfect person for you to meet."

Despite Natalie's plea to divulge the name of the physician, I suggest Natalie give me her business card so I can initiate the introduction. "You know, she may not be open to it, so I'd prefer to speak with her first."

Looking a bit dejected, Natalie hands me several of her cards, perhaps in case I think of other contacts. I bet she's hoping Tom or one of his partners might be interested, though I know my limits with my husband.

Patrick and I are home before eleven. As I begin to head upstairs to change from my warm indoor soccer clothing into something more appropriate for lunch at Parc, Patrick follows me up the steps.

"Mom, did you really watch this time, or did you keep your eyes shut ... like you *always* do?" While he appears to be teasing me, I sense there's a bit more significance to his question.

I pause, sit down on a step, and motion for him to join me. "You know, it's super hard for me to watch you in goal."

"I know, Mom. But you don't need to worry. I'm not going to hurt myself." His voice is sweet; still there's a hint of frustration as if he's tired of telling me the same thing.

"I know, Patrick." I swallow before continuing. "You mean so much to me." I exhale loudly as I take his hand in mine. "The mere thought of anything happening to you, well, it freaks me out."

"Your fears are irrational, Mom. I've never seen anyone get hurt badly in goal." He has a point. Neither have I, but I'm aware it can happen.

"You're getting older, Patrick ... and in less than two years, you'll be off to college ... where I won't be there to protect you." Although I do my best, I cannot prevent a tear from escaping the corner of my eye.

Patrick places his arm around me. "It's only college, Mom ... I promise ... I'll be fine. You don't need to protect me anymore. I can take care of myself. Don't worry ... I love you ... always will." With that, he kisses me on my cheek before standing and sprinting up the last half of the stairs. "I've got some homework to do, but then I told Matt he could come over, OK?"

I sniff slightly before saying, "Absolutely."

It's then I know my son is fine. He's growing up faster than I could imagine. And he loves me. Knowing not every sixteen-year-old is capable of saying these words to his mother, I feel blessed. I wipe my eyes then head to my bedroom to change for lunch.

***

I arrive at the restaurant twenty minutes early. Traffic on the expressway was lighter than normal. Unaccustomed to having extra time, I decide to walk around Rittenhouse Square. Of course, I've walked *through* the square a multitude of times. However, I haven't permitted myself to consciously wander within the small park.

After several minutes of strolling on the narrow walkways, I sit down on a vacant bench, watching those passing by—the young, the old, those in love, and the homeless. Pigeons swoop overhead. One lands at my feet, tilting its head in the most curious fashion, as if to ask what I think of this place.

For as many years as I've spent in downtown Philly, I've never once taken the time to merely sit and watch. People in heavy woolen coats, black down puffies, and green Eagles jackets stroll up and down the paths. A young couple with three boys, all of whom appear under the age of ten, play tag on the dormant grass. A homeless man, propped against a small iron fence and partially sheltered by cardboard boxes, sleeps. This, the good and the sad, is life. Have I become so callous to my surroundings or perhaps afraid of what might be that I've forgotten or refused to look? And by veiling my sight, have I also squelched my innermost feelings, numbing the painful emotions as well as the pleasurable ones?

I cannot deny the answer to both questions is yes. By playing it safe and remaining in my comfort zone, I've avoided the true grit of reality and the tangible feelings that accompany witnessing what truly is. And my fear of watching Patrick in goal was only the tip of this iceberg.

Yet, this past weekend, I was anything but sheltered. I faced Travis, after all of these years, better understanding our relationship and how much we've both grown. And I allowed my vulnerabilities to surface, admitting my deepest concerns to Sophia and Juliette. Then, in the face of all of the trauma with Nicki, Wyatt, and Billy, I somehow opened up to an intuitive spirit I did not know existed. By trusting in myself, I was able to help make a difference in a woman's fate. And I finally finished my article.

The chime from St. Patrick's church alerts me it's now one o'clock. As I leave the solitude of my bench and head down the cement path toward the restaurant, a sense of ease surrounds me. When I arrive at Parc, Sophia is standing by the hostess stand. Within minutes, the hostess seats us in a booth at the back of the restaurant. While a table by one of the huge windows that face Eighteenth Street would have been nice, I appreciate the coziness and privacy our booth provides.

Sophia's glowing, and it becomes evident she's eager to share something with me.

"Marlee," she begins, "I spoke with my partners, and all three were open to adding holistic elements to our practice." She smiles, revealing her perfectly formed teeth. "They do have some reservations regarding the best way to introduce this shift in direction to our patients. However, they recognize the benefits and believe incorporating practices such as Reiki might help us expand, attracting new patients looking for a more balanced medical approach."

"I am thrilled for you," I say as I place my hand on hers. "Has Elena agreed to come on board?"

"She has. In fact, adding Reiki is our first step. The office manager plans to send a follow-up questionnaire to patients after they see Elena. This will provide valuable feedback before we add other practitioners." Sophia's words are committed, strong, and confident.

"Oh, I almost forgot," I say as I search the pocket in my purse for Natalie's business card. "My friend Natalie is becoming certified in Ayurveda. I think I mentioned her when we were at the Poconos. Anyway, she's interested in connecting with an existing practice, you know, in hopes of working with some of their patients. She might be a good match for you and your partners," I say, handing the laminated card to Sophia.

"Thank you, Marlee. I have incorporated Ayurvedic practices into my personal routine, and I would love to speak with Natalie about a possible collaboration."

Could Ayurveda be partially responsible for Sophia's beautiful complexion?

As my mind's contemplating this thought, Juliette approaches the table. Her smile is a mile wide, and there's a glow about her. As she pulls back a chair to sit down, I'm drawn to a sparkle coming from her left hand.

"Michael proposed?" I blurt out as I stare at the gorgeous diamond surrounded by two baguettes. Instantly, I jump from my seat to give her a hug.

"He did ... when we got back ... on Valentine's Day." Her voice is dreamy, somewhat distant.

As Sophia stands to embrace Juliette, I feel compelled to ask, "Why didn't you tell us?" No doubt I sound a bit hurt. And why didn't Tom tell me? I'm sure Michael shared this news with him.

"I wanted it to be a surprise. In fact, I made Michael promise not to share our news with anyone until I was able to tell the three of you in person," Juliette says as she gracefully slides into her chair. Although her physical body is with us, her mind seems elsewhere.

Relieved, my heart settles. I chastise myself for my being so quick to accuse Juliette of keeping her engagement from me. I'd reverted to old ways, instantly assuming something that was not true.

"What did I miss?" Annie asks, a look of confusion on her face as she sits down in the remaining chair.

"Juliette and Michael are engaged," I proudly announce, as if I had anything to do with this. After all, I've known Michael the longest and feel a special connection with him.

"Apparently, we have a lot to celebrate," Juliette says as she places her hand on Annie's still flat belly. "How did Jonathon react when you told him about the pregnancy?" Juliette's eyes widen, excited to hear his response.

"Jonathon's beside himself." Annie giggles. "Since we didn't think we could have children of our own, we've made decisions that now need to be altered. It's exciting, but kind of scary at the same time." Annie pauses for a moment before continuing. "We'll both feel better when I'm farther along."

"Have you seen your doctor?" Sophia asks, raising her eyebrows as if to insinuate she better not wait.

"I saw Dr. Sanchez yesterday. She's amazing. Jonathon and she went to med school together. He holds her in the highest regard." Annie proceeds to tell us she's due the middle of October.

"That means you must have gotten pregnant sometime around Marlee's dinner party." Juliette's direct assumption causes Annie to blush.

"I think you're right," is all she says before shifting the conversation back to Juliette's engagement. "So, tell us, how did he propose?" Annie leans closer toward Juliette, then takes Juliette's hand so she can better see the platinum engagement ring.

Before Juliette can answer, a tall man dressed in black pants and a long sleeve black shirt appears by our table, ready to take our drink order: a mimosa, two Bloody Marys, and a San Pellegrino.

"Well," Juliette begins as soon as the server leaves, "as you know, I drove home last Sunday with Marlee. I think it was a bit after four when she dropped me off at my place." Juliette pauses for a moment before continuing. "Michael had asked me to be ready by seven … said he'd pick me up and we'd go to dinner."

"Did he?" Annie asks, inflecting the word *he*.

Sophia uncharacteristically says, "Shhh."

"Yes. But it wasn't just Michael … When I walked outside of my apartment, there was a limo waiting. At first, I thought Michael wanted to have a few drinks and didn't want to risk driving afterward. But when we headed away from the city, I became a bit suspicious."

"Where did you go?" Annie blurts out, incapable of containing herself.

"Strawberry Mansion ... in Fairmont Park," Juliette whispers, eyes wide as she leans forward toward the three of us. "He rented a private room ... had a catered dinner for the two of us ... The chef made the most exquisite vegetarian meal ... beets stacked with goat cheese, a spiced cauliflower cake made with lemon, herbs, and toasted almonds ... and a tart with heirloom tomatoes and basil." She sits back and looks at her left hand, as if still in shock at being engaged.

"It must have been amazing," Sophia says, tilting her head to the side, as if waiting for more details.

"The entire night felt like a dream."

"*How* did he propose?" Annie's questioning is endless.

"Actually, *that* didn't happen like you'd assume it would. Knowing Michael, you would think he'd be smooth, have the perfect words to ask me to marry him. After all, he picked me up in the limo and took me to this awesome place for a romantic dinner." Juliette's eyes come alive as the palms of her hands press into the table's edge. "I guess he was nervous." She tries to prevent a laugh but she's unable. "After the waiter brought our dessert, a salted caramel and chocolate tart ... with fresh raspberries, Michael started stammering, and I could see sweat begin to form on his brow." Now Juliette's giggling.

"Did you know what was going on?" Annie's eyes are wide with apprehension.

Juliette blushes a bit before answering. "Once he put the small velvet box on the table, I figured it out ... then I started laughing ..." She shakes her head, continuing to giggle.

"You laughed at Michael as he was trying to propose?" Stunned by what I'm hearing, my jaw drops a bit. A part of me feels badly for Michael, yet another side thinks this is exactly how it was supposed to happen. Too many women have swooned at his feet … and Juliette is certainly not one of those.

Juliette bites her bottom lip. "I know, I felt terrible. Then we both started laughing. Before I knew it, Michael opened the Safian & Rudolf Jewelers box, but he didn't say a thing. Then I said, 'So I guess this means you want to marry me?' Speechless, he took the ring out of the box and placed it on my finger."

The server returns with our drinks and we toast … to Juliette and Michael, and then to Annie soon becoming a mom.

"Oh, and to Sophia," I say, as I raise my Bloody Mary. "May I share your good news?" I ask, hoping I haven't spoken out of turn. Sophia only smiles, offering me a wink.

"Sophia's partners have agreed to her idea of adding a holistic element to their practice. Elena is going to join them, offering Reiki to their patients."

Annie takes a sip of her San Pellegrino then says in the sweetest manner, "It's like your dream is coming true."

"Yes … it is." Sophia's delicate shoulders naturally glide down her back as she says, "I am delighted all three partners are open to offering a more balanced approach to our patients. Actually, I am filled with joy and gratitude." It's then Sophia's expression becomes serious before asking, "Marlee, how is your article coming?"

I sit up a bit as I proudly announce I submitted it to my editor yesterday.

Juliette's the first to react. "Did you write about the weekend?"

"In a roundabout way. I know I said I was going to, but then when I sat down to finish the article, I took a new approach. Instead of writing in an objective third-person voice, I decided to share my personal introduction to holistic healing … how I opened myself up to the practices. I also talk about how these experiences allowed me to shift perspectives, view life in a different light, and consider possibilities I would not have entertained before."

"But did you mention the murder?" Annie asks insistently, eyes wide and mouth open. "And my clairvoyance?" By the expression on her face, it's as though she hopes I did.

"I touched on both, only not the people involved … naming individuals seemed inappropriate. And most likely, discussing the actual murder would probably violate some rule of sorts. I felt it better to keep it to me and the changes I underwent. After all, I cannot speak for others. And your gift, well, that's yours to share, Annie … if you choose to." I give Annie a quick wink and an astute smile.

"Are you ready to order?" the server, who reappeared unnoticed, interrupts, but I don't mind. Sometimes I don't like to discuss pieces I've written, especially before they are published.

"If we could have a few more moments," Sophia says.

We pause our conversation so we can choose from the menu. Several moments later, after seeing our closed menus, the server returns with a basket of delicious homemade breads. We each order one of Parc's signature salads.

"So now what?" Juliette asks.

Confused, I look at her, "What do you mean?"

"How do we all stay in touch? I'm not sure how to do this 'girl thing.' Do we agree to meet monthly for brunch?" Juliette gives me a perplexed look, confirming the truth in her words.

"That would be great," I say in response. Still, I don't want to wait an entire month to get together with these awesome women. Cupping my chin in my hand, I ask, "What if we all took yoga together … at Bliss? I'm sure we could find a night that works for everyone." Immediately, Juliette lights up, no doubt thrilled I suggested we do a weekly yoga class at her studio.

After discussing the various options, we all commit to Wednesday's five thirty restorative class, as Annie will be able to participate throughout her pregnancy. Sophia then proposes we plan to have drinks or dinner afterward. "We *could* invite the men"—she gives us a sly smile—"occasionally." There's comfort knowing we now have a designated time to see one another.

While we nibble on the delicious bread, Juliette shares more about their wedding plans. They are looking at dates in late November. Then, once again, she surprises us, asking us to be her bridesmaids. In classic Juliette style, she tries to underplay the importance of this invitation. Yet there's no misreading how much this would mean to her.

"Really, you want us, three older women, to be in your wedding?" I ask, honored she's including us.

"Hell yeah. I wouldn't have it any other way," Juliette says as a mischievous smirk appears on her face. It's then I see the glisten in those turquoise eyes, confirming how important we are to her. After all, we are her friends.

I then look at Annie, who breathes a sigh of relief, perhaps from knowing the wedding will take place after her due date. "Since it's not till the end of November, yes!" Annie's face lights up as she accepts. "If it were earlier, I'd have to decline … don't want to look like a whale in your wedding pictures," she says, laughing aloud. I wonder if she knows how tough it can be to lose baby weight. Nevertheless, I remain silent. No need to cause more concerns for Annie.

Our conversation then transitions to everyday issues. We talk about Sophia's children, Tom's and my plans to show Patrick colleges next month, Annie's effort to cook more meals instead of constantly eating out, and Juliette's aspiration to open a second studio on the Main Line.

"You know, I'm planning to go on a retreat this April … to Costa Rica." She pauses to look around the table at each of us. "By chance, would anyone want to come with me?" Her voice inflects a bit, perhaps in uncertainty to how we will respond. After all, we, the three of us, just committed to being her bridesmaids.

"What is the retreat?" Sophia asks, as if she's truly interested in attending.

"It's called Elevar, and it's taking place at the resort, Nueva Vida, in Nosara. There are going to be numerous practitioners ... like shamans, energy workers, channelers, astrologers ... offering workshops as well as individual healing sessions. And there are yoga and meditation classes each day. Instead of having a set schedule like most traditional retreats do, you can pick and choose what you want to do." She smiles, then explains, "The retreat's titled Elevate because it is meant to help you in your transformation ... to your next phase."

I sit up a bit straighter. Juliette has my full attention.

"I'm planning to attend a bunch of the workshops and sign up for several of the private sessions. However, you can also go there for pure relaxation," she says, looking directly at Annie. "The resort's amazing, and it's only a short walk to the beach. It takes a bit of time to get to Nosara, but it's totally worth the drive. Once you're there, you feel like you're in the middle of the jungle. And you can hear the howler monkeys at night."

Annie flinches at the mention of primates.

"No, the monkeys are harmless. Actually, they're adorable." Juliette grabs her phone and begins searching her photos for a picture of these wiry monkeys. "I've been to this resort before, but not this retreat." Juliette pauses as she passes her phone around. After a bit, she asks, "Would you come with me?" Her tone is serious, and I sense she's hoping we'll all say yes.

Costa Rica's been on my bucket list. Still, can I say yes? Am I ready to take the plunge into deeper modalities of healing, like channeling and shamanism? Immediately, I sense my core become warm, and it is as though butterflies are again swirling inside of my abdomen. Though this sensation is not ominous. It's encouraging, empowering. "I'll go," I say without giving it another thought.

"As will I," Sophia says. "It aligns beautifully with my new business plan. Of course, it is no coincidence you asked us to join you." Sophia briefly arches her eyebrows before a serene look comes across her face. "I suspect I will learn a great deal at this retreat."

The three of us look toward Annie, whose head faces down toward her lap.

"What about you, Annie?" Juliette asks. "Will you come?" There is no hint of pleading in Juliette's voice, only a welcoming and compassionate invitation.

"Oh, I don't think I should, with being pregnant and everything."

Sophia speaks up. "Annie, it is perfectly safe for you to fly. By April, you will be less than four months into your pregnancy. Plus, I will be there, so if you have any concerns, you will have a personal physician by your side."

Annie inhales deeply, holding her breath as if afraid to let go because then she will be required to answer.

"Come on, it will be fun," I say. We hear her let out a loud sigh.

"And it will be good for you. The baby will automatically benefit from all of the healing sessions you attend," Juliette says. "Please." She leans toward Annie and takes her hand.

Annie lifts her eyes then looks at each of us. "OK, as long as my doctor says I can."

"It's settled. I'll email you the information as soon as I get home. Let's book our flights together." Juliette looks as if she's about to elevate off of her chair.

Our salads arrive, and suddenly I am famished. After all, a lot has happened today, and it's not yet two o'clock. Apparently, I've conquered my fear of watching Patrick in goal. And I've taken a pause to witness my surroundings in the park. But most impressive,

I've committed to a week-long holistic retreat in Costa Rica ... with my new friends.

I like how that sounds. As I take a bite of the arugula and pear salad, I look across the table at each of the women. Juliette's glowing; her face shines as brightly as the diamond on her left finger. Annie's equally luminous, and I believe that as her child grows within, so will her self-confidence. Then there's Sophia, who naturally radiates grace, wisdom, and compassion. These three, well, I think I've found what I've been missing.

We most certainly are an unlikely amalgamation of females—a twenty-seven-year-old yoga instructor, a forty-four-year-old psychologist, a fifty-five-year-old physician, and a forty-six-year-old journalist. Yet what makes us different is our bond. Unlike others, it's based on acceptance, respect, trust, and vulnerability. We recognize our differing preferences, personalities, and perspective. And we refrain from making assumptions. Each one of us shows up as our true self, holding space for one another. This is the real thing ... This is friendship. And it's only beginning ... We're headed to a retreat in Costa Rica this April!

ACKNOWLEDGEMENTS

The Invitation is the first of three books in *The Awakening Series*. Never would I have envisioned this trilogy had I not had the privilege of working with the following individuals who introduced me to the concept of energy healing and prompted me to begin my own spiritual journey:

Gabby Warner
Alyssa Lindahl
Sally Brower

While authors may write the words, novels are published because a team of talented people collaborate to create the final product. Thank you to my all-star team:

Julie Swearingen – Editor
Alison Cantrell – Copyeditor
Lieve Maas – Graphic Designer
Katie Dwyer – Beta Reader

And finally, thank you to my family. Without your love and support, I would not possess the courage to share my stories:

Scott Davis
Jack Davis
Grant Davis
Janice Miller

Made in the USA
Middletown, DE
06 December 2021

54460132R00146